Erle Stanley Gardner and The Murder Room

>>> This title is part of The Murder Room, our series dedicated to making available out-of-print or hard-to-find titles by classic crime writers.

Crime fiction has always held up a mirror to society. The Victorians were fascinated by sensational murder and the emerging science of detection; now we are obsessed with the forensic detail of violent death. And no other genre has so captivated and enthralled readers.

Vast troves of classic crime writing have for a long time been unavailable to all but the most dedicated frequenters of second-hand bookshops. The advent of digital publishing means that we are now able to bring you the backlists of a huge range of titles by classic and contemporary crime writers, some of which have been out of print for decades.

From the genteel amateur private eyes of the Golden Age and the femmes fatales of pulp fiction, to the morally ambiguous hard-boiled detectives of mid twentieth-century America and their descendants who walk our twenty-first century streets, The Murder Room has it all. >>>

The Murder Room
Where Criminal Minds Meet

themurderroom.com

Erle Stanley Gardner (1889–1970)

Born in Malden, Massachusetts, Erle Stanley Gardner left school in 1909 and attended Valparaiso University School of Law in Indiana for just one month before he was suspended for focusing more on his hobby of boxing that his academic studies. Soon after, he settled in California, where he taught himself the law and passed the state bar exam in 1911. The practise of law never held much interest for him, however, apart from as it pertained to trial strategy, and in his spare time he began to write for the pulp magazines that gave Dashiell Hammett and Raymond Chandler their start. Not long after the publication of his first novel, *The Case of the Velvet Claws*, featuring Perry Mason, he gave up his legal practice to write full time. He had one daughter, Grace, with his first wife, Natalie, from whom he later separated. In 1968 Gardner married his long-term secretary, Agnes Jean Bethell, whom he professed to be the real 'Della Street', Perry Mason's sole (although unacknowledged) love interest. He was one of the most successful authors of all time and at the time of his death, in Temecula, California in 1970, is said to have had 135 million copies of his books in print in America alone.

By Erle Stanley Gardner
(titles below include only those
published in the Murder Room)

Perry Mason series

The Case of the Sulky Girl
(1933)
The Case of the Baited Hook
(1940)
The Case of the Borrowed
Brunette (1946)
The Case of the Lonely
Heiress (1948)
The Case of the Negligent
Nymph (1950)
The Case of the Moth-Eaten
Mink (1952)
The Case of the Glamorous
Ghost (1955)
The Case of the Terrified
Typist (1956)
The Case of the Gilded Lily
(1956)
The Case of the Lucky Loser
(1957)
The Case of the Long-Legged
Models (1958)
The Case of the Deadly Toy
(1959)
The Case of the Singing Skirt
(1959)

The Case of the Duplicate
Daughter (1960)
The Case of the Blonde
Bonanza (1962)

Cool and Lam series

The Bigger They Come (1939)
Turn on the Heat (1940)
Gold Comes in Bricks (1940)
Spill the Jackpot (1941)
Double or Quits (1941)
Owls Don't Blink (1942)
Bats Fly at Dusk (1942)
Cats Prowl at Night (1943)
Crows Can't Count (1946)
Fools Die on Friday (1947)
Bedrooms Have Windows
(1949)
Some Women Won't Wait (1953)
Beware the Curves (1956)
You Can Die Laughing (1957)
Some Slips Don't Show (1957)
The Count of Nine (1958)
Pass the Gravy (1959)
Kept Women Can't Quit (1960)
Bachelors Get Lonely (1961)
Shills Can't Count Chips (1961)

Try Anything Once (1962)
Fish or Cut Bait (1963)
Up For Grabs (1964)
Cut Thin to Win (1965)
Widows Wear Weeds (1966)
Traps Need Fresh Bait (1967)

Doug Selby D.A. series

The D.A. Calls it Murder (1937)
The D.A. Holds a Candle (1938)
The D.A. Draws a Circle (1939)
The D.A. Goes to Trial (1940)
The D.A. Cooks a Goose (1942)
The D.A. Calls a Turn (1944)
The D.A. Takes a Chance (1946)
The D.A. Breaks an Egg (1949)

Terry Clane series

Murder Up My Sleeve (1937)
The Case of the Backward
   Mule (1946)

Gramp Wiggins series

The Case of the Turning Tide
   (1941)
The Case of the Smoking
   Chimney (1943)

Two Clues (two novellas) (1947)

Bedrooms Have Windows

Erle Stanley Gardner

An Orion book

Copyright © The Erle Stanley Gardner Trust 1949

The right of Erle Stanley Gardner to be identified as the author of this work has been asserted in accordance with the Copyright, Designs and Patents Act 1988.

This edition published by
The Orion Publishing Group Ltd
Orion House
5 Upper St Martin's Lane
London WC2H 9EA

An Hachette UK company
A CIP catalogue record for this book is available from the British Library

ISBN 978 1 4719 0896 5

www.orionbooks.co.uk

CHAPTER ONE

Pick-Up in Reverse

SHE WAS A SMALL, well-formed package of dynamite. A pocket edition Venus—high-breasted, thin-waisted, smooth-hipped—with large brown eyes and taffy-colored hair. She couldn't weigh much over a hundred pounds, but she was perfect, and she was buzzing like an angry hornet.

The suave individual who ran the cocktail lounge was trying to explain.

A girl as perfect as she was, and small, could write her own ticket. The manufacturers of the automobiles that used to be called "medium priced" would have worshiped her as a photographic model. She'd have made an airline stewardess whose large brown eyes would have transferred the butterflies from a passenger's stomach to his heart.

Those eyes were blazing now. She said, "What do you think I am, a streetwalker?"

"It isn't that," the manager of the cocktail lounge assured her. "It's a policy, a rule, a law. Unescorted women are simply not allowed in here."

"You make me sick!" she said. "I've heard that unescorted-woman business until I am absolutely nauseated."

He had been walking as he talked, his hand placed with deferential gallantry on her arm, and now she was in the hotel lobby, safely removed from the confines of the cocktail lounge. The manager didn't have to take any more, and he didn't. He merely bowed, smiled, turned and got out of there, fast.

She stood for a moment in the hotel lobby, undecided and angry.

I had looked up over the top of my paper at the sound of voices. Her roving, angry eyes shifted in my direction.

I started to return to my newspaper, but I wasn't in time. Her eyes caught mine and held them for a long moment. Then she turned away.

Her face became thoughtful.

I folded my newspaper.

She sank into one of the chairs across from me, and, knowing she was about to make a detailed appraisal, I started to study the folded section of the newspaper intently until I felt the big brown eyes had seen all there was to see. Then I put the paper down. She hastily averted her glance and crossed her knee.

I made what appraisal the circumstances permitted.

All of a sudden she switched her eyes to mine, tilted up her chin and smiled. It was a nice smile that showed teeth.

"Hello, escort," she said.

"Hello," I replied, and grinned.

She said, "Frankly, I was debating whether to drop a handkerchief or get up and leave my purse in the chair, or ask you if you had the time. I rejected them all. I don't like beating around the bush."

I said, "So you want in the cocktail lounge?"

"Yes."

"Why?"

"Perhaps I want a drink."

"Perhaps," I said.

"Perhaps I like your looks."

"How nice."

She opened her purse, took out a twenty-dollar bill and said, "Naturally, I'd expect to finance the expedition."

"Will it be that expensive?"

"I don't know."

I said, "We'll talk about that later." I got up and offered her my arm.

She said, "Will this be difficult?"

"I don't think so."

We went back to the cocktail lounge. The manager was waiting right behind the door.

I said, "What's the idea of telling my sister she can't come in here?"

"I'm sorry," he said. "It's a custom, a rule, and a law. Unescorted women are not allowed."

"I'm sorry," I said. "I didn't know. I asked her to meet me here."

He bowed frigidly and escorted us to a table. Then he went over and said something to the bartender.

A waiter came and took our orders.

"Dry Martini," she said.

"The same," I told him.

The waiter bowed and withdrew.

She looked across the table at me and said, "You're nice."

I said, "I may prey on women. Your body may be found all cut up in a vacant lot tomorrow morning. You shouldn't pick up strangers."

"I know," she said. "My mother told me."

She was silent for a few seconds, then said, "I tried to get into an auto camp, and they told me they didn't cater to unescorted women."

I didn't say anything.

"It is," she observed, "practically impossible for a woman to be guilty of immorality *without* an escort."

"You shouldn't have much trouble finding an escort," I told her.

"I didn't," she said, and then added hastily, "but I didn't want to do it that way. You're nice. What's your name?"

"Lam," I said. "Donald Lam."

"I'm Lucille Hart. Since we're brother and sister, we'd better dispense with formality."

The waiter returned and put two drinks down on the table. He also deposited a check and stood waiting.

She pushed the twenty-dollar bill at me under the table. I paid no attention to it but took my billfold from my coat pocket and put out two one-dollar bills. The waiter promptly reached into his pocket and took out two twenty-five cent pieces. I picked up one. The waiter picked up the other.

Lucille lifted her glass, looked at me and said, "Here's to crime."

I extended my glass toward hers, then sipped it.

The drink consisted of sixty percent ice water with perhaps a teaspoonful of gin, a few drops of dry Vermouth, and an olive.

3

Lucille put the drink down, winked at me, made a little face and said, "I guess they don't want us here."

"Apparently not," I said.

"In any event, they don't want us to become intoxicated."

"That's right."

I sat back and sipped the cocktail, looking over the interior of the cocktail lounge casually, trying to find out why it was she had been so anxious to get into the place, yet not really caring.

It was Saturday afternoon. I had tailed the man I was shadowing to this hotel and had been waiting for the night shift to come on, to see if I could pick up more information, but that could wait. I had all night.

They were doing a fair business. A heavy-set, beefy man in the late fifties was having the time of his life, putting his personality across with a platinum blonde in the dubious twenties and hard as a diamond. She hadn't quite made up her mind what to do about him yet, and, while she was smiling at his sallies, her eyes were hard with appraisal.

A foursome was proceeding to wade through the preliminaries of a Saturday night drunk. A young chap with long hair and soulful eyes was pouring forth his political views in an impassioned oration to a good-looking chick who had evidently heard it all before but who admired him enough to keep on listening. A middle-aged man and his wife were making an effort to relieve the monotony of matrimony by "dining out" on Saturday night. Their attempt to be interested in each other was a conscious effort which slipped back occasionally into routine boredom, only to be rescued by a sudden burst of conscious animation.

Then I saw the couple she was interested in.

The man was thirty-two or thirty-three, with an air of grave responsibility about him. His mouth showed that he was accustomed to making decisions. His manner had that certain deferential insistence which characterizes the salesman, and his appearance was worried. He might have been intent upon sedition rather than seduction, from the gravely apprehensive aura with which he surrounded himself.

The girl was five or six years younger, red-headed, gray-eyed, and thoughtful. She wasn't too good-looking, but there was character about her face and her manner was that of one who has decided to undergo a critical operation. There was affection in her eyes as she looked at the man, but it was the quiet affection of respect. There wasn't any passion about it.

I took two more sips of the pallid ice water in the cocktail glass. It was so weak I could taste the flavor of the olive rather than that of the gin. I decided that it was the woman who interested Lucille.

I pushed the cocktail glass back across the table.

"And I can't go mine," Lucille said. "It's nauseating."

The waiter hovered over us and coughed significantly.

"Two more Martinis," I said. "We were interested, talking, and let these get a little warm. I can't stand a warm Martini."

"Yes, sir," he said, picking up the glasses.

"Why do you do that, Donald?" she asked.

"What?"

"Give them a chance to rub it in."

"I don't know," I said. "I guess I'm built that way."

She said abruptly, "Would you have tried to pick me up and be my escort if I hadn't made the break?"

"I don't know. Probably not."

"You're wondering why I wanted to come in here, aren't you?"

"No."

"What?" she asked, startled. "Of course you are."

I said, "It's the redhead, isn't it? The one with the gray eyes?"

She looked at me with just the faintest suggestion of a scowl. Her eyes were big. "Say, who *are* you?" she asked suspiciously.

"Oh, forget it," I said. "I'm sorry I said anything."

"Say, what kind of a frame-up is this?" she demanded.

"Skip it," I told her.

The waiter brought two more Martinis, together with a check. I pulled out two dollar bills from my pocket. He scooped up the two dollars and put down two quarters. I took a dime and two pennies from my pocket, put the assortment on the table and picked up the two quarters.

As the waiter glowered at the twelve cents, I said, "Eat your olive before the water gets to it, Lucille."

5

The waiter scooped up the money, walked over and said something to the manager.

The manager came over to the table. "Everything all right?" he asked.

"Everything's fine," I said. "Did you drive down, Lucille?"

"Yes," she said.

"Then you shouldn't drink more than ten or fifteen of these cocktails."

She smiled and we drank.

The manager waited for me to say something after I'd tasted the cocktail. I smacked my lips, put it down and said, "Delicious!"

He reluctantly moved away.

"Come on," Lucille said. "Come through with the low-down."

I said, "You wouldn't believe me if I told you."

"Don't be coy. What's the answer?"

I took the billfold from my pocket, took out one of my business cards and handed it to her.

She read it: "Cool & Lam, Private Detectives. Presented by Donald Lam."

She started to get to her feet.

"Take it easy," I said. "It's purely coincidental."

"What is?"

I said, "It's Saturday afternoon. I'd finished the last job I was working on and sat down to read the racing news before I went out to dinner. I'm unmarried, unattached, and there's nothing romantic about my job. It's a business. I've never seen you before, and as far as I know, I don't think we have a client that has either. No one's paying me for this and I'm not sending in any report on you. You wanted an escort and you're the one who picked a detective. I didn't even give you the eye."

"You looked—at my legs."

"Who wouldn't?"

"Who's this Cool?" she asked.

"Bertha Cool," I said.

"A woman partner?" she asked.

"That's right."

"Oh," she said, elevating her eyebrows, "it's like that, eh?"

6

"Not like that," I explained. "Bertha Cool is middle-aged, weighs a hundred and sixty-five pounds, has a broad beam, a bulldog jaw, little glittering, greedy eyes, and is just as hard and tough and difficult to handle as a roll of barbed wire.

"She was running the business several years ago, when I was up against it for almost any kind of a job. I've had legal training, and Bertha hired me and worked the hell out of me. Later on I graduated into a full partnership."

"What kind of work do you do?"

I said, "Bertha Cool used to do divorce work, automobile accident stuff, and in addition to that a lot of little things that most of the agencies wouldn't bother with. Now I haven't any way of describing exactly what we do. I'm an opportunist and we've been lucky."

"You mean you've made money?" she asked.

"Yes. That's only part of it. We sharp-shoot."

"What kind of cases?"

"All kinds."

She said, "You're a rotten detective."

I said, "You should know Bertha Cool. You have a lot in common."

"I like that!" she flared. "Broad of beam—bulldog jaw—!"

"Mentally," I said. "When it comes to judging my qualifications as a detective."

She said, "You think I'm interested in the redhead with the gray eyes?"

"Yes."

Her laugh was scornful. "Let's get out of this dump. The only reason I wanted to come in here was because they told me I couldn't. If you want to know it, I've had a heartbreak and had decided to get drunk. The man I was carrying the torch for turned out to be a rat, and the only other man I knew well enough to go out and get cockeyed with would have felt I was trying to make him a second choice. I didn't want him to do that because if I can wait a few weeks he'll start coming around of his own accord and then I'm going to give him a break. I've been a little fool and the taste of my folly is as bitter in my mouth as a chicken liver when the gall bladder has been ruptured by a poor cook.

"The trouble with you detectives is that you have to see murder cases lurking behind every lamp post. When I found I had to have an escort, I thought you looked good. Now you bore me."

"So you're going out and get tight alone?" I asked.

"You're damn right. And as far as you're concerned—No, wait a minute, guess I'll have to vamp you to make up for this outburst. Apparently I can't get tight without an escort. I—come on, let's get out of this dump."

We got up and started for the street door.

"Everything all right?" the manager asked suavely.

"Fine," I assured him. "Two of the best olives I've ever tasted."

"Come back any time you want more of the same," he said.

"I might surprise you," I told him.

We walked past the table where the salesman was talking to the girl with the gray eyes. She gave us a flicker of disinterested appraisal, then suddenly looked at me—hard. The grave man kept on talking.

Lucille didn't show the faintest interest as she swept by.

Out on the street I said, "Well, Lucille, have a good time."

She said impulsively, "Let's go to a place where we can get a real drink. My mouth tastes like a cocktail shaker smells the next morning."

I hesitated.

She put her hand on my arm, said, "It's my party, you know."

"Will you tell me all about your broken romance?"

"Every word," she said. "I'll withhold nothing. I'll be like the girl in the *Arabian Nights* who told stories to keep her lord and master amused. I lost my temper and shot off my big mouth about you being a lousy detective and now your professional pride is insulted. But I need an escort and if I let you go, the other one may be terrible. You're nice as an individual. It's only your detective ability that has a slight odor. So I'll tell you all about my shattered romance and broken heart. Do you want the spicy, intimate version of my romantic entanglement, or would you prefer the psychological reaction motif?"

"The psychological reaction motif," I said.

"Good heavens, you *are* different!" she exclaimed.

"I'm not. You are. Remember, it's entertainment. I was going to a movie but this should be more fun."

"More romantic," she promised. "You see, *I* won't have to submit the script to the Breen office. The movies would."

We went a block and a half to another cocktail bar. These cocktails had liquor in them. Lucille drew on her imagination for a story of lurid romance. The details didn't always jibe here and there, but she took great pains to let me know that, when she went, she went all the way.

She was a nice girl with a good figure, swell eyes, and after the second cocktail I could see she had a plan.

We went to dinner. Lucille wanted more cocktails. Then she wanted Scotch and soda.

She went to the powder room and I saw her manage to slip the waiter a bill and a few words.

I called the waiter over to the table. "What did the girl want?" I asked.

He looked innocent. "Nothing," he said.

"She gave you five dollars," I told him. "For what?"

He coughed apologetically.

I took out my wallet and pulled out a ten-dollar bill.

He grinned and said, "Whenever she ordered Scotch and soda, I was to bring her plain pale ginger ale."

I handed him the ten and said, "Double it."

"You mean you want pale ginger ale too?"

"Yes."

"The prices will have to be those of Scotch and sodas," he warned.

"Certainly," I told him.

We finished dinner and consumed pale ginger ale. She drank hers and pretended to get a little tipsy, watching me like a hawk when she thought I wasn't looking.

I drank my pale ginger ale and pretended to get a little tipsy, watching her when I knew damn well she wasn't looking.

It was a Saturday night. While this was more expensive than a movie, it had more suspense, and, as she had so aptly pointed out, the script hadn't been passed on by the Breen office.

When the floor show started, she started for the rest room,

detoured, glided out of the door and was gone for twenty minutes.

When she came back, she said, "Miss me? I've been ill. I get that way when I try to pour it in too fast."

"Sure I missed you," I assured her, "but there was a strip-tease on. I liked it. She was beautiful."

"Oh, so you fall for the strip-tease numbers."

"Yes."

"The strip or the tease?"

"I guess it's the tease, but I wouldn't like to be teased if they didn't strip."

"However, I suppose you *could* stand the strip if they didn't tease."

I pondered that. "Frankly, I hadn't given the matter that much consideration."

"You would if you were a woman," she said. "Let's have some more dizzy water. I'm getting sober. I won't drink so fast now."

CHAPTER TWO

The Vanishing Venus

LUCILLE HART WAS SMILING AT ME with her best imitation of loose-lipped friendliness.

"I like," she said.

"I like *you*."

She put her hand over mine. "Have a Hart," she said.

"Yes, Miss Hart," I told her.

She giggled. "Know what?"

"What?"

"I've got to go home."

"I'll take you."

"I've got my sister's car. I was s'posed to deliver it by eight o'clock. I guess it's past that now, isn't it?"

"Nine-five."

"Ouch! I didn't know it was so late. Time flies, doesn't it?"

"That's right."

"Look," she said, "you're more sober than I am, aren't you?"

I regarded her owlishly and said, "Fifty-fifty."

She giggled again. "Look, you drive the car. What we do, we drive to my sister's house and then my brother-in-law picks up the car and drives us back."

"Is your brother-in-law going to like me?"

She made a raspberry with her lips.

"What's his name?"

"Dover Fulton."

"Meaning he won't like me?"

"Probably not. He likes *him*. You will, won't you?"

"What?"

"Drive."

11

"Okay," I said. "Where do they live?"

"San Robles."

"That's way out," I told her.

"Not so far. Listen, Donald, you going to let me pay the check?"

"Nope. It's my party."

"It's mine."

"Mine," I said.

I summoned the waiter and paid the check. We walked a block to a parking lot and she gave me the ticket. I walked down with the attendant when he went to get the car and looked at the certificate of registration fastened to the post of the steering wheel. It showed the car was registered in the name of Dover Fulton, and the address was 6285 Orange Avenue, San Robles.

So far everything checked. That bothered me. In keeping with the picture, that car should have been as hot as a firecracker.

We eased the car out of the parking lot, and I opened the door for Lucille to get in.

I didn't like it. I wanted a witness. I stopped at a service station and told the attendant I thought we needed air in the rear tires. I walked around behind the car with him, pushed two dollars into his hand, and said in a loud voice, "Go ahead and drive, Lucille. Since you say it's your sister's car, I'd much prefer to have you drive it."

She shook her head, her chin drooped forward on her chest. "You're all right. You aren't too drunk. You can drive."

"Sure I'm a'righ'. But I ain't gonna."

I didn't buy any gas. The attendant would remember me and remember the argument. I winked at him and said, "Okay, I'll drive if you insist, but I'm doing it under protest."

"It's all right."

"This is your brother-in-law's car?"

"My sister's car," she said. "Dover said it hadda be registered in his name. He's a kind has to be big shot. Otherwise Dover won't play. M' sister's money paid for it—Dover Fulton!" she said, and her voice had a note of disgust.

The attendant washed off the windshield, puttered around

12

the headlights. I snapped on the gas gauge, looked at it, smiled, shook my head, and we went away from there.

I saw Lucille looking me over, studying me carefully.

"You're not tight, are you?"

I said, "Whenever I get my hands on the steering wheel of an automobile I sober up."

"But you can feel the stuff sloshing around inside of you, can't you?"

"Sure."

"That's a' right, then," she said, and settled down with her head on my shoulder.

We went out the freeway and hit the Valley Boulevard. "Slow down," Lucille said abruptly.

"Why?"

"I'm lonesome."

I slowed down.

She crawled up against me, her hands clinging to my arm. She said, "Pull off to the side of the road and kiss me."

I pulled off to the side of the road and kissed her. It was quite a kiss.

Ahead, on the right, I saw the neon sign, *Kozy Dell Slumber Court,* and down underneath it a sign that said, *Vacancy.*

"Drive on slow," she said.

I drove on.

"Stop the car," she commanded. "Right here."

"What's the matter?"

"I don't feel well. I'm— Oh, Donald, I'm *so* lonesome, and I'm afraid I'm going to have a horrible hangover tomorrow. Drive off the road," she said. "Here, drive in here."

"That's an auto court."

"Well?" she asked.

I said, "I just wondered."

"I've got to get off the road. They'll have a rest room here," she said.

I turned the car in to the auto court.

"Go find where the women's rest room is," she said.

I went into the office. The woman who ran the place looked me over with a cold, fishy eye and told me they didn't have rest rooms. They had baths in the cabins. She had a single. Did I want that?

"I'll go find out," I told her.

Her eyes were contemptuous.

I went back to the car and said, "No rest rooms, honey. All the bathrooms are in the cottages. They have one cottage left."

"Okay," she said, heaving herself up out of the car. "Take me into the cottage."

I went back and registered as Mr. and Mrs. Dover Fulton. I gave the address as 6285 Orange Avenue, San Robles, and put down the license number of the car—45S531.

The woman who ran the place showed me where the cabin was. Lucille was slumped down in the seat.

I got the key to the place—cabin number eleven. The woman from the office wished me an acid good night and went back to the office. I helped Lucille into the cabin. She went to the bathroom and made noises of being ill. She came out and lay on the bed.

I sat on the edge of the bed, looking down at her.

"Turn out the lights," she said, "they hurt my eyes."

I turned out the lights. She lit a cigarette.

She said, "I guess I need air."

"I'll open the door."

"No, I want to go outside."

"I'll go with you."

"No, you stay here," she said. "I'm not feeling well. I'm going to be unglamorous. Tell me, Donald, how are we registered?"

"How do you think?"

"I want to know."

"As husband and wife," I said. "You don't think we'd have got the cabin otherwise, do you?"

"You think I'm terrible, don't you?"

"No, I think you're nice."

She said, "Wait here, Donald. I've got some Kleenex in the car. Where's the key?"

I gave her the key. "The car doors are locked, honey."

She said, "I'm glad I was sick. Now I'll feel better in the morning. How do you feel?"

"Swell."

She said, "We shouldn't do this."

"Do what?"

"Stay here."

14

I said, "We're not *really* staying here. Don't you remember, we're taking the car back to your sister. Your brother-in-law is going to drive me back. You only stopped in here because you needed the bathroom."

"Oh," she said, and there was a half twinkle in her eyes. She went out.

I went to the window, pulled up the shade, and sat where I could watch the car.

Nothing happened. She didn't go near the car. She walked out around the houses, getting a breath of fresh air.

Ten minutes later she hadn't returned.

After twenty minutes I went out to look for her. The auto court was on the outskirts. There was quite a bit of vacant property around. The graveled driveway showed as a red path in the light of the neon sign at the front. Cars were whizzing by with considerable regularity on the highway.

I crunched gravel around the auto court. The cabins were, for the most part, dark and silent. There was a party in one of the front cabins where a foursome was making a little whoopee, with occasional bits of giggling laughter. A man's voice told a story which was followed by a burst of merriment.

A married couple, with an Iowa license plate on the car, were having a quarrel in one of the middle cottages. I didn't get all the words. It was something about the way the man was treating his stepdaughter. The woman was talking in a high-pitched, rapid monotone, apparently afraid that something would happen before she had a chance to say all that she wanted to say. In the few seconds that it took me to walk past the place, I heard enough to gather that the man had never appreciated Rose, that he had been unkind to her from the first and made her feel that she wasn't wanted; that Rose was sensitive and shy; and that it was only natural for any girl to resent that kind of treatment; that he owed Rose an apology and that he didn't amount to much anyway; that he was all wrapped up in himself and was inclined to nag and wasn't at all like her first husband; Rose had always loved her father *so* much and respected him because he had been so much of a gentleman and so courteous and considerate; whereas, under the circumstances, you couldn't blame her for being disillusioned and . . .

15

I moved on out of earshot.

There was no sign of Lucille Hart anywhere around the auto court. In one of the cabins a portable radio was turned up loud.

I tried the car. The doors were locked.

I walked around the back part of the houses but I couldn't see anything of Lucille. She might have been lying down somewhere on the ground, perhaps putting on the second scene in her act of being drunk. I made a wide circle through the vacant lots.

No Lucille.

When I was starting back, I heard a sound that could have been the backfire of a motor.

I waited and listened. There were two more sounds that *could* have been caused by a truck backfiring; but I couldn't see any truck at the moment.

I went back to the cabin I had rented and looked it over. Lucille had left a package of cigarettes and a book of matches. The match book carried the ad of the *Cabanita Night Club*. I put it in my pocket. I picked up the package of cigarettes. It was two-thirds full. The Cellophane wrapper had been torn off the top of the package and a folded piece of heavy white paper thrust down between the Cellophane and the package.

I unfolded the paper.

It was part of a menu. On the reverse side was written in pencil: *Kozy Dell Slumber Court—Valley Boulevard.*

There was nothing else.

I put the cigarettes, the paper, and the matches in my pocket. I looked around and couldn't see anything else.

I carefully polished all fingerprints off the doorknobs and off of anything I had touched. I didn't bother the bathroom. Only Lucille's fingerprints were in there. I *might* want them.

I wiped all fingerprints off the key, put it on the inside of the door, covered the doorknob with my handkerchief and pulled the door shut. I couldn't get my fingerprints off the steering wheel of the automobile because the car doors were locked.

The radio in the nearby cabin was still blaring.

I detoured the office and walked to the highway. I didn't try to hitchhike. I kept as far as I could to the side of the road so that the headlights of approaching automobiles wouldn't show me clearly.

I came to a little roadside restaurant that was still open.

There was a telephone booth. I dropped a nickel and dialed the number of Bertha Cool's apartment.

It took a couple of minutes before Bertha answered. I could see she didn't like the idea of being disturbed.

"Well," she snapped, "what is it?"

I said, "It's Donald, Bertha. I want you to pick me up."

"Well, I'll be a dirty name!" Bertha said. "Of all the crust! So you want to be picked up, do you? You—"

I said, "It may be important. I'm out on the Valley Boulevard in a small roadside restaurant. I don't want to be seen here. I'm going out and wait in front. Get out here just as fast as you can."

"The hell with that stuff!" Bertha said. "Get a taxicab!"

"If I get a taxicab to come out here," I said, "the driver will remember it and you'll see my name in the papers."

"Get your name in the papers and see who gives a damn!" Bertha screamed into the telephone.

I said, "It will have a bad effect on the reputation of the agency."

"The hell with reputation! What's reputation? That's just what a lot of fools say about you. It—"

"And will cause us to lose money," I said.

Bertha stopped screaming as fast as though I had put my hand over her mouth. She waited three or four seconds without saying anything. I knew she was there because I could hear her heavy breathing over the phone. Her indignation had used up the reserve oxygen in her system and she sounded as though she'd been running upstairs.

"Well?" I asked.

"Okay, lover," she said. "What's the address?"

The spluttering began all over again when I gave it to her so I hung up.

CHAPTER THREE

Very Smart or Very Dumb

IT WAS A GOOD THIRTY MINUTES before Bertha Cool showed up and she was mad enough to have bitten her initials on an iron fence rail.

She slammed the car to a stop, and I walked around behind, came up on the right-hand side, opened the door, got in beside her and sat down.

Bertha had her chin pushed forward like the prow of a battleship. Her little beady eyes were glittering angrily.

"What the hell have you been into now?" she asked.

"I don't know."

"Well, this is a fine time to start finding out."

"Isn't it?"

She jerked the car through the gears, drove savagely to the first intersection, watched her opportunity, and swung the car in a U turn that wore rubber off the protesting tires.

"Nice weather we're having for this time of year," I said.

"You go to the devil!" she told me.

We drove on in silence.

After a while her curiosity got the upper hand. "Well," she said, "Tell me about it. What is it all about?"

I said, "Let's go back to the beginning. Do you remember this afternoon when I was working on a shadow job?"

"That's right," she said. "Someone wanted us to find out the name and identity of a man who was selling some sort of stock. Have any trouble?"

"Not a bit," I said. "It was almost a setup. I picked this man up exactly where I was supposed to find him and followed him without the least bit of difficulty. He went directly to the Westchester Arms Hotel, walked up to the desk and

18

got his key. I made discreet inquiries and found out that he was Thomas Durham and that he had been registered in the hotel for the last two days. No one seemed to know exactly what he did.

"There was a change of shifts due at six o'clock and I thought I'd wait for the new shift to come on and see if I could get any more information. I only had a little over half an hour or so to wait."

"Damn it," Bertha said, "don't tell me all the sordid details. My God, I've worn out my fanny sitting around hotel lobbies, waiting for the night clerk to come on. If you're in a jam, there's a girl mixed up in it someplace. Who is she?"

"I don't know for sure," I said.

"Another damn redhead, I presume. You can't ever seem to leave them alone."

"This one's a molasses taffy, smooth-as-silk—"

"My God," Bertha said, "If I ever go in business with another partner, I'll get one past sixty who—"

"That won't buy you anything, Bertha," I told her. "The boys at sixty are peculiarly susceptible. A good-looking girl would tie them in knots and—"

"Past seventy," Bertha amended.

"That wouldn't do you any good, either. A clever baby would remind them of their childhood sweethearts. You'll have to get past eighty, and by that time their eyesight will be bad."

"That's the worst of it!" Bertha said angrily. "Some damn woman is always upsetting the apple cart. Well, tell me about this broad. What did she do?"

I said, "I keep going back to this Tom Durham case because I'm not entirely certain that my waiting in that hotel was purely the result of an accident."

"What do you mean, an accident?" Bertha said, and then added parenthetically, "Damn that guy, if he doesn't get his headlights down. Here, you mug, take *that* and *that* and *that!*"

Bertha angrily clicked the foot switch which sent the lights on the agency automobile bouncing up and down.

The other driver never did lower his lights, and Bertha Cool rolled down the left-hand window. As he swept on past, she shouted epithets at the top of her lungs, then rolled the window back up. "What are you beating around the bush for?" she asked.

I said, "I was sitting in this hotel when a girl who said her name was Lucille Hart showed up. She pretended to have been driving an automobile which she said belonged to her sister, but which was registered in the name of her brother-in-law, apparently a chap who wants to be important in the family."

"Husbands always want to be important," Bertha said. "What happened?"

"When we walked out of the last joint, where we'd had drinks and dinner, the car very fortuitously was parked only a block away."

Bertha grunted.

"And shortly before that she'd gone by-by and been out of the picture for twenty minutes."

I saw Bertha was getting ready to explode so I hurried on. "One thing led to another and—"

"My God," Bertha told me, "I know the facts of life. You don't start making women in hotel lobbies and restaurants. Well, damn it, yes, that's where you *start*, but the start's always the same. So's the finish, as far as that's concerned. Tell me what the hell happened in the middle."

I said, "We went out along this road. I was going home with her and then her brother-in-law was going to take us back to town, then drive the car back again."

"Humph!" Bertha snorted.

I said, "She had been drinking a lot of ginger ale. She said she was ill and wanted to find a rest room. She told me to stop the car because she couldn't go any farther. It was right near an auto court."

Bertha slowed the car long enough to look at me pityingly. "For God's sake," she said, "what does a girl have to do with you? Hit you over the head with something?"

I said, "I got a cabin and by that time she thought she needed air. She walked out and I never saw her again."

Bertha said, *"You're* the one that needed the air! She gave it to you. I've told you a dozen times, Donald, that women go nuts over you, but you can't keep turning them down the way you do. You get some jane all worked up and then wind up being a perfect little gentleman. My God, I'll bet she was

20

sore at you. It's a wonder she didn't take a wrench out of the car and club you over the head. Why didn't you take the car— or did she take it?''

I said, "It was all locked up. The last I saw of her, she had the keys. I have a very strong suspicion she may have telephoned the police, stating that the car was stolen and asking them to be on the lookout for it. I'm not at all certain but what I was roped in as a fall guy for something, and it bothers me.''

"Well,'' Bertha said, "we're trying to run a detective agency. God knows, it's bad enough when I have to go around at night playing taxicab for you. I can't lose sleep listening to all your wenching troubles, and I can't go along to hold the script and read your lines for you. Next time take your own car, or carry a walkie-talkie so that when she makes you walk home, you can at least call a taxicab.''

I said, "I didn't think I wanted a taxicab. I didn't think it was advisable for me to be seen out there. Just as I was ready to leave the auto court, I heard a sound very much like the backfiring of a truck.''

"How's that?'' Bertha asked, suddenly rigid with attention.

"Just like the sound of a truck backfiring,'' I said, "only there wasn't any truck.''

Bertha slowed the car and looked me over.

I said, "I think the place to start is back at that Tom Durham case. The person who contacted the agency on that case talked with you. Tell me about it.''

Bertha said, "She was a girl by the name of Bushnell, pretty easy on the eyes. I remember thinking at the time that it was a Godsend I got her. If she'd gone to you, she'd have vamped you into taking the case without any retainer and you'd have turned the office upside down. As it was, I collected two hundred bucks in advance.''

"What did she want?''

"She said that her aunt, the only living relative, and a little bit indisposed at present on account of an automobile accident, had been seeing quite a bit of a relatively young man lately. She had an idea the man might be a slicker who was trying to talk dear auntie out of some money. This Bushnell girl had questioned the maid, trying to find out who the young man was. The aunt got in a huff, said she was fully capable of handling her own business, and didn't need her niece's interfering. The niece's pretty much worked up about it. She wanted the agency to find out all about the man. She wanted something that would cramp his style.''

"Do you think she was afraid he might have dishonorable intentions?"

Bertha snorted. "She paid two hundred bucks. Do you think any dame would part with two hundred smackers to keep a guy from making passes? She's afraid the thing may get serious. Suppose he should propose matrimony? The aunt's rich and the niece is the sole heir. That's the two-hundred-dollar angle, lover.''

I said, "There's just a chance the whole thing was a plant. Did she want me to work on the case personally?"

"I guess perhaps she did," Bertha said, "but don't be so damn conceited. Everyone in the world isn't thinking about you.''

I didn't say anything, and Bertha went on after a minute: "She told me how important it was that the thing be handled so skillfully that the man would have no idea he was being shadowed or that anyone was checking up on him. In case he got wise, he'd report back to the aunt and then there would be the devil to pay. If the aunt thought the niece had hired private detectives, there'd be a real estrangement.''

"Meaning the niece wouldn't inherit the aunt's money under a will?"

Bertha said, "When I say an estrangement, what do you think I'm talking about? Of course it'd mean the loss of an inheritance. I told her it would be as smooth as a cake of wet soap on the bathroom floor. I guaranteed no one would know there was a thing in the wind.''

"You didn't warn me to be *that* careful," I said.

"Why should I? You're supposed to know your way around. Anyhow, she paid in advance.''

"I just wanted to get it straight," I said.

"Well, you've got it straight now.''

"And so you told her I'd take over the case?''

"That's right. I told her I'd have you handle it personally; that it would cost more money that way, but that you were the best operator in the city.''

Bertha waited a few minutes, apparently thinking that over,

then frowned, and said, "When you come right down to it, something is screwy at that. This Bushnell babe wasn't at all bad looking."

"How old?"

"Right around twenty-three."

"What's her first name?"

"Claire."

"Where does she live?"

Bertha said angrily, "I'm not a card index. Get me up in the middle of the night to come and bring you back from your philandering and expect me to give you the address of every client that ever came to the office."

I didn't say anything, and Bertha fought it out for a while in silence, then she went on, as though there had been no digression on her part: "With a babe like that, who knew that I had a young, brainy partner to handle the case, the normal reaction would have been for her to have gone to him to make the business arrangements, but this chick did nothing of the sort. She said she had unlimited confidence in my ability, that she knew all about our reputation, and she pulled out a checkbook. She seemed only sort of half interested— Now, when you come right down to it, that's funny on the face of it."

"It's a little screwy on the face of it, even if you don't come down to anything," I said. "Specifically, how much did the girl tell you about her family?"

Bertha said, "Look, Donald, that's where you and I differ. You always want to go into all the insignificant details that don't make a bit of difference in the case."

"In other words," I said, "she didn't really tell you anything about her aunt."

"I got her aunt's address," Bertha said. "She told me this personable slicker had an appointment with the old gal for four o'clock in the afternoon."

"But she didn't tell you much about the aunt's affairs, her history, her preferences? You didn't ask about her love history?"

"Damn it," Bertha said, "she signed her name on the bottom of a check for two hundred bucks! Don't talk to me about what I should have done."

"I won't," I said. "I just wanted to do a little thinking."

23

"I see," Bertha said sarcastically. "I suppose now you're going to bed and dream of some little babe who had to draw you a diagram. My God, you were driving her home, way out in the suburbs! Then her brother-in-law was going to drive you back! How nice! How cozy! You went driving along with both hands on the wheel. I suppose you were talking about books, or astronomy, or some of the good shows you'd seen lately, and the poor thing finally had to take that auto court and—"

"She did, for a fact," I interrupted.

"Well, let that be a lesson to you."

I said, "When you're driving through town, go along Seventh Street. I want to stop at the Westchester Arms Hotel. I think I'll begin to give Mr. Thomas Durham a little highly specialized attention."

"You be damn careful you don't let the cat out of the bag," Bertha said. "The whole thing sounds to me as though you'd spilled the beans. If Durham knew he was being followed—"

"If he knew I was following him," I said, "he's a mind reader and a veteran crook. I did a pretty smooth job."

Bertha snorted. "He dragged out his red herring within ten minutes of the time you trailed him to the hotel."

"Not ten—twenty."

"Okay, twenty. Just time enough for him to get on the phone, call some frail that he knew had plenty of this and that and these and those, and turn her loose on you. I tell you, the guy could take one look at you and tell you'd be a push-over for a bit of fluff—and then she had to stop the car in front of an auto court and tell you she was feeling ill! My God!"

I didn't say anything. There was nothing to say.

Bertha drove down Seventh Street, pulled the car to a stop in front of the Westchester Arms Hotel.

"Don't stay right here," I said. "Drive on half a block down the street and park. I'll catch you when I'm ready."

"The hell you will!" Bertha said angrily. "I'm going home and get some shut-eye. This is your job. I went out and picked you up, when you couldn't get a taxi, but all you have to do here is step out and grab yourself a cab whenever you're ready to go. And be sure you itemize it on the expense account so I can collect it from the client as necessary traveling expense.''

I closed the door. Bertha slammed the car in gear and took off, leaving behind her a trail of exhaust gas.

I went into the Westchester Arms.

There were a few people around the lobby. I looked the place over and made certain Durham wasn't there. I looked in the cocktail lounge. He wasn't there. I went over to the house telephones and said, ''I'm looking for a man by the name of Jerome K. Durham from Massachusetts. Is he registered here?''

She waited long enough to thumb through some records, then said, ''No, he isn't here.''

''That's funny. Are you certain?''

''Yes.''

''Do you have any Durhams at all?'' I asked.

''Not at present,'' she said. ''There was a Thomas B. Durham staying here for a couple of days, but he checked out about an hour ago.''

''Thank you,'' I said. ''That's all I wanted to know,'' and hung up.

I started a quiet investigation with the bellboys and the doorman. Durham had checked out. He had a bag, a brief case, and a suitcase that had two little brass padlocks on it.

The bellboy had taken the baggage to the doorman. The doorman remembered it being there. He'd been busy getting some people loaded in taxicabs, and the three pieces of baggage had vanished by the time he'd turned around to see if their owner wanted a cab.

The doorman was certain Durham hadn't taken a cab. I asked if a private car could have picked him up. The doorman thought not. I asked where Durham could have gone and the doorman merely grinned and scratched his head.

The entrance to the cocktail lounge was within a few feet of the hotel entrance but I hardly thought the manager would appreciate being questioned.

Neither did I think he'd have welcomed Durham if he'd entered the place lugging a brief case, a bag, and a suitcase.

In other words, Tom Durham had disappeared without a trace.

He'd either been smarter than I thought he was or I'd been

even dumber than Bertha had thought I was. I'd have sworn he hadn't known I was following him to the hotel.

I looked at my watch. It was late, but there was one other possibility I could explore.

I went into the telephone booth, found a suburban directory, looked under San Robles, and ran down the pages until I found a Dover Fulton residing at 6285 Orange Avenue. Evidently, then, that much of the story had been true.

From a phone booth, I called the Fulton number. A few moments later the operator told me to deposit twenty cents for three minutes. After the dimes had trickled into the coin box, I heard a sleepy feminine voice at the other end of the line.

"I'm very sorry to disturb you at this late hour," I said, "but it's quite important that I get in touch with Mr. Dover Fulton. Is he there, please?"

"Why, no," the woman said, "he's not here right now. He's been detained in the city. I'm expecting him home almost any time."

"Could you take a message for him?" I asked.

"Yes."

"Is this Mrs. Fulton?"

"That's right."

"Then you'll pardon the question, Mrs. Fulton, but do you have a sister?"

"A sister?" she echoed.

"Yes."

"Why, no."

"A Miss Lucille Hart?" I answered. "Isn't she your sister?"

"I never heard of her. She's certainly not my sister. I tell you, I have no sister."

"I'm very sorry, then. There's been some mistake," I said, and hung up before she could ask for any explanation.

CHAPTER FOUR

Situation with Angles—
and Curves

THE MORNING PAPERS HAD THE STORY. They'd had to throw it in at the last minute. It was a routine double-suicide death pact, the way the papers sized it up, but it had "angles." If these developed, it could be a whale of a sex scandal. The papers wanted to be free to play it up or to drop it, whichever way the cat jumped.

Headlines said: SAN ROBLES BROKER IN DEATH PACT . . . KILLS FORMER SECRETARY, THEN TURNS GUN ON SELF . . . LOVE TRYST IN MOTOR COURT TERMINATES IN TRAGEDY.

The story followed the usual line, but emphasized that there were certain "peculiar circumstances" which police were investigating.

The dead woman was Mrs. Stanwick Carlton, who had been Dover Fulton's secretary for a period of years. She had left his employ about three years ago to marry Stanwick Carlton, a mining man, and had been living in Colorado.

Two weeks ago she had told her husband she wanted to "visit relatives in California." She had driven her own car on the trip, arriving ten days ago. During those ten days she had apparently been in company with Dover Fulton on several occasions. The proprietor of the Kozy Dell Slumber Court remembered that the same couple had rented a cabin there the week before under the name of Mr. and Mrs. Stanwick Carlton.

The thing which puzzled police, however, was that while the proprietor of the Kozy Dell had insisted the parties to the tragedy had arrived in the Colorado car, Dover Fulton's own automobile was found parked in the driveway of the auto court. The car was locked both inside and out, but the car

27

keys were not found on Dover's body. A woman's coin purse was on the floor of the car. It contained about ten dollars in small change and a "business card."

To further complicate matters, police had received a call just a few minutes before the time of the shooting, advising them that Dover Fulton's car had been stolen.

The time of the shooting was fixed as being between ten and ten-thirty in the evening. Several occupants of adjoining cabins had heard the sound of the shots but had thought they were caused by a car backfiring. The bodies were discovered when occupants of an adjoining cabin complained of the blaring radio next door.

One point which police were trying to clear up was why *three* shots had been fired. Apparently Fulton had killed his mistress with one shot through the back of the head. He had then turned the gun on himself, but two witnesses insisted there had been three shots, and after some considerable search, police found where the third bullet had entered a suitcase identified as belonging to Mrs. Carlton.

Stanwick Carlton, husband of the dead woman, had, as it turned out, arrived in the city by plane only an hour or so before the shooting. He had, he explained, "Felt something was wrong." He was "stunned" when located at a downtown hotel and advised of his wife's death. Dover Fulton, a prominent broker in San Robles, left a widow, Irene Fulton, and two children, one a girl four years old, one a boy of six. He had apparently been happily married and Mrs. Fulton "was at a loss to account for his actions," refusing at first to believe that he could possibly have been the person who had committed suicide. Not until she was confronted with the body did she believe what had happened.

Perhaps the strangest thing of all, however, was the fact that while Dover Fulton and Mrs. Carlton had registered as Mr. and Mrs. Stanwick Carlton and had been assigned cabin number three, it appeared a second couple had rented cabin number eleven in the name of Mr. and Mrs. Dover Fulton, and these people had given the license number of Dover Fulton's Buick sedan, which was found parked and locked in front of the cabin which had been assigned to them.

The woman who ran the place described the girl as being a beautiful blonde who appeared somehow to be intensely nervous; the man with her, according to the best recollection of the woman who managed the motor court, was of medium height and weight, with dark, wavy hair, and what the witness described as "expressive eyes." She said she had felt certain "there was something phony" about this second couple.

The newspaper account stated: *While apparently there can be no question but what the tragedy was a routine version of a death pact by people who had found themselves in love, but who were separated by marital entanglements, there are certain phases of the case which the police are investigating.*

The paper then went on to state that police had given Stanwick Carlton a severe grilling and were not entirely satisfied with his answers. They were investigating his movements after getting off the plane and going to the downtown hotel where he had registered.

The revolver from which the shots were fired was a .32 caliber revolver owned by Dover Fulton. Mrs. Fulton stated that her husband had been working almost every evening for the past ten days and that about ten days ago he had opened the drawer, taken out the small caliber revolver, and had been carrying it with him ever since. She was prostrated by shock.

The newspaper had photographs, pictures of Dover Fulton and of Minerva Carlton, pictures of the bodies, of the interior of the cabin. This last picture showed the sprawled figures, the open bathroom door, a double towel rack with two hand towels on the upper rod, a bath towel on the lower.

I folded the newspaper back into place and did a little floor pacing. No matter how I looked at it, the thing was completely cockeyed.

I rang Bertha on the telephone. "Seen the newspapers?" I asked.

"Don't be a sap!" Bertha yelled back at me. "I haven't seen anything. I'm trying to get some sleep—that is, I *was* trying."

"Take a look at the morning newspaper," I told her. "Late edition. Front page. Lower right-hand corner, with a continuation over on page three."

"What the hell's it all about?" Bertha asked.

"Something you should know," I said. "Call me back

when you've finished reading it. Be careful what you say over the phone. Good-bye.''

I could hear Bertha Cool's indignant sputtering in the telephone receiver as I dropped it back into its cradle on the bedside stand.

It was a full fifteen minutes before she called me.

Apparently she had made up her mind to put me in my place by not calling back, but when she read the news it was so disturbing she had forgotten her anger.

''Donald,'' she said, ''what's up?''

''I don't know.''

''You're the one who drove that second car—''

''Careful!'' I interrupted.

''And the name—well, it's in your handwriting?''

''That's right.''

''Why the hell did you sign *his* name?''

''Because I didn't want to sign mine.''

''You put down the right license number?'' Bertha asked after a second or two.

''Yes.''

''Why?''

''Reasons.''

''Did you think any questions were going to be asked later on?''

''I considered it as a possibility.''

''Well, you've got yourself in a nice mess,'' she said.

''You don't know the half of it,'' I told her. ''There's a chance that 'business card' in the coin purse was mine.''

''The hell it was!''

''I don't know. It could have been. Now you just keep completely out of it and tell me where I can find this Claire Bushnell. I want to talk with her.''

Bertha said, ''I wrote her address on a sheet of paper and stuck it under the corner of my blotter.''

''Any telephone number?''

''I don't know, lover. I don't think so. It came in too late to file, so I just took the data and left it all under the blotter on my desk. It was Saturday morning, and—''

''You cashed the check?'' I interrupted.

''Don't be a fool. Of course I cashed the check.''

''And it was good?''

30

"I had you go out there, didn't I? If the check hadn't been good I'd have had the little tart thrown in the can. Do you think it'd be smart to go to the police and tell them the whole story?"

"Not yet," I told her. "Later on perhaps. When we tell the police, I want to have something to work on."

"They'd have something to work on if we told them now, wouldn't they, lover?"

"Yes," I said. "Me!"

I slipped the receiver back on the cradle and went up to our office building. I signed the register the janitor kept in the elevator, and he took me up to our floor. I walked down to the offices where the frosted glass bore the legend *Cool & Lam,* and down in the lower left-hand corner: *Investigations. Walk in.*

I entered the office, swung past the door to my private office and on into Bertha's private office. Every piece of furniture was stamped with the individuality of Bertha Cool, from the creaky swivel chair back of her desk to the locked cash drawer over on the right-hand side—a drawer which locked with a separate key from any of the other drawers in her desk. It was always a safe bet that Bertha had everything under lock and key. She didn't trust the secretary, the janitors, or, for that matter, her partner.

I sat down in Bertha Cool's swivel chair.

The squeak seemed to have been built into it, a peculiar squeak which came just at one place whenever I moved.

I raised the blotter.

The memorandum was there.

I studied it. The address I wanted was 1624 Veronica Way.

Down underneath that, in Bertha's strong masculine handwriting, appeared the words, *Wants her aunt shadowed.*

Then Bertha had crossed out the *aunt* and inserted *stock salesman* in place of *aunt.*

Below that, Bertha had started doodling, evidently while she'd been talking with Claire Bushnell.

Bertha had started out writing *one hundred dollars* in words. Then she had made *$100.00* in figures. Then she had written *one hundred dollars* two or three times. Then she had crossed out all of the *one hundred dollars* and written *one hundred and fifty dollars.* Then she had written, *thinks* *stock salesman might be boy friend—thinks some cause for alarm here—something she is not telling us—wants Donald.*

Then Bertha had gone doodling again and this time the figure was $175.00, after which appeared the words, *Donald personally.*

Then there was more doodling, then the words, *Aunt's address, 226 Korreander Street.*

Then there were more doodlings of aimless lines, then in Bertha's handwriting: *Aunt's name, Amelia Jasper; man who is trying to swindle her: Age 35, well-dressed, thick-chested, double-breasted suits, mostly gray; dark-complected, long, straight features; nervous laugh, smokes cigarette with long, carved ivory holder, a chain smoker, smoking one right after the other; good profile until he laughs, then the mouth seems cruel; laughter harsh; profile beautiful.*

There were more doodlings, then Bertha, as an afterthought, had got the things I'd been trying to impress on her for the last three years, an accurate description of the man she wanted shadowed: *Height 5 feet 11; weight 195; dark hair, gray eyes.*

Once more Bertha had written *one hundred and seventy-five dollars,* then crossed it out, put in *two hundred dollars,* then more doodling, then: *Subject has appointment for four o'clock in afternoon. Have Donald shadow, picking up subject at 226 Korreander.*

Down underneath, in firm, angular strokes, appeared the one thing which, so far as Bertha was concerned, terminated the interview: *Received check, $200.00.*

It was all written on three sheets of legal foolscap which Bertha had clipped together and pushed under the blotter of her desk, intending later on to dictate a memo to go into the case-history file, but since the client had come in just before noon on Saturday, Bertha hadn't had a chance to get at the dictation.

That was where I'd taken over. Bertha had called me in and I'd staked out at 226 Korreander, a well-designed but small stucco house.

I'd waited out there and the subject had come in exactly on the dot, just as specified, smoking a cigarette in a holder, wearing a double-breasted, well-tailored gray suit with blue stripes. He'd remained for approximately an hour and ten minutes.

I'd tagged along behind when he left, keeping in the blind spot where his rear-view mirror couldn't pick me up, noting the license number of the car he was driving, watching the traffic, dropping as far behind as possible when I knew I couldn't lose him, then crowding up close on him. He hadn't given the slightest indication of being interested in anything that was going on behind him.

Yet the man had checked out of the hotel that night after I'd tailed him there. He *must* have been smarter than I had thought, *must* have known he was being followed. I couldn't figure out any other answer at the moment, and that answer bothered me, was bad for my self-respect—that which Bertha would have referred to as my damn conceit. I had always flattered myself on being able to tell when a subject knew he was being followed.

I made up my mind I'd be a lot more cautious with Mr. Thomas Durham in the future—in the event there was going to be any future.

It was typical of Bertha's memo that she had boosted the price a hundred dollars while she'd been talking with the client, and a clinical record of Bertha's mental processes was preserved on those sheets of legal foolscap, but she hadn't even bothered to find out whether the client had a telephone, or anything about the client's history. She'd received two hundred dollars, and that was that.

I looked under the name of Bushnell in the telephone directory and couldn't find anything. I got hold of Information, and Information either couldn't or wouldn't help me, so I went down to the garage and got out our old agency car "Number Two."

Agency "Number One" was a new job and Bertha usually managed to use that on her business. Agency "Number Two" was a nondescript, stout-hearted little jalopy that had rubbed dents in its fenders being loyal to the agency business. For over a hundred thousand miles it had trailed other cars, shadowed married men who were explaining to cuties that their wives didn't understand them, worn out tires digging up witnesses and chasing down clues in an assortment of murder cases.

I got the motor warmed up and waited until most of the rattles and bangs had ceased to be quite so noticeable before pushing the car in gear and starting out for Claire Bushnell's place.

1624 Veronica Way turned out to be an apartment house. I looked over the cards and saw the name Claire Bushnell, cut from a visiting card and inserted in a little holder over the button.

I pressed the button.

Nothing happened.

It was Sunday and she might be loafing around or she might be out taking a walk. From the name on the card, she evidently didn't have a husband, so I decided to be informal. I played a little tune on the bell, a long, two shorts, a long, a short, a long, a short, then a long followed by three quick shorts.

That did the trick. The buzzer announced the door was being opened.

I took a look at the number, saw it was Apartment 319, and went inside.

It was a gorgeous day outside, with beautiful clear sunlight, and the air had a nice fresh tang to it that had made me want to take the agency car way out on the highway, park under some trees, and watch the birds. Inside the apartment house the air was stuffy and stale. After the bright sunlight outside, it was difficult to see things down the hall.

The owners of the apartment house must have decided to conserve electricity so the big industrial users could have all they wanted.

I finally found the elevator, and rattled and banged up to the third floor. It didn't take me long to locate Apartment 319.

The door wasn't open.

I tapped on the panels.

Nothing happened.

I tried the knob and went in.

It was an ordinary furnished apartment, the kind that used to be medium-priced. It was an old building with something of rambling incoherency about its design, and the apartments had been figured out, not on a basis of the greatest efficiency, but on a sort of hit or miss basis. I gathered perhaps the building had at one time consisted of flats or larger apartments, and had been cut up.

There was water running in the bathroom, and as I closed the door behind me, a woman's voice called out, "It's a wonder you wouldn't have shown up with the car earlier. It's a nice day outside and . . ."

I walked over to a chair by the window and sat down.

When I didn't say anything, the voice from the bathroom quieted down, and then the water shut off and a door opened.

Claire Bushnell, wearing a bathrobe and slippers, her eyes wide with startled curiosity, came shuffling into the room.

"Well, I like *that!*" she exclaimed.

There was a Sunday paper on the table. I'd already seen all of it that interested me, mostly about the mess out at the Kozy Dell Slumber Court, but I thought it was a good time to appear nonchalant. I picked up the paper and said, "Don't let me interfere with your bath. Go ahead and get your clothes on."

"Get out!" she said.

I lowered the paper and looked up over the top of it with mild surprise registered on my face.

"What's that?"

"You heard what I said. Get out!"

"But I want to see you."

"Get out. I thought you were—"

"Yes?" I asked as she hesitated.

"Who *are* you?"

I said, "Didn't you want a detective agency to shadow—?"

"No!" she screamed at me.

"I think you did."

"Well, you're completely wrong. I never hired a detective agency in my life."

I put down the paper, took my card case from my pocket, extracted a business card, got up out of the chair, walked over and handed it to her.

She took the card, read it, looked at me suspiciously for a moment, then said, "Oh!"

I went back to the chair and sat down.

She looked at the card again.

"You're Donald Lam?"

35

"That's right."

She thought things over for a moment, then said, "Got anything on you to identify you?"

I showed her my driver's license and my license as a private detective.

She said, "I was just taking a bath."

"So I gathered."

"Well," she said, "no use telling you to make yourself at home. Do you have this much assurance with all your clients?"

"I knocked at the door," I said. "You didn't answer."

"I left it unlocked. I thought you were—a girl friend."

"Well," I said, "I couldn't help that. I didn't want to stand out in the hall and shout my identity for the benefit of your neighbors."

"No," she admitted, "I suppose not. All right, I'll get some clothes on."

There evidently was a bedroom on the other side of the bath. She went through the bathroom, pulled the door shut, and I heard the bolt shoot into position. She trusted me about as much as a canary trusts a house cat.

I waited for about fifteen minutes; then she came back.

Bertha Cool was right. She was a slick-looking chick, easy on the eyes.

She had nice lines, lively black eyes, which probably could twinkle with humor on occasion, hair so dark that it seemed almost blue-black in some lights, and a very, very neat figure.

She looked cool, clean, and comfortable as she sat down and said, "Suppose you tell me what it's all about. What have you found out?"

I said, "I'd like to have you fill in a few details."

"I gave Mrs. Cool all the information."

I said, "You probably did, at that, but she didn't write it down."

"Why, yes, she did. She was sitting there with a pencil and a pad, making notes of everything."

I said, "Bertha Cool was mainly interested in the fee. She wrote down the amount of money we were getting quite a few times, but—"

Claire Bushnell threw back her head and laughed.

I said, "First, let's find out something about your aunt. According to Bertha Cool, she's Amelia Jasper, and she lives at 226 Korreander. You're the only living relative she has."

"That's right."

"What else?"

"What do you want to know?"

"Everything."

She hesitated for a moment, looking me over as though trying to decide how much to tell me. Then she said, "My uncle died a few years ago and apparently left my aunt some money. No one knows how much."

I simply sat there.

She started choosing her words, and I knew she was being careful, trying to say exactly what she wanted to say. "My aunt is now fifty-two. During the past few years I am afraid she has become inordinately vain. She is a very young-looking woman for her age, but she carries it to extremes and is getting positively silly. She has developed a passion for asking people to guess her age—well, you know how that is. Nothing seems to be too absurd for her. As I say, she's fifty-two. If a person guesses her as forty-five, Aunt Amelia gets just a little bit frosty. If it's forty, she'll smile. But if they put her down around thirty-seven, Auntie will simper and beam and really warm up and say, 'Darling, you never would guess it, but I'm actually forty-one.' "

"Her hair?" I asked.

"Henna."

"Disposition?"

"Coy."

I said, "In other words, you're afraid this man who's calling on her may have honorable intentions."

She met my eyes for a long moment and then said, "Exactly."

"How are you and your aunt? Friendly?"

She said, "Let's not misunderstand each other, Mr. Lam. Suppose you were fifty-two and wanted people to think you looked thirty-five, and you had a young niece hanging around who was—well, how old do you think *I* am?"

I looked her over carefully and with a long, steady appraisal. "Thirty-eight," I said.

37

Her eyes flashed hot anger; then she threw back her head and broke out laughing.

"I'm twenty-four."

"Well," I told her, "after the lecture you'd given me on—"

"My God!" she said. "Do I really *look* past thirty?"

"No," I told her. "I figured you as about seventeen, but, since you'd explained the psychology of the thing, I thought—"

"Oh, nuts!" she interrupted.

I sat there and waited.

"Well, anyway," she said after a moment, "you can figure how it is with Aunt Amelia. She is friendly enough so she likes to have me there when no men are around. Particularly since this man has been calling on her, Auntie has let it become apparent that she'd just as soon have me phone before I come. In other words, be sure that I don't come when the gentleman with the dark hair and the beautiful profile is there."

"Have you ever been there when he's there?"

"Once," she said, "and Auntie got rid of me so fast that it wasn't even funny."

"Your aunt introduce you?"

"Don't be silly!"

"Then you never met him?"

"No."

"Think he'd know you if he saw you again?"

"Yes."

"He only saw you for a few minutes?"

"A few seconds."

"Just that once?"

"Yes."

"But he looked you over?"

"His eyes burned holes in my clothes."

"He's that way?"

"I think so. His eyes are."

"Any idea what he's after—with your aunt?"

"I think he's selling her something."

"You told Bertha Cool you were afraid he was selling her stock."

"You seem to have the right answer," she said.

38

"You wouldn't mind if he nicked her for a little money on a stock transaction?"

She said, "Mr. Lam, if that man could be given an opportunity to swindle Aunt Amelia out of twenty or thirty thousand dollars, I—I'd almost tell him all I knew about Auntie's psychology so he could go ahead. What I'm afraid of is that's what he *started* to do and now I'm afraid he's trying to sell her merchandise that's going to cost her more and will be a lot less valuable to her."

"You mean he's trying to sell himself?"

"Yes."

"Would your aunt remarry?"

"I think so, under proper circumstances. She's—well, she's carried this business of being flattered to a point of where it's making her sort of—well, I hate to say it, but—"

"You don't have to say it," I said.

"What have you found out?" she asked. "What happened yesterday?"

"I picked up this man and shadowed him."

"Who is he? Where does he live?"

"His name is Thomas Durham, and he was staying in the Westchester Arms Hotel. He checked out late yesterday night."

"Checked out!"

"Yes."

"Where did he go?"

"I don't know."

"You're a fine detective!" she flared.

I said, "Wait a minute. The instructions that I had were to shadow this man and find out who he was—that was all. You didn't want a twenty-four-hour shadowing job, and you didn't pay for one."

"Well, I wanted to find out something about him."

"You're going to," I told her. "I'm working on it."

"Why did he check out?"

"I don't know. I intend to find out. In order to find out, I've got to get a little more information."

"Well, go get it."

"I want to get some here."

"What about?"

"Let's start with you. You've been married."

39

"Yes."

"What happened to the marriage?"

"It went on the rocks."

"Who was the man?"

"A Mr. Bushnell," she said. "A James Bushnell. Mrs. Bushnell's little boy, Jimmie, you know."

"Oh, yes," I said, "Jimmie—good old Jimmie! Well, well, well! And what was wrong with Jimmie?"

"A little bit of everything."

"How long have you been on your own?"

"A year."

"Alimony?"

"Go fly a kite."

"I was just asking."

"I was just answering."

"Are you dependent on your aunt financially?"

"No."

"Any other relatives?"

"No."

"In other words, you're the sole heir?"

"If she should die, I presume I would be, but, of course, she has the right to do anything she wants to with her property."

I said, "You're not being very helpful."

"I'm answering questions."

"You're not volunteering anything."

"I hired *you* to get *me* information."

"Your attitude toward your aunt seems a little detached."

She said with feeling, "I'd like to be closer to her. She's my only relative. At times she misses me. Then she gets these boy-struck ideas. But so far she's always drawn the line at matrimony. She's been afraid someone would get her money. She's tight as a new shoe. When she's lonely she loves me and wants me to come stay with her. A few weeks ago she had an auto accident. Since then she's had attacks of sciatica. She thinks they were caused by injuries received in the accident. She makes a great to-do over it, rests on an air cushion in a wheel chair and all that."

"And the insurance company?"

"Thinks the accident was her fault."

"And she's a little man-crazy?"

40

"That's putting it mildly!"

"Too bad," I said. "She might get over it with a little financial pruning."

"She might—I can't see what she's trying to get. I simply can't understand her—yes I can, too. I understand and I sympathize, but I can't—"

"Condone?" I asked.

"Who am I to condone?" she asked.

"Well, suppose you quit trying to justify yourself to yourself, and start telling me the facts."

"My parents died when I was three. They perished together in a shipwreck. Aunt Amelia took me to raise. I can't even remember my parents. I can remember Aunt Amelia, all of her virtues, which are many, and all of her faults."

"Go ahead," I said.

"Aunt Amelia was a very, very beautiful woman," she went on. "She married Uncle Dave out of pity, and was disillusioned. She didn't believe in divorce. She learned after a few years that the man to whom she was married had an incurable ailment. She desperately, passionately, tried to keep herself young so that when Uncle Dave died she could—well, keep as much of her youth as possible. She wanted to begin all over again."

"That's understandable," I said.

"Then Uncle Dave died and she met Uncle Fred. By that time I think Aunt Amelia had become shrewdly calculating. I only know that the first memories of my childhood are of Auntie standing in front of mirrors, studying herself carefully from every angle, turning me over to a nurse; then to a governess; then I was shipped away to a private school.

"You can see what happened, Mr. Lam. During those years when Auntie was waiting for the man she had married to die, trying to keep herself young, she had formed a habit of thinking of herself exclusively, dreaming about her youthful appearance. That was the primary thing in her life. If Aunt Amelia could only be jarred out of that, she'd be a very wonderful woman. She's witty, intelligent and—selfish."

"She's been injured?"

"Yes, this automobile accident. Only minor injuries, but she's trying to keep them alive. Every so often she has a relapse and takes to her wheel chair."

41

"Who pushes it?"

"Susie Irwin, maid, housekeeper, companion, cook, and chauffeur."

"Any other help in the house?"

"No."

"Your aunt is stingy?"

"Both stingy and secretive."

"Rich?"

"I tell you, no one knows. She inherited some money. She's made investments. She always seems to have money, but she hates to spend it and if you *really* want to make her mad, ask her one question, just one single question about her financial affairs."

"Tell me about the accident."

"Oh, it was one of those street intersection things, with each party claiming the other was in the wrong."

"Settled?"

"Auntie sputtered and fumed for a while, but the insurance company decided she was in the wrong and made a settlement with the owner of the other car. He had three witnesses with him. Auntie was driving alone. She was furious. She canceled her insurance with the company because of it."

"Taken out any since?"

"No, she swears she'll carry her own insurance. She feels the other people should have been sued and made to pay. She may have been right. Auntie's very careful and observing and her reactions are quick, but, as I said, the other car had three witnesses. They might have been coached by a phonograph record, the way they told their story."

I said, "Let's be frank with each other, Mrs. Bushnell—"

"I go under the name of Miss Bushnell."

"All right; then, let's be frank with each other, Claire."

She said, "You work fast, don't you, *Mister* Lam?"

"Not so fast," I said. "I just don't think we have time to waste getting acquainted. Let's get down to brass tacks. This is a medium-priced, furnished apartment. You—"

"You ought to pay the rent on it if you think it's medium-priced."

"I know, but it's in that general classification. You haven't a car. You probably have some income, perhaps alimony. You have good clothes, as cheap an apartment as one can live in comfortably and still have a little elbow room. You don't have a telephone. You aren't rich. You don't have any big income."

Her eyes were angry.

I said, "But you gave Bertha Cool two hundred bucks in order to find out about the man who is hanging around your aunt. That two hundred dollars didn't come easy."

"Well, it *went* easy," she flared.

I nodded, said, "You're not getting my point. It took quite a motive for you to part with two hundred dollars. You didn't do it simply because you were suspicious of a man who was dancing attendance on your Aunt Amelia."

"I said he was trying to sell her something."

"Bertha Cool talked with you for quite a while. Then she made the two-hundred-dollar price and you didn't argue with her. You didn't try to bargain—"

"Was I supposed to have done so?"

"Some of them do."

"Then what happens?"

"They get the worst of it. But I'm not talking about Bertha. I'm talking about you."

"So it would seem."

"In other words," I said, "you had some motive that you haven't told us."

She bounced up out of her chair, said angrily, *"Will* you get busy and do what you're paid to do, instead of hanging around here and insulting me?"

"I'm trying to get information so I can help you."

She said sarcastically, "Believe me, Mr. Lam, if *I* had known the answers, I certainly wouldn't have paid your estimable, grasping, avaricious Bertha Cool two hundred dollars in order to get those answers for me. When I turned that money over to your partner, I was foolish enough to think that I could get someone who would go out and start collecting information for me, not hang around my apartment on a Sunday morning, making passes—"

"I haven't made any passes," I told her.

"I know," she said, "but you will."

"Want to bet?" I asked.

She looked at me scornfully, then said, "Yes."

"How much?"

43

"Two hundred dollars," she said, and then added hastily, "No, wait a minute. You'd—I'm talking about the way you came in when I was taking a bath, the way you—I mean for two hundred dollars you wouldn't.''

"Make it a hundred."

"No."

"Fifty."

"No."

"Ten."

"That's a go," she said. "It's a bet. You'd be a gentleman for twenty, but you'd be willing to lose the ten if you thought you could get to first base."

I said, "Okay. You've made a bet. Now, let's get back to the case."

"What do you want to know?"

I said casually, "Ever lived in Colorado?"

"No."

"Don't happen to know a Dover Fulton?"

"No."

"His wife?"

"No, never heard of them."

"Don't happen to know a Stanwick Carlton?"

Her eyes became round. "What does *that* have to do with it?"

"Nothing, perhaps. I wanted to know."

"Why, I—I know Minerva Carlton. I've known her for years. She's a close friend. I don't know her husband. I've never met him."

"Where does Minerva live?"

"In Colorado."

"Heard from her lately?"

"No."

"Read the papers?" I asked.

She said, "The comic section and the magazine part. What on earth does Minerva have to do with all this?"

"I don't know," I said. "You're a close friend of hers?"

"Yes, very close."

"When did you hear from her last?"

"Oh, I don't know—a month or so ago. We write constantly."

"Don't happen to have her picture, do you?"

"Why, yes, I've got a photograph she sent, and I have some snapshots taken when we were at the beach this summer."

"Let's take a look at the snapshots."

"But why?"

"I want to see them."

"But what does that have to do with this man who's been calling on Aunt Amelia?"

"I don't know. I want to take a look at the pictures."

She said, "You're the most arbitrary man I think I ever knew, outside of—" She hesitated.

"You mean Mrs. Bushnell's little boy, Jimmie?"

"Exactly," she said.

I said, "Okay, get the pictures and we'll call it square."

She went to a closet, rummaged around in a drawer, came out with an envelope of the kind put out by concerns that specialize in developing and printing pictures. There was a pocket on one side for films, a pocket on the other for prints.

She took out the prints and started running through them. A half smile played around the corners of her mouth as she hastily put six of the prints back in the pocket. Then she handed me two.

I looked at the photographs. They were good, clear photographs of Claire Bushnell and another girl in very skimpy bathing suits. The pictures showed that Claire Bushnell had a neat little figure. The girl with her was the one I'd seen in the cocktail lounge the night before, the red-headed girl with the contemplative eyes.

"That's Minerva Carlton?" I asked.

"The one with me, yes."

"Nice figure," I said.

"She gets by."

"Yours, I was looking at."

"Is this part of the service I get for two hundred dollars, or do you throw this in?"

"I throw this in."

"You can throw it out, as far as I'm concerned."

"What are the other pictures?"

She shook her head. "When two girls have a camera and get to playing around on the beach, you can't tell just what will happen."

45

"You have the films for these pictures?" I asked.

"Yes."

"Give me the films for these two, will you?"

"Why?"

"I want them."

She hesitated a moment, then took films from the pocket on the other side. She walked over to hold them up to the light so she could identify the ones she wanted. She had her back to me. I watched her shoulders move, watched the semi-opaque films coming up to the light.

She picked out the films I wanted, handed them to me.

"Got an envelope?" I asked.

By the way of answer, she dumped the rest of the films out and handed me the empty envelope.

I looked at the films. They were good and clear, two and a quarter by three and a quarter. They'd enlarge nicely.

"Nice exposure," I said.

"Cut the personal stuff, please."

"I was referring to the shutter timing," I said.

"Oh!"

I studied the films. "And well developed."

"That corner drugstore has done my developing for three years."

I said, "That time I wasn't referring to the films. I was talking about your figure."

She made as if to throw a book at me, but she couldn't keep the twinkle out of her eyes.

"So you haven't heard from Stanwick Carlton?" I asked.

She smiled and shook her head and said, "I suspect Stanwick doesn't like me. After all, I'm linked with Minerva's purple past."

"Did she have one?"

"Don't be silly. He's jealous, possessive, and suspicious."

I said, "You might read the rest of your paper."

"Why?"

"Minerva was found dead in the Kozy Dell Slumber Court, an auto court about eight or ten miles outside of the city. She—"

Claire Bushnell dashed to the little smoking stand, whipped the paper open, tossing the comic section and the magazine part to the floor. I pointed to the account of the love-pact slaying.

While she was standing there in stupefied bewilderment, or the best imitation of it she could assume, I picked up the rest of the films, slipped them into my pocket and walked out, quietly closing the door behind me.

She didn't even hear me go. The last I saw of her as I closed the door, she was standing with wide, horror-stricken eyes, reading the account of Minerva Carlton's death.

The elevator wasn't on the third floor and I didn't wait for it. I took the stairs two at a time, climbed in the agency heap, and got out of there.

Four blocks down the street I stopped the car to look at the films I had.

Two of them were nudes. In the other four, the girls wore bathing suits, but there was a man with them. Minerva Carlton's head was resting on his bare torso. They both looked happy.

I put the films all together in the pocket of the envelope. The print order was on the front. *Three each on glossy*, it said.

CHAPTER FIVE

The Personal Touch

I STOPPED THE AGENCY CAR at the address on Korreander Street and bustled up the steps of the white stucco bungalow.

A gaunt woman in the fifties, moving with awkward, swinging stride, came down the corridor. I could see her through the locked screen door. The inner door was open.

She stood tall and unsmiling, surveying me through screen.

"What are you selling?"

"Nothing."

"What do you want?"

"To see Mrs. Jasper."

"What about?"

"An automobile accident."

"What about it?"

"I want to find out how it happened. Her insurance company paid off on it."

"What do you want to know about it?"

"I'll tell her when I see her."

She didn't say, "Wait a minute," or "I'll see," or "Excuse me," or anything else. She merely turned on her heel and I watched her long, angular figure as she strode unhurriedly down the hallway.

I heard the sound of voices. Then the woman was coming back, her long, thin legs swinging easily from the bony hips. Once more she stood in the doorway. "What's your name?"

"Lam."

"What's your first name?"

"Donald."

"Are you with an insurance company?"

"No."

"What's your interest in the accident?"

"I'll tell Mrs. Jasper when I see her."

"Have you talked with the people on the other side?"

"No."

"Talk with the insurance company?"

"I prefer to give my information to Mrs. Jasper."

"Well, she prefers to have you give it to me."

I said, "Tell her if she wants to let that outrageous settlement stand, all she has to do is to refuse to see me. If she wants to be vindicated, she'd better talk with me."

"What do you know about it?"

"A lot."

Eyes as black as though they had been coated with Japanese lacquer surveyed me from deep sockets. Then she turned once more, walked back down the corridor, this time was gone for about a minute and a half, then returned and unlocked the screen door.

I went in.

She locked the screen door behind me.

"Which way?" I asked.

"Down the corridor," she said. "First door to the left."

I walked down the long carpeted corridor, turned to the left, and entered a living-room.

The woman who sat in the wheel chair was good-looking. Her hair was a rich shade of henna. The face was relatively unlined. The eyes were quick, alert, and intelligent. If it hadn't been for a little sag under the chin, she could well have been a lot younger than her years.

"How do you do, Mr. Lam," she said. "I'm Amelia Jasper."

"Mrs. Jasper." I bowed. "It is a pleasure. I regret the intrusion at this hour, and on Sunday, but, you see, it's the only day I have to gather material for the work I'm doing."

"And what is your work, may I ask?"

I said, "I'm a free-lance writer."

Her lips retained that fixed smile, but her eyes lost their cordiality. "A writer?" she asked coldly.

I said with some feeling. "I'm writing some articles on insurance and the way automobile insurance companies are operated. One thing I am attacking is the way they put a premium on committing perjury. When an accident takes place involving a car where one person, no matter how reputable, is the sole witness on one side, and several people on the other side are manifestly lying about what happened, the insurance company rarely takes the trouble to fight it out and—"

"Are *you* telling *me?*" Amelia Jasper interrupted, her eyes blazing with indignation. "I was never so humiliated in all my life. I take it you know about my accident."

"The general circumstances only," I said. "I understand you were riding alone."

She hesitated a moment, then said, "Yes."

"And there were three or four people in the other car?"

"Four people," she said. "Ignorant boors, people of exactly the type one would expect to find distorting the facts in order to obtain a paltry settlement of a few dollars."

"It happened at an intersection?"

"Yes. I was coming into the intersection. I looked over on the right and saw no one coming. I glanced hurriedly to the left, assuming that I would have the right of way over any vehicle on the left and that I needed to concern myself only with some vehicle on the right."

"What happened?"

"These insufferable people ran into me. They were coming from the left. They were coming so fast that they entered the intersection long after I got there, but they had the consummate nerve to tell the insurance adjuster that they were already in the intersection when they saw me coming, that I was driving at such terrific speed I couldn't stop, that *I* ran into *them.*"

"Did you?"

"My car struck theirs, if that's what you mean."

"Then they didn't run into you. You ran into them?"

"They put their car *directly* in front of mine," she said.

"I can understand how the insurance company would have looked at it."

"Well, I can't," she flared, "and don't expect any cooperation from me if you're going to start sympathizing with that insurance company."

"I'm not sympathizing," I told her. "I just was trying to find out what happened."

I had taken a notebook and pencil from my pocket. Now, without even having opened the notebook, I put book and pencil back in my pocket, and bowed. "I am very happy to have met you, Mrs. Jasper, and thank you so much for having consented to see me."

"But I haven't told you all about the accident."

I shifted my position uneasily and said, "Well—I think I understand the circumstances."

She said angrily, "Simply because there are four people on the other side, you're adopting the position that I must be in the wrong."

"Not at all," I told her. "I simply felt it wasn't a case that would be interesting to the editor of the magazine for which I'm planning to do the writing."

"Why?"

I said, "What I want to show is the danger inherent in compromising cases, where the insured party is actually in the right but where the insurance company feels that defending the case would involve too much effort. Therefore they let a majority of witnesses on the other side commit perjury and—"

"Well, why isn't that exactly what happened in my case?"

I hesitated. "Were you seriously injured?"

"My left hip was injured."

"Is it nearly healed now?"

"Yes. I'm able to walk now, but ever since the accident I've had spells of sciatica. I'm having a bad one now—air pillows, aspirin, and pain."

"I'm sorry," I said sympathetically.

"And what's more, I'm afraid that this accident is going to leave one leg shorter than the other, permanently."

"That will be all right as soon as the muscles adjust themselves—in time."

"In *time!*" she exclaimed scornfully.

I kept quiet.

She studied me for a moment, then said, "My legs have always looked—well, rather nice."

She hesitated just the proper amount of time to make it appear that the desire to convince me had overcome her modesty, and then raised her skirt, showing me her left leg.

I whistled.

She jerked the skirt back down indignantly. "I didn't show you that for you to whistle at!"

"No?" I asked.

She said, "I was simply proving a point."

"Proving a curve, I would say."

"You're nice; but think of my other leg so much shorter it will be disfigured." Tears came to her eyes.

"It won't be hurt in the least."

"It's shorter now. My hip is pulled up. And it's getting thinner than the other as I fail to use the muscles. And I'm—well, I'm not as young as I used to be."

I smiled tolerantly.

"I tell you I'm not. How old do you think I am?"

I pursed my lips, went through the motions of disinterested appraisal. "Well," I said thoughtfully, "you're probably *past* thirty-five, but it's not fair to ask me that question now, because a woman always looks older in a wheel chair. If you were walking around I'd—well, I guess perhaps you *are* around thirty-five, at that."

She beamed at me. "Do you think so?"

"Right around there."

She said, "I'm forty-one."

"What?" I exclaimed incredulously.

She simpered at me. "Forty-one."

"Well, you certainly don't look it!"

"I don't feel it."

I said, "Well, I'm going to call on the insurance company and get all of the facts in your case. I think perhaps, after all, it's something that would go well in an article."

"I'm satisfied it will, and I *do* wish you'd write an article like that. I think it needs to be published. Insurance companies are altogether too conceited, too cocksure of themselves."

"They're corporations," I told her. "They tend to wind themselves up in a lot of red tape."

"I'll say they do."

I motioned toward the morning paper which was lying on a reading table near her wheel chair. "Read about the murder?" I asked.

"What murder?"

"The one out in the Kozy Dell Slumber Court."

52

"Oh," she said casually, "that's one of those love murders and suicide things. I remember seeing the headlines."

"You didn't read the article?"

"No."

"Some folks from Colorado," I said. "I believe the man's name was Stanwick Carlton—no, wait a minute, the man who was killed was Dover Fulton. He's from San Robles. Stanwick Carlton is the husband of the girl who was killed in the tragedy—Minerva, I believe her name was."

Mrs. Jasper nodded absently, said, "I'd like very much to have you get in touch with the insurance company. Ask for Mr. Smith and get him to give you his version of what happened. Then I'd like to know just what he tells you. Do you suppose you could get in touch with me and let me know?"

"I might."

"I'd really appreciate it. So you're a writer. What do you write?"

"Oh, all sorts of things."

"Under your own name?"

"No, mostly under pen names and sometimes anonymously."

"Why do you do that?"

I grinned. "I write lots of true confession stories and—"

"You mean to tell me those things aren't true?"

"The ones I write aren't."

"But I thought they were."

"Oh, I get facts out of real life and then I dress them up and tell them in the first person. I'm always interested in divorces and murders, and things of that sort."

"That's why you asked about that murder?"

"I guess so, yes."

She said, "I've always wanted to do some writing. Is it difficult?"

"Not in the least. You just put yourself on paper. It's surprising how easy the words come."

"But if it's easy, why aren't more people writing?"

"They are," I said.

"Well," she said, "you know what I mean—selling things to the magazines."

"Oh, *selling!*" I exclaimed, and shook my head. "That's

53

terrible! The writing's easy. You just go ahead and write the stuff. But trying to sell it, that's where the rub comes."

She laughed then and said, "You *do* think of the most humorous things, Mr. Lam. Won't you sit down and talk with me a little longer?"

"I hate to presume on—"

"Well, after all, it's Sunday and I'm here alone, and—of course, I don't want to take up *your* time."

"Not at all," I told her. "It's a pleasure. . . . I'll bet there'd be some red faces on the adjusters in that insurance company if I should uncover some new witness who would show that the accident absolutely was the fault of the other side. I think the insurance company knows what I'm doing and resents it, and are going to try to pin something on me so I can't go ahead."

"Well, I like *that!* Don't you let them do it!"

I said diffidently, "I started to call on you yesterday, and then got frightened away." I smiled, and then let my smile grow into a laugh of polite deprecation for my own timidity.

"You were *frightened* away?"

"Yes."

"What frightened you?"

"A young, well-dressed chap I thought was a detective."

"Why, what ever happened, Mr. Lam?"

I said, "He was tall and was wearing a gray double-breasted suit and was smoking a cigarette. He got out of his car just about the same time I did, and looked me over. Then he walked past me and came up the steps and rang the bell here at the house. I drove around the block and parked where I could watch his car. I waited for him to come out. I thought—well, I felt sure that he was a detective working for the insurance company and checking up on me. I almost passed you up. But your case was exactly typical of the cases I wanted to investigate, so I decided to make another try."

"He wasn't a detective," she said, *"surely* he wasn't a detective. He's—why, he's a nice young man, just the same as you are."

I laughed, and said, "Well, that's a load off my mind. He's a friend, then. You've known him for a while?"

"Not *too* long."

I waited.

She said, "He's nice. A *nice* young man."

I said, "He looked like a detective to me."

She frowned.

"How did you meet him?" I asked.

She said, "Well, you might call it accidentally. He's a rich chap, has an interest in some mining properties so he doesn't have to work. He's what you'd call a playboy, I guess, although what a man like that can see in me is more than I can tell."

She simpered.

"He can see what I can see, can't he?"

"Mr. Lam! You forget my age. The man can't be over—well, he's a lot younger than I am."

"I'll bet he's older."

"Why, Mr. Lam! How you talk!"

"You know I'm right."

She tried to look demure. "Why such an idea never occurred to me. Mr. Durham was just trying to be nice to me."

I smiled knowingly.

She looked as satisfied as a bird preening its feathers.

I said, "Well, I'm sorry. I hope you'll pardon me."

"For what?"

"For getting so personal."

She said archly, "Women like men who get personal."

"Do they?"

"Don't you know?"

"I—I guess I just never stopped to think of it."

"Well, that's what they want," she said. "Remember it."

"I will."

She looked at me somewhat wistfully. "Will you be back?"

"Oh, yes. I'll have to come back several times. I'll make an investigation and then I'll have to come back and ask you some more questions."

"I wish you would. I'd like to do something about that insurance company."

I got to my feet. She raised her voice and called, "Susie."

The maid popped into the room with suspicious alacrity.

"Mr. Lam's leaving," she said. "He'll be back from time to time. I'll see him any time he comes, Susie, any time."

The woman merely nodded her head.

She stood to one side in the passageway, and I walked out ahead of her.

I unhooked the screen door and opened it. She stood in the doorway.

"Good-bye, Susie," I said, and smiled.

She glared at me and said, "You've fooled her. That doesn't mean you've fooled me," and slammed the front door hard.

I thought that over while I was walking across the street to where I'd left the agency car. I'd parked off the pavement, on the side of the road, and when I noticed the tracks of flat-heeled, feminine shoes around the license number, I was glad that we took the precaution of keeping the car registered in the name of a dummy.

CHAPTER SIX

Something Is Cockeyed

I DROVE THE AGENCY CAR to the parking space we rented by the month, got out, locked the bus, and started toward the building where our office was located.

I saw a flicker of motion from across the street, then a big police car came out of a parking lot, driving fast. Sergeant Frank Sellers of Homicide grinned from behind the wheel and said, "Hi, Master Mind!"

"Hi, yourself," I told him. "What's on *your* mind?"

He said, "I just wanted to talk with you. You're a hard guy to catch. Bertha told me you were out working on a case."

"That's right, I am."

"What case?"

"Don't be silly. You know I can't tell you that."

"You'd have to if I asked the question in the right way."

"Well, that wasn't the right way."

"I've been trying to get you for two or three hours, Lam. You must have started out pretty early this morning."

"Early is a relative word," I said, "depending on whether you're working for Bertha Cool or the taxpayers."

He didn't see the humor of that. He pulled the catch and pushed the door open. "Get in."

"Where are we going?"

"Places."

"For what?"

"Never mind. Get in."

I got in. He slammed the door shut and poured speed into the car.

"Can't you tell me where we're going?" I asked.

57

"Not now. I don't want to question you, and I don't want any statements from you until I'm sure of my ground. When I'm sure of it, I'm going to give you a chance to come clean."

I settled back against the cushions and yawned.

Sergeant Sellers turned on the siren, and we really started making time through the frozen traffic.

"Must be an emergency," I said.

He grinned. "I just hate to plod along behind a stream of Sunday drivers. It does them good to hear a siren once in a while. Makes 'em get over. They— Damn the guy!"

Sellers whipped the car into a skid, barely avoided a chap who had swung out, trying to pass another car.

Having missed the collision, Sellers slammed on his brakes and was skidding to a stop when a road patrol car flashed out of line and the man at the wheel shouted, "I'll get him!"

"Throw the book at him!" Sellers yelled. "Give him the works on five counts."

The officer nodded.

Sellers stepped on the throttle once more, saying, "Guys like that should be locked up and *kept* locked up."

"That's right," I told him. "Here you are tearing out on a matter of life and death and—"

He flashed me a sidelong glance. "Better save your sarcasm. You may need it later on."

"Okay," I said, "I'll save it. I probably *will* need it."

Another three minutes, and I knew where he was taking me. I braced myself for what was bound to happen and sat tight.

The Kozy Dell Slumber Court seemed drab and shoddy by daylight. At night, the neon signs in front had been arranged so that it gave a certain colorful glamour to the front. The motorist could see the sweep of the curved gravel driveway, the red and green lights, the cottages arranged in neat, orderly rows, with lights illuminating only the white stucco fronts and showing the neat whiteness of the gravel. But by daylight the backs of the cottages were apparent and the white stucco showed that it was badly in need of paint and repair, chipped here and there, grimy with dirt.

Sergeant Sellers swung the car into the driveway. "Come on in, Lam," he invited.

I followed him in.

The woman who ran the place looked us over.

"Ever seen him before?" Sellers asked.

I met her eyes.

"That's the one," she said.

"What one?"

"The one I was telling you about, the one who came here in Fulton's car. He's the one that wrote 'Dover Fulton, 6285 Orange Avenue, San Robles.' That's his handwriting."

"What about the girl with him?"

She sniffed, and said, "Some little tramp. And if you ask me, this man is grass green. My God, he came here with a stall about this dame being sick and needing a rest room. I told him we didn't have rest rooms, that we had cabins and that the cabins had baths and toilets, and asked him if he wanted one. And what do you suppose he said?"

Sergeant Sellers was regarding me speculatively. "What the hell *did* he say?"

"Said he'd have to go and ask *her.* "

Sellers grinned.

"I almost didn't rent it to him," she said. "It's people like that who give a place a bad name. I wish now I'd followed my inclination and kicked him out. A couple of little amateurs, that's what they are. After all, I'm not running a place for kids."

"He ain't a kid," Sellers said.

"Well, he acts like it."

"What about the babe that was with him?"

"I didn't get a good look at her," the woman said, and then added wearily, "I never do with that type. Some of them stand right out brazen as can be, but, for the most part, the amateurs keep back out of the way, sitting in the car and trying to look disinterested. They make me sick!"

"Come on," Sellers said, "you must have had something of a look at her. Was she a red-headed girl with—"

"No, she was small, and she was blonde. I saw that much. I've told the police all about her already."

"Then what happened?"

She said, "This man registered. I took them down and showed them the place, collected the rent money, and went back. I had three more cottages. I rented them within about

59

an hour and a half. On the last one there was this complaint about the radio in the other cabin, so I—"

"Did you hear the shots?"

"I thought it was a truck backfiring. I had no idea—"

"Three of them?"

"Three."

"After these people had rented the cabin?"

"Yes"

"How long after?"

"I don't know—perhaps fifteen minutes—perhaps not that long. Perhaps only ten."

"Longer than fifteen minutes?"

"I tell you it could have been. I don't keep the time on those things. If I'd known they were shots I certainly would have noticed the time. And if I'd known this man was going to make me all this trouble, I never would have rented him anything in the first place. I'm not a fortune teller."

"No, I suppose not," Sellers agreed. "What happened after that?"

"I didn't rent the last cabin until around eleven o'clock. That was the cabin that was right next to this one. It was a double cabin, and the way it's arranged it's a white elephant. A party of four showed up and wanted the place. I took them down to get them located, and when I did, I noticed that the lights were on in this other cabin and the radio was playing."

"You hadn't had any complaints before that?"

"No, I don't think any of the other cottages would have noticed it so much. But this vacant double was right next to it and you could hear plenty plain. The four people said they were tired and wanted to get to sleep, so I said I'd get the party next door to quiet down."

"Go ahead," Sellers said.

"I've told all this before."

"Tell it again."

"I went over and knocked on the door. Nothing happened. I knocked louder. Nothing happened. I tried the door. It was locked from the inside. I got mad and punched the key out and used my passkey to get in. There they were, lying on the floor. Blood all over my carpet, and me trying to run a decent place! I'd put in a new carpet there only three months ago, trying to keep the place attractive. That's the way it goes and—"

"And you called the police?"

"That's right—and while you're here I wish you'd tell me something—I'd collected the money for that double cabin from the four people. They got angry when they heard the police cars and all the commotion, and insisted that I give them their money back. I told them they'd rented the cabin and that if they were decent people with clean consciences, they could go to sleep, and a little noise of automobiles coming and going wouldn't hurt anything. They said they were going to have me arrested if I didn't give them the money back. Can they do that?"

"No," Sellers said.

"Well, that's what I thought. I'm glad you told me so."

"What happened?"

"They pulled out about one in the morning. Said they wouldn't sleep in a place that was next to a killing. They went on down the road somewhere. I hope they never did find a place to stay."

I looked at Sellers. Sellers said, "Get me the dope on that party. Let me see how they registered. Give me their license number and—"

The woman started pawing through a file of registration cards. "Not now," Sellers said hastily. "I'll be back in a few minutes. You get that stuff for me. Write it all out, and I'll come back and pick it up."

Sellers took my arm, piloted me outside. "Suppose you start talking, Donald?" he asked.

I shook my head.

"Come on," Sellers said. "You'd better come clean."

I said, "I can't. It's a job I'm working on."

"A job, my eye!" Sellers said. "I've already checked with Bertha on that angle."

"I still tell you it's a job. A woman paid me two hundred dollars. She wanted her—"

"Go on," Sellers said as I stopped.

I shook my head, and said, "I can't do it without betraying the confidence of a client. I'll have to get her permission before I can say anything."

"You can give us a lift on this thing, Donald. I want it cleared up and off the books."

"No I can't Frank. I tell you it's a job."

"Phooey! You were out with a jane on your own. Bertha herself says so. You try pulling this sort of stuff, and you'll lose your license. I'll try to make it easy on the partnership because Bertha's been a square shooter, but as far as you're concerned, you've always cut corners."

I said, "I tell you I was on a job. It had to do with Dover Fulton, but it didn't have a darned thing to do with the killing."

"You're supposed to cooperate with the police. Remember that."

I said, "Look, Frank, this is a suicide, frustrated love. They were both of them nuts. They chose that way out. It's their business. As far as the police are concerned, the case is closed. You know that as well as I do."

"It has some funny angles. The department wants them cleared up."

I said, "There's nothing to investigate. They're both dead. It's the same old suicide pact stuff."

"But that automobile being here. The whole thing is cockeyed. I want the straight of it."

"If I told you all I knew about it, it would still be cockeyed."

"Who's your client? Who are you working for?"

I shook my head.

Sellers said, "Wait here."

His heavy feet crunched on the gravel as he went back into the office of the auto court. He was in there about five minutes, then came out, folding a paper. He climbed into the police car, said, "Okay, we'll take another ride."

This time we went to San Robles.

6285 Orange Avenue was a post-war job that had been knocked together out of such materials as were available and such labor as had been willing to work. It was a Monterey-type house, neat enough on the outside, but the builders had been up against a problem of cost per square foot and had tried to make the square feet as few as possible.

Fifteen years ago the place would have been an architect's model, a miniature house used for a real estate office or an oversized doll house. Now it was two bedrooms and bath, twelve thousand, seven hundred and eighty-five dollars.

We went through a little gate.

Sellers rang the bell.

The woman who opened the door had been crying until she had realized crying wouldn't do her any good. Now she was in the dazed condition of trying to adjust herself to a whole new set of circumstances on which she hadn't figured.

"Know this man?" Sellers asked.

She shook her head.

"I'm sorry to intrude," Sellers said, "but we want to come in."

Mrs. Fulton stood to one side and held the door open for us.

"Where are the children?" Sellers asked.

"One of the neighbors came and took them," she said. "I guess it's better to have them out of the house, what with the way people have been trooping in here and everything."

Sellers said, "I guess so. We won't stay long."

He settled himself in a comfortable chair, crossed his legs, pulled back his coat, shoved the thumbs in the armholes of his vest, said, "I don't want any run-around. You're absolutely certain you haven't seen this man before?"

She looked at me and shook her head.

"You didn't hire him to shadow your husband?"

"No! Heaven's sake, no! I didn't think for a minute there was anything wrong."

"You thought your husband was working at the office?"

"Not at the office, but out on a job somewhere."

"Did he seem as devoted to you the last two weeks as he had before that?"

"Yes—even more so. Just a few days ago when Dover came home I was thinking how fortunate I was. He was complimenting me on the way I looked and—well—it must have been yesterday. It seems like it was ages ago."

Sellers looked at me.

"How about the insurance?" I asked.

Sellers said to me, "What's the idea, Master Mind?"

"Nothing," I said. "Only you've been around here churning up the woman's feelings, and I thought it might be about time you did something constructive for a change."

63

"Well, *I'll* do the thinking," Sellers said.

Irene Fulton said, "I had him take out insurance just a few months ago. The way the cost of living has been going up he couldn't save anything—well, not enough. So I had him take out something that would give us protection, fifteen thousand apiece for the children, to put them through school, and ten thousand for me."

"That's good," Sellers said.

"How long ago?" I asked.

"Last fall—and I called up the insurance people and they told me the policies were no good in case of suicide within one year from the date the policies were issued. I get back the first premiums and that's all. And that's going to be every cent I'll have."

"How about the house?" Sellers asked.

"We own it subject to a big mortgage. I suppose we could get something out of it for our equity. But that would take time—and I've got to live somewhere. And then the children—"

She stopped for a moment to appraise the situation.

There was sheer panic in her eyes. "What am I going to do now? How am I going to—good heavens, there won't be any monthly income at all! There won't be—there won't—!"

"Take it easy," Sellers said.

"Those policies," I asked, "were they straight life insurance?"

"Yes. They provided for double indemnity in case anything happened to him. You know, in case he died in an automobile accident or anything of that sort. Until he took them out I hadn't been able to sleep nights wondering what would happen to the children and me in case anything should—well, then it was a load off my mind—and now they won't pay."

"That's right," Sellers said, "they don't pay off in case of suicide. Not when it's within one year."

There was silence for a moment, then Sellers said, "I'm awfully sorry, Mrs. Fulton, but you're going to have to take a little ride with me. You're going to have to go to see a person."

"Well, if I have to, I have to," she said. Her voice sounded as though she welcomed the chance to get away.

"You can leave the house all right?"

64

"Yes, I'll just lock up. The children are over at the neighbor's."

"Okay," Sellers said. "Get ready and come on."

He glared belligerently at me and said, "And I can get along without any of your comments for a while, Master Mind."

"Okay by me," I said. "I can tell you right now you're going to draw a blank."

"Never mind the comments," he said angrily. "I don't know exactly what I'm going to do about you. I—I wish it had been a murder, then I could have thrown you in the hoosegow."

I didn't say anything. Sellers wasn't in any mood for argument.

Mrs. Fulton got her hat and coat, dashed cold water in her eyes, put on some makeup, and joined us.

Sellers drove to the Kozy Dell Slumber Court. The woman came out, looked at Mrs. Fulton and shook her head.

"No?" Sellers asked.

"No," she said. "The woman who was with him was smaller, a well-formed pint-size kid, with long hair, high cheekbones, big, darkish eyes, and very full lips."

"You're sure you weren't fooled, not seeing her get out of the car?" Sellers asked.

"Not a chance in the world," the woman said. "This woman—well, *she* knows her way around. She's married. The other one was slinky, well, a little bit frightened. She'd done a little playing around, but she wasn't accustomed to spending the night in auto camps."

"Thought you said she was a tramp," Sellers said.

"Well—put it this way. She was a damn little hypocrite, and she was frightened about something that was due to happen. I thought it was about maybe getting caught on an all-night party. I don't know. It was something."

"How do you know this woman's married?" Sellers asked.

"I can tell 'em as far as I can see 'em. This woman's settled down. She'd quit thinking of herself. She's got a home, a kid, probably a couple of 'em. This little tramp last night hadn't got her man yet and she wasn't thinking of anybody but herself."

Sellers said, "You talk like a mind reader."

"I am," the woman said. "In this business you've got to be."

"How old was this girl last night?" Sellers asked.

"Younger than this woman, a lot younger."

"Smaller?"

"Smaller."

"Lighter?"

"A whole lot lighter."

Sellers sighed and started the car. "Okay," he said wearily. "That's just the way it goes. You have to investigate all of these angles."

While we were driving back to San Robles, I said casually to Sellers, "What time do you figure the shooting took place, Sellers?"

"Right around ten-fifteen, as nearly as we can determine. You know how it is in a case of that kind. No one pays enough attention to look at the time, and then they have to approximate it afterward, but it was right around ten-fifteen."

"Checked up on everybody?" I asked.

"Uh huh," he said wearily.

"How about Mrs. Fulton?"

"What about her?"

"Checked up on her?"

"What are you getting at?" Mrs. Fulton said.

Sellers cocked a quizzical eyebrow at me.

I said, "You must have had quite a shock last night, Mrs. Fulton. When did you learn your husband was dead?"

"About one o'clock in the morning. The police came and got me out of bed."

"That's tough. Of course," I said, "you thought you had insurance. That must have helped soften the blow."

"Yes," she admitted, "I thought I had insurance until I talked with that insurance man. What's all this about checking up on me?"

"He just wants to know where you were," Sellers said, grinning. "He's taking an indirect way of finding out."

"Where I was! Why, I was home, of course."

"Anyone else with you?"

"Certainly not. My husband was away. I was there with the children."

"Where were the children?"

"In bed."

"I mean at ten-fifteen."

"That's when I mean."

Sellers glanced over at the woman, then looked at me again. "Lam," he said, "you do get some of the damnedest ideas."

"Don't I?"

Sellers said, "Okay, Mrs. Fulton, I hate to rub it in, but just for the record, you *could* have slipped out of the house, gone down to the Kozy Dell Slumber Court, found your husband down there, made a scene, and—"

"Oh, bosh!" she interrupted.

"And that scene," Sellers went on, "could have been the thing that caused your husband to shoot his sweetheart and commit suicide."

"Don't be a sap."

"There's *something* cockeyed about it."

"In the first place," she said, "how would I have got down there? I didn't have a car."

"How do we know you didn't? You told us that your husband was out working and had his car, but—by God, Lam, I believe you've got something! Dover Fulton *didn't* have the car with him. He'd left the car at home. His wife got in the car, beat it down to the Kozy Dell Slumber Court, made a scene, and the scene terminated in a shooting, and she was afraid to drive the car back. She—"

Seller's voice trailed off into silence.

"Running out of ideas?" Mrs. Fulton asked sarcastically.

"No, just getting them," Sellers said. "You got any way of showing where you were at ten-fifteen? Any way at all?"

She hesitated a moment, then said, "Certainly I have."

"What is it?"

"A man called up just about ten-fifteen," she said, "and ask me if my husband was home. Then he said something about a Lucille Hart, who was supposed to be my sister. I told him I didn't have any sister. And then he hung up. But all we have to do is to find that man and—"

"Nice stuff," Sellers said sarcastically. "All we have to do is to find one guy out of the three or four million phone subscribers who are within reaching distance."

"Well, it seems to me it would be easy. If you'd let it be known in the paper—"

"We might at that," Sellers interrupted. "You answered the phone personally?"

"That's right."

"Talked with this man?"

"Yes."

"Think he'd recognize your voice?"

"He should—he should be able to tell it again. In any event, he can tell that some grown woman was at my address and answered the telephone. That would certainly seem to dispose of this wild theory you have."

Sellers drove for a while in silence.

"And how do you think I got home after the shooting?" Mrs. Fulton asked.

"You probably hitchhiked," Sellers said. "You'd locked the car up when you went there and you were afraid to— Now, wait a minute. Donald Lam's card was in there, and— Where's your coin purse?"

"Right here in my bag."

"Let's take a look at it."

She opened her bag, and Sellers pulled the police car over to the curb to a stop. He looked at the coin purse Irene Fulton handed him, said thoughtfully, "That doesn't prove anything."

"Neither do you!" she snapped, then said suddenly, "Isn't it enough that I have all these troubles without having you coming along and adding to them?"

"Yes, I suppose so," Sellers said, and eased the car out from the curb. But all the way to San Robles he was scowling as he watched the road. He didn't use the siren, and he was driving so slowly that a couple of times I was afraid we'd be pinched for blocking traffic.

Mrs. Fulton didn't say anything, either. She sat with her face hard, white and strained, looking straight ahead through the windshield. She had thoughts for company, and they weren't nice thoughts.

We got to the house in San Robles and Sellers said, "I guess I'll just take a look through the place. You can show me where the kids were sleeping and where the phone's located."

I made motions in the rear seat, and Sellers threw over his shoulder, "You sit right there, Lam."

I settled back and smoked a cigarette.

Sellers was gone about ten minutes. When he came out, he had a cigar in his mouth that he had chewed into frayed wreckage.

He adjusted himself behind the steering wheel, slammed the car door, turned to me and said, "Damn it, Lam, there are times when I could knock your teeth right down your throat."

I looked at him innocently. "Why?" I asked.

"I'm damned if I know," Sellers said angrily, "and that's what makes it so damned irritating."

69

CHAPTER SEVEN

"My Wife Was a Tramp!"

SELLERS TURNED ON THE SIREN when he was halfway to town and we started speeding again.

"You can take me back to the office," I told him.

"I'm not done with you yet."

"Where to now?"

He said, "You'll find out," and pushed down harder on the throttle.

We screamed through the Sunday traffic, pulled up at length in front of the Beaverbrook Hotel.

A plain-clothes officer gave a nod of his head as Sellers stalked in.

Sellers moved over to him, said, "What's he doing? In his room?"

The man nodded.

"Alone?"

"That's right."

"Telephoning?"

"Only to room service."

"What's he doing."

"Getting plastered."

"That suits me fine," Sellers said. He jerked his head in my direction and said, "Come on, Lam."

We went to the elevator, and got off at the eleventh floor. Sellers already knew the way. He walked on down the corridor and banged his knuckles on the door of 1110.

"Who is it?" a voice called from behind the panels.

"Come on," Sellers said impatiently, "get it open."

There was the sound of motion from within the room, and then the door was opened by a tall, thin individual with good shoulders, flat stomach, and an air about the way he wore his clothes which showed he knew he was good-looking. He had dark, wavy hair, a long, firm mouth, wide-spaced gray eyes, and a skin that was tanned to a hard bronze.

He'd been drinking, and his eyes were red. Whether all the redness came from the liquor was not readily apparent.

"Well, well," he said, "the estimable Sergeant Sellers. Good Old Homicide, himself! Come on in, Sellers. Who's the guy with you?"

Sellers didn't wait for the invitation. He pushed his way into the room, and I followed.

Sellers kicked the door shut.

"Know this guy?" he asked.

The man looked me over, shook his head. "Who is he?"

"Donald Lam, a detective."

"What's he want?"

"He doesn't—I do."

"What do you want?"

"I want to know all about him."

"Ask somebody else."

"Why not introduce us?" I asked.

The man said, "I'm Stanwick Carlton."

"Oh," I said.

Sellers walked over and sat down in the most comfortable chair in the place.

I put my hand out to Carlton and said, "Glad to know you, Mr. Carlton."

"What did you say your name was?"

"Donald Lam."

We shook hands.

Carlton said, "Sit down and have a drink, Lam. Might as well. There isn't anything else to do. The boys are nice to me. Tell me to do anything I want to, go anywhere I want to, just don't leave town. Every time I leave the damn hotel some cop picks me up and trails along with me."

"You don't know when you *are* lucky," Sellers said.

"Perhaps not, but I could stand with a little less good luck, if that's what you call being lucky."

Sellers said, "You *could* be behind bars."

"For what?"

Sellers couldn't think of the answer to that one.

71

"I'm the subject of morbid curiosity," Carlton announced. "I'm the husband of a tramp, a tramp that got caught in the meshes of her own illicit love affair and got killed. Are you married, Lam?"

"No."

"Have a drink, then. Don't get married. You get all wrapped up in someone. They're your very life. And then the first thing you know, they get killed in an auto camp. Have a drink. What do you want? Bourbon and 7-Up? Scotch and soda? Ginger ale and rye? Or—"

"Scotch and soda," I said.

Carlton walked over to the dresser, said to Sellers, "You can't drink, you're on duty. That's your hard luck."

He splashed liquor into glasses with an unsteady hand, said, "Anyhow, the guy's civilized. He drinks Scotch and soda."

Sellers said, "You *could* have hired this man to shadow your wife."

"That's right," Carlton proclaimed, "I sure as hell could. There's lots of things I could have done. There's lots of things I could do. I'm on the eleventh floor. I could make a parachute out of a sheet and jump out of the window. Want to see me try it?"

Sellers didn't say anything.

Carlton grinned, and said, "What's your angle in the racket, Lam?"

"No angle," I said. "Old Beagle over here just picked me up and is taking me along to let people look me over. He thinks he's going to discover something."

"I may, at that," Sellers said, watching the whiskey with hungry eyes.

"Why don't you break down and be human, Sellers?" I asked. "After all, you can't stay on duty twenty-four hours a day. And as far as *this* investigation is concerned you're all finished."

"Who says I'm finished?"

"I do. You're up against a brick wall."

Carlton tossed down his drink, said drunkenly, "I don't want any sympathy. All I want is to be left alone. I don't know what the hell I came to California for, anyway. I was

72

just lonesome. I wanted to see my wife. I saw her—stretched out on a slab in an undertaking parlor.

"Everyone knows about it. They read it in the papers. A cheap, sordid little affair out at an auto court. My God, I don't think it was even a first-class dump. Okay, I'm the fall guy. I've got to arrange for her burial. I've got to go down and pick out the coffin. I've got to go to the funeral. I've got to listen while some concealed voice sings *The End of a Perfect Day* to organ music. I wish to hell I'd have been the one to—"

"Take it easy," I said. "Little Pitchers, over here, has big ears."

"So he does," Carlton said, turning to Sellers. "I'd almost forgotten about you."

Sellers said, "Someday, Lam, I'm going to take you to pieces just to see what makes you tick."

Sellers heaved himself up out of the chair, crossed over to the bureau, poured bourbon into a glass and then dumped in ginger ale.

"Attaboy!" Carlton said. "I knew you had a human streak in you."

"What the hell did you come to California for?" Sellers asked.

"I tell you, I wanted to see my wife. I was lonely."

"Why didn't you let her know you were coming so she'd be meeting you?"

"I'm damned if I know," Carlton said. "I just had a hunch that something was wrong, that she was in some sort of a jam."

He sneered into his drink and said, "The old subconscious. Good old mental telepathy. Thought she was in trouble and needed a helping hand from her husband!"

Sellers said, "Damn it, you came here because you had a hunch. You've admitted that you were suspicious of Dover Fulton. You started looking him up. You found out that he was with your wife. You trailed them to that auto court. You busted in there and did some talking and told them you were through; that as far as Dover Fulton was concerned, he'd taken your woman and now he could keep her. You stalked out.

"Your wife didn't really care for Fulton, except as someone to play around with. She loved you, but she wanted just

73

a little variety. So when she went on her vacation, she wanted to do a little playing. She—"

Carlton came up out of the chair. "Damn you," he said, "watch what you're saying! I don't give a damn if you are a cop, I'll throw this drink in your face!"

"You do it, and you'll be flattened out as though a steam roller had gone over you," Sellers said.

Carlton hesitated for a minute. "You keep a decent tongue in your head when you're talking about Babe."

Sellers said, "Just the same, you went out there, Carlton. It stands to reason you did."

Carlton, quivering with anger, said, "God-damn it, let's not misunderstand each other, Sergeant. If I'd gone out there and caught her with that son-of-a-bitch I'd have killed him so dead he never would have—"

"And then killed your wife," Sellers said.

There were tears in Carlton's eyes. "Not Babe," he said. "I'd have booted her. I'd have kicked her. I'd have given her a black eye, and then I'd have said, 'Get your clothes on and come home, you little tramp!' And when I'd got her home I'd have loved her—just like I always will love her. Now then, keep your filthy mind on something else for a change, flat-foot."

Sellers said, "You're drunk."

"You're damn right I'm drunk," Carlton said. "Want to make something of it?"

Sellers got up and came to stand facing Carlton, chin to chin. "You watch yourself," he said, his broad hulk making Carlton seem even more slender and fragile. "I could slap you real hard and break you in two. I could pick you up by the back of the neck and give you a good shake, and all of your teeth would jar loose. I know how you feel, and I'm making allowances for it, but don't crowd your luck too far."

"*You* know how *I* feel!" Carlton said sarcastically. "You and who else?"

"I just want to know one thing," Sellers said. "Did you hire this guy?"

"No."

"Did you ever talk with him?"

"I've never seen him in my life."

Sellers finished the rest of his drink, put down the empty glass, said, "Come on, Lam."

"Stick around and talk to me," Carlton said. "I'm lonesome. Don't leave."

I saw instant suspicion flare in Sellers's eyes.

I shook my head and said, "Not that way, Carlton. This guy's trying to find out who hired me. If you act as though you want to talk in private, he'll have you nominated on the first ballot."

"Who hired you to do what?" Carlton asked.

"That's what Sellers wants to know."

Carlton stepped back and squinted his eyes as though trying hard to get me in focus. "Say," he said, "maybe I do want to talk with you, after all."

I went over to the door, opened it, stepped out in the hall.

"All right, then," Carlton called after us angrily, "go to hell if you want to, and see who cares."

Sellers came barging out into the hall and pulled the door shut behind him.

I said, "You keep leading with your chin, Frank. Why don't you stay home and read the funnies? This is a hell of a way to spend Sunday."

"Ain't it," Sellers said grimly. "And I haven't finished spending it yet, either. There's one more thing I want to investigate."

"What's that?"

"You'll find out."

We went down in the elevator. Sellers called the plainclothes man in the lobby over to him and said, "I guess that's all. He's burned up and we may as well let him go. He isn't doing us any good the way he is."

The plain-clothes man nodded. "Quitting when?" he asked.

"Now," Sellers said. "Turn in your report. This is quitting time."

The plain-clothes man grinned, and said, "That's a break. I'm on my way. I had a date to take the wife and kid to the beach, and I've been in the doghouse ever since I phoned her you'd staked me out up here."

"Okay, get out of the doghouse," Sellers told him, and took me out to the police car.

This time we went to a parking lot.

Sellers said to the man who ran the place, "Dover Fulton keeps a space here by the month, huh?"

"That's right."

"His car in here last night?"

"It was yesterday afternoon. Say, that's too bad about him. I had no idea he was in it that deep."

Sellers paid no attention. "What about the car? Who got it. Fulton?"

The man shook his head.

"Come over here and take a look at the guy with me," Sellers said. "Get out, Lam."

I got out.

"Ever see this guy before?"

The man who ran the parking station shook his head.

"What about Fulton's car? Do you give him a check for it?"

"Not the regular tenants. We know them. They have stalls that are assigned to them by number and can come and go whenever they want to. They usually keep the cars locked. I don't know whether Fulton kept his locked yesterday or not. It was the jane who got it."

"The jane?" Sellers asked, surprised.

"That's right. The one who was found in the cabin with him, I guess."

"What did she look like?"

"I don't know. I didn't see her too well—just a trim little package came bustling on in here as though she knew right where she was going, and evidently had the keys to the car. I watched her get in. The way she acted, fumbling around at the door for a minute, I felt certain she had the keys."

"Why didn't you say something to her?"

The attendant grinned, and shook his head. "Not with the regular clients. Not with a guy like Dover Fulton you wouldn't. If he sent some babe down after the car, you'd not go over and ask any questions, not if she had the car keys."

"How did you know she wasn't making off with the car?"

"They don't do that. Not in this locality. But I know it was okay. She had one of Dover Fulton's cards with an 'OK' scrawled on it."

"How do you know?"

"She gave it to me when she went out. I wouldn't have stopped her, but she waved the card at me."

"Let's take a look."

The attendant said, "I don't know where I put it. I knew it was all right. Wait a minute, I think I stuck it in the bottom of the cash register. I remember now, I did."

He went over and opened the cash register, pulled up the weight which held the bills in place in the currency drawer and took out one of Dover Fulton's cards. On the back of it was simply written the initials *OK*.

Sellers looked at him pityingly. "This Fulton's handwriting?"

"I presume so. It's his card."

"A business card. He passes 'em out by the dozen."

The man grinned. "You should have seen this doll."

"Redhead?"

"I don't rightly know the color of her hair. She may even have had a hat on. It was her eyes that I noticed—great big dark-brown eyes, about the color of ripe dates. I guess I was thinking of dates and thinking how lucky Fulton was. Lucky! That shows all I know about it. The poor sap was up to his necktie, and sinking deeper."

"Say, wait a minute," Sellers said. "I don't think that's the girl that was in the place with him. Would you know her picture if—?"

"Probably not her picture. But I'd sure know her."

"And this chap wasn't with her?" Sellers asked, jerking his head toward me.

The man shook his head.

"You watched this jane get in the car?"

"I'll say I did—and believe me, there was something to watch."

"You're a lecherous old goat," Sellers said.

"I guess I am, for a fact," the attendant admitted sorrowfully.

"Why don't you grow up?"

"Hell, that's the trouble, I have grown up. The missus is like an old shoe. I wouldn't trade her for anything. She's got a form like a sack of potatoes, but she cooks like nobody's business. She grabs the paycheck as soon as I get it and she bawls hell out of me every so often. But—hang it, I don't know, Sergeant, a man needs a little inspiration once in a while. Just watching a cute little trick like that, as supple as the greased cable out of a speedometer—damn me, it wasn't so long ago that the wife was quite a dancer. We used to go out and hoof it—"

"Not very long ago," Sellers said impatiently. "Thirty-five years is all."

The attendant furrowed his forehead. "It ain't as bad as that—twenty-two—twenty-three—about twenty-four years, and—"

"Okay," Sellers said, "save it. Get back in the car, Lam."

Sellers was thinking all the way back to the office. He let me out in front of the office building and said, "This is where I came in. Go on and resume the even tempo of your life, and remember I'm keeping an eye on you. If you try to pull a fast one on this, I'll break you so fast it'll make your head swim. I don't care what Bertha says, I'll bust you."

I yawned, and said, "I hear that stuff so much it sounds like a radio commercial. Why don't you get someone to put it to music so you could be like the smart boys on the radio and have a singing commercial. It wouldn't tire the audience."

Sellers glared at me, slammed the door of the police car, and went away from there fast.

CHAPTER EIGHT

The Third Bullet

I RANG THE BELL ON BERTHA'S APARTMENT. Bertha's shrill whistle came screaming down the speaking tube. "What is it now?"

"This is Donald."

Bertha grunted under her breath and pushed the buzzer which unlatched the front door.

I climbed the flight of stairs and turned to the left, tapped on the panels of the door, and Bertha yelled, "Come in, it's unlocked."

I opened the door and went in.

Bertha was sprawled out in typical Sunday splendor, wearing loose-fitting pajamas, a robe, her hair pulled straight back and stringing down back of her ears. The big easy chair in the middle of the floor was the center of a litter of Sunday papers. On a coffee table by the side of the chair was an electric percolator. Nearby was a cup, saucer, cream and sugar; a big cigarette tray was all but overflowing with the ends of cigarettes and matches.

On the other side of the big easy chair was a table with an electric toaster, a plate of bread, some butter, and a plate containing butterhorns.

It was typical of the way Bertha spent her Sundays. From time to time she'd feed a piece of bread into the electric toaster and butter it when it came out a golden brown. Then she'd pour more coffee from the big electric percolator which held half a gallon, and put in lots of cream and sugar. She'd drink coffee, nibble toast, read, and snort comments at the news stories.

Bertha looked up over her shoulder, her little beady eyes

glittering angrily. "What the hell," she said. "Frank Sellers has been camped on my doorstep. He showed up shortly after you telephoned. What the hell's the idea?"

I said, "I gave that girl my card."

"So I gathered," Bertha said. "God, but you're dumb, for a detective."

"It seemed like a good idea at the time."

"Lots of things do when you're dealing with a babe on a Saturday night."

I said, "I can't tell whether she deliberately left it as a cross, or whether it was an accident."

"Does it make any difference?" Bertha asked.

"It might."

Bertha said, "You should get yourself a good name to go philandering under. Just because you're not married you think you can pass out cards. My God, I don't know why it is that a brainy little guy like you can be so damned naïve."

I waited until she had sputtered herself into silence, then said, "I want to get something on the Cabanita Club."

"What do you want?"

"Some low-down," I said. "You know the master of ceremonies there, don't you?"

I knew that was a safe bet, because Bertha knew them all. There was a streak of the showman about Bertha, and somehow she managed to know half of the night club entertainers in the country.

"Let me see," Bertha said, "I think Bob Elgin is down there now."

"I'd like to talk with him."

"He wouldn't like to talk with you."

"He might."

Bertha sighed, and said, "Open that drawer over there in the bureau, lover. Get me that red notebook in there on top of the cigarette cartons. Better toss me out a fresh package of cigarettes while you're about it, too."

I got her the notebook and the cigarettes.

Bertha said, "What's Sellers got on his mind? Wasn't it just another suicide pact?"

"Looks like it," I said, "only there are some things that don't fit in. They're bothering Sellers. I think now he's crossed the thing off the books."

"Well, if he's crossed it off, that's all there is to it."

"Perhaps."

Bertha said, "What the hell are you getting at?"

I said, "If a man's made a suicide pact, why should he miss the first shot?"

Bertha's glittering little eyes sharpened with avaricious interest. "Anything in it for us, Donald?" she asked.

"I don't know."

"Come over here and sit down. Pour yourself a drink. What do you want? Coffee? Beer? Or whiskey and soda? I have coffee here, but you'll have to get yourself a cup. There's soda in the ice box and—"

"I'll take a cup of coffee," I said.

I went for a cup and saucer. Bertha put on a slice of toast for me, ran through the little red-backed notebook and said, "Bob Elgin's apartment telephone is Cornwall 6-3481. Why do you think he missed the first shot, lover?"

I said, "I don't know. There were three shots, all right."

"The third shot went into a suitcase?"

"That's right. Into the woman's suitcase, right near the handle. For a while police couldn't find the bullet. They were wondering about that third shot. Then they opened the suitcase and found where the bullet had gone through, leaving a neat little hole and embedding itself in the clothes."

"It didn't go all the way through the suitcase?"

"About halfway."

"What's in it for us, lover? What's the angle?"

I said, "He carried forty thousand dollars' worth of insurance, double indemnity, at that. He'd had it for less than a year. If he killed the woman and then himself, the insurance is void. If the man was shot first, then he was murdered and the insurance company would be nicked for eighty thousand dollars."

"But the gun was in *his* hand," Bertha said, her eyes greedy.

"It was when they found the bodies. Someone *could* have tampered with the evidence—not much, just eighty thousand dollars' worth."

"But the woman was shot in the *back* of the head," Bertha said.

"That's right."

"She couldn't have done that to herself, could she?"

"Probably not."

Bertha said angrily, "You're the most exasperating person in the world!"

"A percentage of eighty thousand bucks would be a lot of dollars."

Bertha beamed. "You get busy on that angle, lover."

"There are a couple of things for you to do, Bertha. Go see the widow, get her to employ us."

"Suppose she popped him?"

"There are children. If we did work for their benefit a court would give us a fee, *if* the guardian employed us. The mother's the guardian right now."

"I'll tie her up," Bertha said with determination.

"Always remember that she could have done the shooting," I pointed out. "She's the logical suspect."

"Well, damn it all," Bertha said angrily, "don't go taking up my time building air castles and then letting me down to the ground. Haven't you anything that makes you think—"

"The only thing is that I called up the wife to find out where her husband was. I also asked about her sister. I didn't look at the time, but that was after we'd got back to town and I'd checked on this Durham man in the Westchester Arms Hotel. He'd checked out a short time before. I telephoned the wife to ask if she had a sister and she said no."

"Well, what about it?"

"She told Sergeant Sellers that call came in just about the time the police fix the hour when the shots were fired. But my call must have been a good hour and a half later."

"What was her idea in saying that?"

"Perhaps she was trying to get an alibi. Perhaps she was sleepy and didn't know what time it really was."

"Any other thoughts?"

"Lots of them. Some of them Sergeant Sellers shares. He doesn't like the idea of Stanwick Carlton, the husband who was being betrayed, coming here from Colorado just in time to check in at the hotel, look around, and then go out somewhere at about the time the shooting took place."

"I don't like that, either," Bertha said. "Wait a minute, I like it a lot. If it was murder we could make something of that."

I nodded.

"What makes the police think suicide?"

I said, "The door was locked from the inside. The bodies were lying on the floor. There was no sign of a struggle. It was the guy's own gun. It was held loosely in his hand when the police found the bodies."

Bertha frowned, and said, "You'd have a hell of a time selling the insurance company eighty thousand dollars' worth of theory when the facts are like that."

I nodded.

"Door locked from the inside?" Bertha said.

"That's right. The woman who owned the place had to punch the key out of the door on the inside before she could open the door with her passkey. I think there was a window open."

Bertha frowned. Slowly a look of disappointment came over her face. She said, "You can't make it stick, Donald, no matter how you try. The door was locked from the inside and it was his gun. That sews the case up."

"But there were three shots."

"Well, he missed one."

"Which one?"

"The first, probably."

I said, "The woman was shot in the back of the head."

"Well?"

I said, "All right, he missed the first shot. What happened then?"

"How the hell do I know?" Bertha said. "You're putting the thing together. You tell me what happened next."

I said, "If the woman had had her back turned, she'd have swung around at the sound of that shot to see what happened, wouldn't she?"

Bertha nodded.

I said, "In that event, if he'd shot her again he'd have shot her in the forehead, right while she was looking at him."

Bertha said, "She looked at him for a second, saw what he had in mind, and turned and started to run. Perhaps she was trying to get to the door. He shot her in the back of the head."

"While she was running?"

"Why not?"

83

I said, "If he missed the first shot while she was standing still, he must have improved his shooting a lot between the time of the first and second shot while she was running."

"Perhaps the woman turned her back to him, knowing he was going to shoot her. It was a suicide pact and she couldn't face the gun, or perhaps he couldn't get up his nerve to shoot her in the forehead."

"That's logical," I said, "but then why did he miss the first shot, and why did he miss it that far?"

"What do you mean that far?"

I said, "A woman who's standing up has her head over five feet above the floor. A suitcase on the floor isn't more than eighteen inches high. If he was shooting at her head, and missed, and hit the suitcase—"

"I get it!" Bertha said. "I get it!" Her little eyes blinked rapidly. She let her lips soften in a smile. "Donald," she said, "you're smart—at times—damn smart. Now, what can Bertha do to help?"

I said, "You can ring up Bob Elgin and tell him your partner wants to talk with him. Tell him that you'd appreciate it if he'd give me an hour."

"Hand me the phone," Bertha said.

I handed Bertha the telephone. She dialed the number she wanted, and sat there waiting, her little beady eyes blinking rapidly as she thought things over.

Abruptly Bertha cupped her hand over the mouthpiece of the telephone, looked up and said, "Ten G's in it for us, lover?"

"That depends," I told her. "There *could* be plenty."

Bertha nodded with smug complacency. "Now you're talking," she said. "I knew I could depend on you to—"

She jerked her hand away from the mouthpiece and said in her most seductive tones, "Hello . . . hello . . . hello, Bob? Bob, this is Bertha Cool. . . . Now, Bob, I know you work late, but after all it's time *anyone* should be up. I sleep late, myself. . . . Look, Bob, I have a favor I want you to do for me. Now be a lamb and do what Bertha wants."

There was an interval of silence during which Bertha frowned at the telephone, then she apparently interrupted, to say, "Now don't be like that, Bob. Here's the setup. I have a partner, Donald Lam, and he's working on a case, trying to find somebody who evidently has had some contact with the Cabanita. Now, Bob, if you could give him just half an hour—just talk with him. . . . No, no, you don't need to dress, just stick around in your pajamas. Just talk with him, that's all. . . . No, it isn't doing anything that will give your place notoriety. . . . I tell you, it's just giving my partner a little help. . . . All right, he'll be right over. . . . You still at the same address?

"Thanks, Bob, darling. Bertha loves you for that."

Bertha hung up the telephone and said, "The son-of-a-bitch!"

"What's the matter?" I asked.

"Half grouchy," Bertha said. "After all I've done for him, too."

"But he's going to see me?"

"He'll see you," Bertha said, "but he could have been a lot nicer about it."

"What's the address?"

Bertha took a piece of paper, scribbled an address on it, said, "His apartment is 825. It's one of those places where you have to be announced. Private switchboard and all that kind of stuff. Just wait until the next time Bob Elgin wants something out of me."

I said, "Perhaps he was just grouchy at being disturbed by the telephone."

"He tried to stall us," Bertha said. "Fancy that, lover, the nerve of him trying to stall Bertha Cool!"

"Perhaps he wanted to go back to sleep."

"Well, it's time for him to get up. I've done too damn much for him."

"What did you ever do for him, Bertha? It might help if I knew."

"I squared a rap for him once, and believe me, it took some squaring. I damn near lost my license over that. But that's something you don't need to know. It's better if you don't. You beat it on up there, lover."

I said, "Okay, here's something you can do while I'm gone."

"What?"

I said, "The police are closing the case. They're giving everyone a clean bill of health. Now this suitcase with a bullet in it belonged to Minerva Carlton. I want you to get hold of Stanwick Carlton and persuade him that, as the husband of the dead woman, he should demand that suitcase from the authorities. When he gets it, persuade him that you want to take it for a little while for evidence.''

"What for?" Bertha asked.

I said, "I want to follow the course of that bullet.''

Bertha's eyes glittered. "I get you," she said.

I said, "Stanwick Carlton is a big, tough guy, but he isn't half as tough as he thinks he is. He'd love to have someone pull a mother act with him.''

"I'll clutch him to my bosom and let him sob his heart out," Bertha said.

"Be a mother to him," I told her. "You won't mind putting on a mother act, will you, Bertha?''

"Hell," Bertha said, "If it'll bring us in any money, I'll be his *grand*mother.''

CHAPTER NINE

Gag Man At Home

THE APARTMENT HOUSE had originally been built to cater to the type that wanted to make an impression. The front of the place looked like a million dollars. There was an ornate lobby with a desk and a private switchboard. A solemn-faced clerk took care of both and there was even an elevator boy clad in blue livery with gold braid and the crest of the apartment house embroidered on the collar and sleeves.

The clerk looked up as I came in. I said, "Mr. Elgin, please."

"Robert Elgin?"

"Yes."

"Is he expecting you?"

"Yes."

"Your name, please."

"Lam."

The clerk turned to the switchboard, stabbed a plug into one of the receptacles, waited a moment until the light went off, then said, "A Mr. Lam to see you. He says you're expecting him. . . . Thank you."

He pulled out the plug, slipped off the earphones, said, "You may go up. Apartment 825."

The elevator boy took me up, stopped the elevator, and indicated the apartment.

The place was just as I had expected it would be, plenty of swank in front and all cut up into small apartments. Bob Elgin stood in the doorway, wearing a dressing gown, pajamas, and a look of complete, utter weariness. I don't think I have ever seen a man who looked so thoroughly tired, not the fatigue of exhaustion, but simply a complete and utter weariness with himself, his surroundings, his life, and his job.

He had a cigarette dangling listlessly from loose lips. It was as though the mouth simply didn't have the strength enough to hold the cigarette up, but let it dangle at an angle that emphasized the utter weariness of his features.

"You're Lam," he said.

"That's right." I extended my hand.

"Bertha Cool's partner?"

"Right."

He gave me a listless hand. For a moment there was a slight tightening of the fingers, then his hand became putty.

I dropped the hand, and Elgin said, "Come in."

Technically, it was a double apartment. If the bedroom could be judged by the living-room, it was just about big enough to hold a bed, a dresser, and the door to the bathroom. The living-room had a davenport, two chairs and a table, a badly worn carpet, dejected lace curtains, and a few pictures. At one end was a miniature breakfast nook, an electric refrigerator, and a small electric range. Above that were some cupboards.

The sinkboard held a few dirty dishes, and there were two glasses on the table in the living-room. The half inch of water in the bottom of each glass could have been left by ice cubes that had melted during the night. The ash trays were filled with cigarette stubs and the open window hadn't been able to get the atmosphere of stale tobacco and liquor fumes out of the room. There was a copy of *Variety* on the table, and another one on the davenport. The Sunday newspapers, still folded, were also on the davenport, as though Elgin had picked them up right after he had answered Bertha Cool's telephone call but had decided not to read them.

He was, however, shaved, and his hair was combed. Glossy black hair, combed straight back.

"Sit down," he said, "make yourself at home. The place is a mess. I had a couple of drinks last night before we rolled in."

I nodded, and sat down.

He was around fifty, hollow-cheeked, pinch-waisted, fairly broad-shouldered. He had high cheekbones, and his black eyes were spread far apart. He had a trick of lowering the lids over those eyes, tilting his head back and looking out from half-closed eyes. It gave him a peculiar expression of not giving a damn about anything.

I said, "I suppose you have to keep pretty late hours."

"It's pretty close to daylight before I get home." The weariness of the voice showed how he felt about it.

"I understand you put on quite a show at the Cabanita," I said.

He made a little gesture of disgust, sucked deeply on the cigarette, blew out twin streams of smoke from his nostrils, said, "It's a job."

"You own the place?"

"I lease it."

"You have a steady trade?"

"Steady business, not steady trade. You want to buy the dump?"

"No, I was just interested in the way it runs."

"We see a lot of the same faces," Elgin admitted, "but with a place like that, you try to build it up so it has a reputation. I put on an act of fast talking, slip in some double-meanings so fast it takes them a while to get it, and go right on without waiting for the laughs, until I get my first titter. Then I stop and look surprised, and that usually brings down the house."

"Women go for that stuff?" I asked.

"They eat it up."

"The first laugh usually comes from a woman?"

"The fast talking, double-meanings get the women," he said. "Usually some dowager who knows all the angles titters hysterically. Then I stop talking and look at her in surprise. By that time the joke in the situation has caught up with the rest of the audience and they start laughing.

"On the jokes that are a little more raw, there's usually some loud-voiced guy gives a belly laugh first. I don't pay any attention to him, simply go on talking, and then stop when the general laughter develops. It's a job of timing. The main thing is never to stop long enough for the audience to catch up. Some of them might get shocked if you did. Just keep on going."

"They fall for it, eh?"

"I tell you, they eat it up. Women who would slap your face

if you tried to say anything off-color in private sit out there right in front of the whole damn dining-room and laugh their heads off at stuff I tell them that's just as close to the border-line as I can get by with it. What the hell *do* you want?"

"I wanted to find out something about a woman."

"Oh, my God!"

"What's the matter?"

"Getting me up at this hour over a woman. God, I can give you the names and telephone numbers of five hundred of them."

"You know a lot of them?"

"I know every hustler in town."

"This may not be a hustler. She has been in the Cabanita recently."

"What about her?"

I said, "She's a pocket edition—warm eyes, light hair, very small, but perfectly formed. High cheekbones, full lips. Sort of a baby stare, and—"

He interrupted me, to make a motion with his hand, a lazy motion which pivoted at the wrist, much as a swimming seal would casually twist a flipper.

"Know her?"

"Hell, yes. I know a hundred of them. They all come in. They all look the same. It's a model you're describing, not an individual."

"This one's an individual."

"Well, we've got lots of them. I can't help you on that. You'll have to look the joint over for yourself."

I said, "This little number has lots of fire, quite a bit of individuality."

"Know her name?"

"I know the name she gave me—Lucille Hart."

"Don't know her."

"I think the 'Lucille' may be okay," I said. "The 'Hart' may or may not have been made up."

He said, "Wait a minute. I want to think."

He took another drag at the cigarette, then pinched it out and dropped the butt into an ash tray that was just about full. I noticed other cigarette butts in there with lipstick smears on them.

"Lucille," he said almost musingly.

90

He waited a while, his eyes on the faded carpet, then he tilted his head back so that he could look down his nose at me through half-closed lids. "What's it to you?" he asked.

"I want to find her."

"So I gathered," he said dryly. "Professional or personal?"

"You might say it's a little of both."

"Tell me about the personal angle."

"She took me to a motor court, then stood me up and left me holding the sack."

Elgin yawned.

There was silence in the room. A fly was buzzing around in sleepy circles, looking for a patch of sunlight and not finding any.

Elgin reached for another cigarette. "Want one?"

"No, thanks."

"What's the professional angle?"

"I don't know. She may be mixed up in a case I'm investigating."

"What sort of a case?"

"Suicide. A love tryst. It's in the paper," I said, jerking my hand toward the folded newspapers.

"Never read that kind of crap," Elgin said. "I look at the foreign news, then study the sporting pages, particularly the horse race stuff. Lots of times you can get a chance for a good gag on a horse race."

"You don't read the funnies?" I asked.

"Good God, no. When you have to be comical three shows a night, seven days a week, you don't want to even think of some guy who tries to be funny every day in a comic strip. I have to be funny. It's a business. He has to be funny; it's his business. I sympathize with him too much. What else do you want to know?"

"Suppose this Lucille hangs around your place? How would I be apt to find her?"

"Just by hanging around the dump. I wouldn't ask any questions, though, if I were you."

I said, "Here's a folder of matches from the Cabanita. Is this the latest type you're using?"

"That's right. Never have used any other. Only the one folder."

I said, "There was something folded on the inside of a cigarette package that went with it."

I took out the torn slip of cardboard, on the back of which were the words, *Kozy Dell Slumber Court*.

Bob Elgin looked it over.

I said, "Look at the front of the thing now. What do you make of it?"

I pushed the torn scrap of cardboard over to him. I said, "I think this may have come from your place."

He turned it over and said, "I think so, too."

I said, "You'll notice on the torn part there's a place where it says, 'Minimum check $5.00 per person.' " Over on the other corner appeared the words, *A la Cabanita, special*.

I said, "That looks to me as though it had been torn from a menu in your place."

"So it does."

"Any ideas?"

"No."

"You're not being very helpful."

"I'm here. I've got the place open. I'm talking to you. I'm answering questions. This Lucille of yours may be a regular patron. She may have been someone that just dropped in. I'm sorry I can't give you any more help. It isn't because I don't recognize her description. I do. I told you before, there are a hundred of them who answer that description."

"Where do they all come from?"

He shrugged his shoulders and said, "Where does dust come from when the wind's blowing?" and then abruptly said, "How many men do you know who have really beautiful wives?"

"What does that have to do with it?" I asked.

He said, cynically, "A beautiful woman doesn't want to go through life bending over a washtub. A beautiful woman doesn't want to spend her time scrubbing floors. You don't see a really beautiful woman get enthusiastic over darning socks. They don't want to do any of those things. They know it's going to impair their beauty. They've learned to live for their beauty. They can't preserve it past a certain point. The lucky ones become picture actresses and the grass widows of wealthy husbands. They live on alimony and opportunity.

"The ones that aren't so lucky make a pass at alimony. They get cheated out of it. They have to live. They have a lot of self-discipline when it comes to watching their diet. You'll find them hovering around any night club, sometimes with one escort, sometimes with another, sometimes temporarily not escorted. They're the slinky type with the smooth hips, the full lips, the ready smile, and the watchful eyes. I get so I hate the bitches.''

The bedroom door opened. A smooth, slinky blonde, wearing well-tailored powder blue slacks, a blouse cut so low in front that the V stretched almost to the belt, sandals which showed crimson toenails, came gliding into the room.

The slacks had been tailored across the hips so that every seductive motion, every wiggle showed to the greatest advantage.

"What the hell *is* this?" she asked. "What's coming off here?"

Bob Elgin bowed. "My dear," he said, "may I present Mr. Lam. Lam is a private detective."

He turned to me and said, "My wife, Mr. Lam."

She looked me over with calculating eyes that started with my face, went down to my feet, then back up again. She twisted the full lips in a smile, and gave me her hand. "How do you do, Mr. Lam," she said.

I noticed her left hand. There were no rings on it.

"Darling," she said, rolling the r's. "Aren't we going to have some coffee?"

"Yes, dearest, I'll put some on right away."

He walked over to the kitchenette, poured water into a coffee percolator, dumped in coffee, and switched on the electric stove.

"You should have done that long ago," the blonde said.

"Yes, dear."

She regarded me with cool gray eyes that were impudently frank in their appraisal.

She took a cigarette from a package, tapped it gently on the arm of the chair, placed it between full red lips and tilted her head back to wait for my light.

I crossed the room, struck a match, and held it to the tip of her cigarette. She reached up with her hand and held it cupped over mine, furnishing guidance for the flame.

She held the hand longer than was necessary.

I blew out the match. Her eyes met mine.

"Thanks," she said throatily.

I went back over to the davenport and sat down.

In the kitchen, I could see Bob Elgin's back and hear the rattling of cups and saucers. Bob Elgin said, "Want to join us in a cup of coffee, Lam?"

"No, thanks. I've been drinking coffee off and on all day."

"What are you detecting, Mr. Lam?" the blonde asked.

"I was just trying to get a line on a cute blonde."

"So many people do," she assured me.

"This one is a pocket edition—short, well-formed, high cheekbones, dark brown eyes, not much over five feet tall, and her first name may be Lucille."

She sat absolutely rigid for a moment, then she looked out toward the kitchenette and said, "Do we know her, Bob?"

"We don't," Elgin said.

"I'm sorry, we can't help you."

I said, "You might also try this one. A man about thirty-five, about five feet eleven, long, straight nose, good features, dark hair, gray eyes, weight a hundred and ninety-five, wears gray double-breasted suit, smokes cigarettes through a long carved ivory cigarette holder. Know him?"

From the kitchenette I heard the clatter of crockery.

"What was that?" the blonde asked.

"A cup, my dear. I'm sorry."

"Bob, you've got the jitters. You drank too much last night."

There was the sound of running water.

"*Now* what are you doing?" she asked.

"Washing a cup. I broke the last clean one."

She turned to me and smiled wearily.

I said, "This man could go by the name of Tom."

"We don't know him," Elgin said from the kitchen.

"I'm sorry, we can't help you."

I waited for Elgin to come back from the kitchenette. Then I opened the Sunday paper which was lying on the davenport, found the section which gave the account of the mysterious suicide pact in the Kozy Dell Slumber Court.

The pictures were fairly good.

"How about these people?" I asked.

An exclamation burst from the woman's lips. "Bob," she said impulsively, "that's the same girl who objected to having her picture taken last week!"

94

Elgin's elbow nudged her so hard I could see her head move. "What girl?" he asked.

The blonde said vaguely, "You know, the girl we saw while we were walking in the park. No, I guess it isn't, either. I thought for a minute she was the same person, but she isn't."

"Ever seen either of them around the Cabanita?" I asked.

"Not around the Cabanita," the blonde said hastily. "I haven't seen them anywhere. I thought I had for a minute, something about the girl's eyes."

"We were walking in the park. This girl was seated on a bench and someone had a camera. She didn't want any pictures taken."

"This girl?"

"No, I'm certain it wasn't the same one. I just thought it was for a minute."

"Do you," I asked the blonde, "spend a good deal of time at the Cabanita?"

She nodded, looked over at Bob Elgin.

Bob Elgin said, "My wife does an interpretive Egyptian dance. She's on the program. The rest of the time she sort of mingles around and helps keep the party moving."

"I see," I said.

Elgin looked at me. The blonde smiled.

"Anything else?" Elgin asked.

"Not a thing," I told him. "You've been a great help. Bertha will certainly appreciate it."

The blonde shook hands with me. "Better stay for some coffee," she invited.

"No, thanks, I'm going to try and get some rest for the balance of the day. I've been putting in enough of my Sunday on work."

"Yes, it would seem so," Elgin said. He was reading the account of the love-tryst, suicide-pact in the newspaper.

"What is it, Bob?" the blonde asked with languid disinterest.

"Just the same old murder-suicide business in a motor court."

"My God," she drawled, "why do the men have to kill 'em?"

"Because they love 'em," Elgin said.

Her comment consisted of one word.

I said, "Well, I'll be going."

"Nice to have seen you," the blonde said. "Come to the club sometime, Mr. Lam. I'd like to have you see my dance."

"Thanks, I will."

Bob Elgin walked to the door with me. I shook hands. The blonde's impudently appraising eyes met mine over Elgin's shoulder.

I took the elevator down and went over to the clerk's desk. "Do you," I asked, "have any vacancies coming up?"

His smile was a weary attempt at being pleasant. "Not a thing," he said.

I took out my billfold and picked out some bills. I started counting them casually. "Not a thing?" I asked.

He eyed the money avariciously. "Not a thing. Gosh, I'm sorry!"

I fingered through the money and said, "If I could get an advance tip on some apartment that was going to be vacated I—"

"Just a minute," he said.

He moved over to the switchboard.

I saw that the call was coming from Bob Elgin's apartment.

"Just a moment," he said. "What was that number again?—All right, I have it—Waverly 9-8765."

He made a note of the number, then dialed, after a moment said, "Here's your party," made the connection on the telephone, and came back to the desk. "I'd like to be of help," he said. "I might have a tip on something later on."

"Later on isn't going to help," I said. "I'm in a jam."

His mouth fairly watered as he saw the outside bill. "I—gosh, I don't know of a thing. I might get in touch with some of my friends and—"

I said, "I have another lead—in fact, I think I can get a place in another apartment house but it isn't as desirable as this. This is a nice place."

"We try to keep it so."

I sat around and chatted with him until Elgin's call was completed. There weren't any more calls, so I went out.

CHAPTER TEN

Butter and Leg Girls

IT WAS AFTER NINE O'CLOCK when I located the girl who had the photographic concession at the Cabanita. Her name was Bessie and she lived in a trailer. She worked several of the night spots, going from one to the other in the trailer which also served as a darkroom. Just now it was at the Red Rooster, a country roadhouse joint about three miles from the Cabanita. It was out away from things and rumor had it the place capitalized on its isolation to put over things that wouldn't get by elsewhere.

I went in and looked the place over. It was easy to spot the girl with the camera. She was all teeth and legs, curves and affability.

It was Sunday evening, and since the place was way out in the outlying factory district it was pretty well deserted, but the photograph girl got four orders. After she'd shot the pictures and started out, she picked up a raincoat from the girl at the hat check concession, threw the coat over her shoulders and then dashed for the trailer.

I fell into step beside her. "Want to sell some pictures?" I asked.

She looked at me out of the sides of her eyes. "Nudes?"

"Customers."

"Sure."

I said, "Last week you had a little trouble with a couple over at the Cabanita. They objected to having their pictures taken. Remember it?"

"Who are you?" she asked.

"My name is Cash," I told her. "My parents christened

me *E. Pluribus Unum*, but folks got to calling me Cash for short. My nickname is Long Green."

She looked at me and smiled, and said, "There *was* a little trouble over one of the pictures I took. I'm busy now. When can I see you?"

"Right now."

She said, "I have to get this stuff in the trailer and start getting it developed."

"I'm an expert photographer."

"I know," she told me, "guys get lots of lines. They like to go in the darkroom with me. In the dark they have a tendency to—"

"I won't," I said.

"Oh, well, come on," she told me. "We have to take a chance sometimes."

She unlocked the door of the trailer. I followed her inside. She closed the door, locked it, and pressed a button. Almost immediately the trailer began to move.

She said, "My partner drives without jerks so I can get these pictures finished before we get to the next place. It's a job. I have to rush them through."

She set an electric timer with a luminous dial, turned out all of the lights and for a while we were standing there in absolute darkness, save for a very faint illumination given by a red bulb at the far end of the trailer.

After a moment my eyes accustomed themselves to the dim red light and I could see her moving around, her hands quick blurs of efficient motion.

I said, "You must have quite a job keeping all the stuff straight."

"It's not bad," she said. "I put these things in a developing frame and as soon as the electric timer indicates—"

The electric timer contributed its share by ringing a bell at that moment.

She lifted the container out of one tank, put it into another, said, "We have two minutes now. Then I put them in a chemical bath which gets rid of the hypo and then we wash them in alcohol, dry them, and while I'm in the next place my partner, who's driving the car, will make the prints. There's a number on each of the films."

"Tell me about what happened last Saturday."

She said, "Every once in a while we run into something like that. I don't know why. Usually I never take a picture until I've verified it, but this time it looked so much on the up-and-up that I fell for it."

"What happened?"

She said, "This couple were sitting there, eating. Very quiet, very subdued. Just like people who have been married to each other for a long while. Ordinarily I don't even waste time with them. It's the gay blades and the visiting firemen who want to have a picture of the cutie with them to show the boys back home that give me my business. Sometimes a family party."

"Go on," I said.

She kept her eye on the electric clock with the luminous hands.

"Someone asked me if I'd take a picture of the people at that table. I thought this person had been sitting at the table. I guess I was a little careless. I explained to her that we require a minimum of four prints at a dollar apiece and she said that was all right. She said the parties were having an anniversary dinner and she'd like to get some pictures to present to them later on. She said she'd take care of all the charges."

"So what happened?"

"I went over to the table, smiled, and waited until they looked up. Then I snapped the picture. The man wanted to know what that was for and I told him it was to be a present for him; that it wasn't to cost him anything. The girl got excited and then he got mad about it and said he hadn't ordered any pictures taken. I told him I knew, that it was a friend of his who was trying to arrange a surprise, and then one thing led to another and he wanted the manager."

"Who's the manager?"

"Bob Elgin. He's the master of ceremonies, and he runs the place. He came over and we had a little powwow. I told them that it was all a mistake and that I'd give him the negative and he could destroy it."

"Did you?"

"Hell, no," she said. "I had an order of four bucks for that negative. Do you think I was going to throw that away?"

"So what did you do?"

"Gave him the next negative that was in the camera, pulled it out and pulled the slide out of the plate holder. Elgin took the film and passed it over to the girl at the table and asked him if that satisfied her, and she said it did, so that was all there was to it, as far as those people were concerned."

"And as far as you were concerned?"

She said, "I found my party. I told her the price of prints had gone up to ten dollars a print. She said that was too steep. She offered me twenty-five dollars for the lot. I felt that was all I could get. I told her I'd mail them. I didn't dare make delivery that night."

"And the negative?"

She said, "Just a minute while I put these films in the water."

She transferred the films, and I heard the rush of running water, then she pulled the top off another tank and I smelled alcohol. She sloshed the films around a minute, then took them out and placed them on hangers to dry. She said, "I could make four more prints for twenty-five dollars."

"How soon?"

"I'll put it next on the list. My partner will make the prints while I'm in this next club."

The trailer came to a stop, evidently at a traffic signal. She reached up, switched on a light, consulted a book which had a lot of numbers in it, opened a drawer in a little filing system and took out an envelope which had a negative.

I took out two tens and a five from my billfold and handed them to her. "When do I get them?"

"Soon as I finish this run in here," she said. "Want to go in the club and watch me work?"

"No, thanks, I'll stay here and watch your partner do the printing. Can you tell me anything about the person who ordered the pictures?"

"Cute blonde," she said, "nice figure but unusually small."

We started on again, rode for about five minutes, then the trailer lurched to one side as the car turned off the pavement and into a graveled driveway.

"This is my next stop," she said. "You sure you don't want to come along?"

"No, I'll wait."

She took her camera and a supply of flashbulbs, pulled the raincoat to one side, straightened her stockings, fluffed out her scanty skirt, said, "How do I look?"

"Like a million dollars."

"Thanks."

"Who's driving the car?" I asked.

"My partner."

"Boyfriend?"

"Don't be silly. She's a girl—homely as a mud fence but a good photographer and a good driver. A man would want to be the whole thing, both in the business and in my private life. Us two girls get along fine. We share living expenses and split the earnings fifty-fifty."

I heard steps on the outside of the trailer. Someone tried the knob.

My friend on the inside said, "Okay, Elsie, I'm coming right out."

She unlocked the door.

The woman who came in looked at me with angry disapproval. She was sallow-faced, angular, with a firm, determined mouth and steady, steel-gray eyes.

"It's all right, Elsie. It's a business deal. He wants picture number 45228, four prints—twenty-five bucks."

Elsie said, "Good. We're making money on that negative. You don't want it thrown away, I take it."

"Don't be silly."

"When do I get the four prints?" I asked.

"Right quick," Elsie said.

"There are four more negatives in there to be printed, four of each."

"Okay, Bessie," Elsie said, "I'll get them."

Bessie gave me one swift look over her shoulder, then, with the camera in her hand and the raincoat buttoned, entered the circle of white lights around the building. Elsie rolled up her sleeves and started working. She pulled a printer toward her, connected it up, laid out five negatives in a pile, a pile of printing paper, and started work, slipping the negatives into the printer, slamming the paper in on top of them, latching the printer cover down, making the exposures and jerking out the paper, putting the exposed sheets in a pile by themselves.

"Know anything about photography?" she asked.

"Some."

"Ever done any of this stuff?"

"Developing and printing, you mean?"

"Yes."

"Uh huh."

She said, "Start running that bunch of paper through the developer. It works pretty fast. Don't figure on time; just watch it in the red light. When the prints begin to show, stick 'em through that washing tray and into the hypo. It's a concentrated developer and it works fast."

I started running the prints through. Elsie watched me with an expert eye, checking my timing. After she saw I knew what I was doing, she didn't pay any further attention, but kept on printing the pictures.

By the time she had her pile finished I was caught up with her. I ran through the last of the prints, and Elsie started taking the bottom ones out of the hypo. She sloshed them around for a minute in plain water, then put them in a water containing a chemical to dissolve the hypo, then washed them once more and put them in a dryer.

"Which ones are mine?" I asked.

"There's a number on them," she said. "It'll tell. How about the twenty-five?"

"I paid your partner."

"She didn't say so."

"She will when she gets back."

She said, "Okay, you'll have to wait."

"It's all right," I told her.

Elsie saw that the prints were dry, then she took photographic mounts from the big pasteboard box that was under the shelf in the darkroom, mounted the pictures, and again switched on the white lights.

It was a neat trailer. There was a kitchenette in front, a bedroom in back that had twin beds. It was a big trailer, but everything was remarkably compact.

"I take it you girls live here all the time."

"Sure. Why not? Why should we be moving things back and forth into an apartment when we already have an apartment on wheels."

"You rent space in a trailer lot?"

102

"That's right. Only it isn't in a trailer lot, it's in back of a private residence. We drive in there, park under a tree, hook up the electricity, sleep until noon, then have breakfast. We eat again about seven-thirty, then start out to work, and usually wind the business up about three o'clock in the morning."

"Looks like a nice business," I said.

"The other person's racket always does," she commented dryly. "Seen the evening paper?"

"No."

"You may as well take a look at it. We may have to wait for Bessie. She's pretty good at hustling business."

"Let's have a look at the pictures."

"Don't make any mistake. I don't know that you've paid the twenty-five bucks yet," Elsie said.

"I won't take them. I just want to look."

The pictures had a certain muddy, drab look about them. But considering the circumstances under which they were taken, they were a pretty good job. And the folders classed them up a lot. One was of the redhead who was now lying on a slab in the morgue. The other was Tom Durham.

It was a good twenty minutes before Bessie came back.

"I've got a load for you, Elsie," she said. "I'll start putting them through while you go to the next place. But you'll have to finish them. I got nine pictures in there."

"You mean nine separate jobs?"

"That's right."

"Gosh!" Elsie said in a tone of awe. "And it's Sunday night, too!"

"I kidded them along and got everybody feeling good," Bessie said. "Did you give this man his pictures?"

"Did he give you the twenty-five?"

"Yes."

"Okay," Elsie said, handing me four prints. "You get the pictures."

I said, "What about the four prints that you'd taken? To whom did you deliver them?"

"The one that ordered them, of course," Bessie said.

"You mean Lucille?"

"That's right. . . . Say, you know about her?"

"Uh huh."

103

"Where do you fit in on it?"

I said, "I was just picking up some more prints and trying to check up on what happened. You don't happen to have Lucille's address, do you?"

"You don't happen to have another twenty-five bucks on you, do you?"

I said, "You girls seem to be always looking for the side of the bread that has the butter."

"What's everyone else always looking for?" Bessie asked.

"You tell me," I said.

She grinned, and said, "Virtually everybody tips me a dollar, making it an even five dollars for the four pictures. Some of the smart ones try to add fifty cents or a dollar to it and want to own you."

I said, "All I'm looking for is an address."

"Give it to him, Elsie," she said.

Elsie extended her hand.

I gave her another two tens and a five, mentally groaning at the thought of what would happen when Bertha saw my expense account.

Elsie opened the book again and gave me the address: "Lucille Hollister, 1925 Mono Drive, care Mrs. Arthur Marbury."

Elsie asked me casually, "You got a card with you, Mister?"

"Sure," I said.

She held out her hand.

I said, "That'll be ten bucks."

"Where do you get that noise?"

I said, "I figure you'll sell that for twenty-five to the next person that comes along. I'm willing to leave you a fifteen-dollar profit."

The girls looked at each other, then laughed.

Bessie said, "Come on, Elsie, get started. I've got to start running those pictures through. It's going to be a mess. Looks like we're going to make a killing tonight. We've got to get back to the Red Rooster and deliver that twenty dollars' worth of pictures and then get back here fast. We won't have time to make the Wishing Well."

I said, "Okay, I'll ride over with you, then bail out."

"I wish you'd give me your name," Bessie said wistfully.

"I know you do."

She laughed and said, "You're nice. Since you won't tell us who you are, you can help me with this batch of pictures on the way."

"With *both* hands," Elsie said acidly.

CHAPTER ELEVEN

Scheming Blonde

I PICKED UP THE AGENCY HEAP at the Red Rooster.

Rolling along toward Mono Drive, I noticed headlights in the rear mirror. They were quite a ways behind. I stepped on the throttle a bit and moved along at a pretty good clip.

The headlights kept behind at just about the same distance, too far really to be following me.

I got more speed out of the car.

As a matter of driving habit, I glanced at the gas gauge on the dashboard.

The hand showed the tank was empty; yet I'd filled up before starting out for the Red Rooster.

Of course, it *could* have been that the gauge had developed trouble. In any event, this was a good time to use up what gas I had as fast as it would flow through the carburetor.

I put the throttle down to the floorboards.

I was on a lonely stretch of road cutting across the back part of the city. It traveled through an industrial center with a few factories scattered around, spur tracks crossing the highway at intervals, vast vacant spaces—little traffic and lots of darkness.

The agency car coughed and went dead, picked up again for a few seconds, then coughed, sputtered, and this time quit for keeps.

I had the door open by the time the car came to a stop. There was no traffic anywhere along the road, but behind me those steady, persistent lights kept coming with dogged purpose.

I looked around and didn't like what I saw. Over to one side was a factory, standing dark and silent, surrounded by a high fence that had signs placed along it at regular intervals: *Keep Out*. There was a spur track, with some box cars standing on the siding just clear of the road. Farther down, I could see a storage yard with a high board fence blotting out all view of what was inside of it.

The logical thing of course was to stick around the car and beg some motorist for a push to the nearest gasoline station.

I didn't feel that it was advisable to do the logical thing.

I looked around for a good place to hide. There wasn't any.

I ran across the road and climbed under the rods of one of the box cars. I huddled up in the shadows.

It was a damn poor hiding place.

Headlights danced shadows along the road, then the car that had been rolling along behind me came to a stop. I heard doors open and slam shut. A man's voice called, "Hello, what's the trouble? Everything okay?"

In the night silence I could hear the smooth running of the other motor.

A second voice, a woman's voice, said, "He's around here someplace. He must have run out of gas. He was right ahead of us."

I kept stiffly silent under the freight car. The pair prowled around. I could see their shadows and occasionally get a glimpse of their legs. The man's legs were stocky and muscular; the feminine voice went with a pair of legs that would have made a swell stocking ad, but her voice was hard.

The man said, "That's the damnedest thing I've ever seen. He was right ahead of us, wasn't he, Babe?"

"Yes. It must have been this car. He can't have gone far. How about those freight cars?"

"Why the hell would he jump out of his automobile and crawl in a freight car?" the man asked irritably. "Naturally he'd do what anyone else does when he runs out of gas. He'd have stood by the car and waited for someone to come along. When he saw our car coming he should have flagged us down and asked for help."

"Well, he didn't do what he should have done," the woman said, and then added, "Guess why?"

"We weren't close enough to him for him to get frightened."

107

"Then he's still in the car," the woman said sarcastically.

I could hear the man climbing up the iron rungs on the freight cars. Then I heard his steps along the runway on the roofs. The woman went along on the ground, looking in between the cars.

I slid out from my place of concealment, kept close to the shadows, and sprinted forward along the cars.

I could hear the motor on their automobile purring away with a sound that was smoothly reassuring.

From behind me, I heard the man say, "Well, let's start looking *under* the cars. He isn't on top."

"He has to be around here somewhere," the woman said angrily. "He couldn't have climbed one of the fences, and— Hey, there he is!"

The man yelled, then both of them started to run.

I jumped in the other car, slammed the car door shut, snapped the transmission in gear, and started rolling.

I'd gone almost fifty yards before I saw a series of luminous pin-pricks in the darkness behind me. Then suddenly the window in the back radiated into myriad cracks and the rear-view mirror didn't do me any good.

I slowed down when I hit the first crossroad, turned to the left, then turned to the right on the next crossroad. I wound up in a residential district and located a streetcar before I abandoned the automobile. Then I took the precaution of looking at the license number and the registration certificate which was attached to the steering post.

The car was registered in the name of Samuel Lowry and the address on the certificate of registration was 968 Rippling Avenue.

I flagged the streetcar, rode on it until I saw a taxi standing by the curb. I got off the car and picked up the taxi. I gave the taxi driver the number of 1810 Mono Drive.

When we got out there the house was dark and the cab driver wanted to wait, but I assured him that my friends would be home shortly, paid him off, and, after he had gone, walked the block and a half down to 1925.

The homes in this vicinity had cost money to put up. It wasn't the swanky neighborhood of extreme wealth, but it was definitely above the average. It was a new subdivision. The houses were modern, with lots of glass, and were, for the most part, low, one-storied affairs that had sweeping curves, intriguing designs and patios. They weren't quite in the private-swimming-pool class, but they were getting close to it.

The house I wanted had curving lines around the living-room, then the house swept back to a garage. On the other side there was a long wing which stretched out to protect a patio.

I thought I'd like to have a look at that patio before I went in.

There was a bit of lawn, some ornamental shrubbery, and a hedge.

I walked along the edge of the hedge, crowded past the shrubbery, skirted around back of the garage, and came to the patio.

I wished I'd had a spotlight to help me find my way. Part of the patio was cement, part of it was where someone had recently planted a lawn. I blundered into the soft soil before I realized where I was and backed out to the hard cement.

The house was so constructed that out here in the patio there was absolute privacy, so far as the bedrooms on this wing of the house were concerned. The girl who was stand-ing in the lighted bedroom hadn't bothered with the shades on the bedroom windows.

It was modern construction, with steel sash, leaded glass French doors, wide steel-framed windows which opened and closed by simply turning a crank on the inside. It was a bed-room designed for a maximum of sunlight and fresh air. Pri-vacy could have been insured by running heavy drapes across the entire side of the bedroom, but now these drapes were to one side, neglected.

The taffy-haired blonde who was standing in front of the mirror, surveying her partially clothed figure with quite evi-dent approval, was the girl who had picked me up the night before as her escort, and had taken me to the motor court.

I hesitated a moment, then decided it was time for a show-down and kept on walking.

She heard my steps on the cement when I was close to the little balcony which led out to the patio, the balcony on which the French doors opened. She raised a hand mirror, caught reflected motion, and whirled, surveying me with wide eyes. She started to scream and then checked herself.

With incredulous dismay, she watched me climb the four brick stairs which led to the little balcony.

"May I come in?" I asked.

Wordlessly, as though in a hypnotic trance, she opened the French door. "How—how did you find me?"

I said, "It took a little work. Want to talk?"

"No."

"I didn't think you would but I think you'd better."

She said, "I—I've been thinking of you," and then suddenly raised her finger to her lips and motioned me to be quiet. "My sister can hear us if we talk loud," she said. And then, with a little nervous laugh, she picked up a robe that was on the foot of the bed and slipped it over her shoulders. "I'm afraid," she said, "I'm making up in scenic generosity for anything I—"

"Deprived me of last night?" I prompted.

"Yes," she said, and smiled. "I guess you thought I was a terrible heel."

"It isn't what *I* think; it's what the police think."

"The police? What have they to do with it?"

I said, "You played it pretty carefully. You went to the parking lot and got Dover Fulton's automobile. Then you started looking for a fall guy. You picked on me. You got me out to the Kozy Dell Slumber Court. You knew that I would register under the name of Dover Fulton. You knew that Dover Fulton and Minerva Carlton were in one of the cottages. You pretended to be drunk. You—"

"I was drunk."

"You're lying."

She flushed.

I said, "Don't be silly. We were both playing a game. You gave the waiter five dollars to bring you straight ginger ale every time you ordered Scotch and soda. I gave him ten dollars to tell me what your game was and bring me straight ginger ale every time *I* ordered Scotch and soda."

"Why, you—you—you—"

"Exactly," I said.

She sat down on the edge of the bed. Suddenly she laughed. I came over and sat down beside her. She reached over and took one of my hands. "Donald, please don't be angry," she said. "It wasn't the way you're thinking it was."

I didn't say anything.

She crossed her knees. The robe slid away from the smooth flesh. She made no effort to pull it back, but sat there kicking her foot back and forth, a few inches at a time, nervous, seductive, trying to think, the robe sliding provocatively each time she kicked.

I said, "The truth will be a lot better for you right now than any lie you can think up. You have just one stab at rehearsal and then you're going to be talking to the police."

"Not to the police, Donald."

"To the police," I said.

"But what have *I* done, for the police to bother me?"

"Murder, for one thing."

"Murder?" she exclaimed, and then suddenly put her hand over her lips, as though to push the word back in when she realized how loud her exclamation had been.

"Donald, you're crazy!"

I said, "You left me there in the auto camp. You went out and prowled around the place until you found the cabin you wanted. You knocked on the door. You went in and started to make a scene. Dover Fulton pulled his gun and took a shot at you. You—"

"Donald, you're crazy! Absolutely stark crazy!"

"All right," I said, "suppose *you* tell *me.*"

"All right, I will," she said. "I'm going to tell you the truth. You'll hate me for it. I don't want you to hate me, Donald. I—I like you. I—"

"Yes, I know," I said. "Another scene of well-modulated seduction. You have a sweet little body. It's done a lot of work for you. It gets you what you want as you go through life. You gave me a great come-on last night. Let's try the truth tonight."

I reached across over the bare flesh, picked up the end of the robe. She sat motionless, waiting, not resisting. I pulled the robe back up and tucked it under the leg.

She laughed. "You can't take it."

"No," I said.

"You're a funny boy."

111

"I suppose I am. I'm quaint. I'm old-fashioned. I like to hear the truth once in a while. Legs confuse the issue."

She said, "All right, I'm going to tell you the truth because—because—damn it, because right now I can't think of any convincing lie. Your presence disturbs my equanimity as much as my legs disturb yours."

I said, "Go ahead. Shoot the works while you're in the mood."

She said, "I'll give you the whole story. My real name is Lucille Hollister. I've been married. I didn't like it. I had a property settlement from my husband when we split up. I have money and—"

"Never mind the biographical sketch," I told her. "Get down to what happened last night. You're sparring for time. That makes me more and more suspicious. If you wanted to tell the truth you'd plunge right into it."

"I *am* telling the truth, Donald, but I want you to understand me. I want you to—I like you more than I've liked anyone in a long time. You—well, you give a girl a break. You were wonderful to me last night."

I said, "Let's quit stalling and start talking."

"But that's what I'm trying to explain—that it's not a stall."

She twisted her position slightly on the bed. Her hand was on my shoulder. Her eyes were pleading up at me. "Donald," she said, "please, please believe me."

"Give me something to believe," I said, "and let's have it fast. The police are on their way out here."

"The *police!* On their way out *here!*"

I nodded.

"Donald, they can't. . . . You wouldn't do that to me."

"It isn't what I'm doing; it's what you've done to yourself."

"But, Donald, what can I do?"

"For one thing," I said, "you can tell me the truth. Then *perhaps* I can help you."

She said, "You're going to think I'm a bitch."

I didn't say anything.

She said, "All right, here it is in chunks. My sister has never been married. Her name is Rosalind Hart. We're from Colorado. We've been visiting here for the last three or four weeks. My sister is four years younger than I am. She's a sweet little thing. She doesn't—well, she doesn't play around. She's romantic, intense, and she's been in love with Stanwick Carlton ever since she met him, absolutely *crazy* in love with him. They were engaged at one time. He was the first man in her life, the first one who wakened her to the fact that she had grown up and was a woman. She loves him. She loves him too much.

"You know how it is, Donald. When a girl really goes all out for a man, after a while he gets tired of it. There's a sense of assurance that he has—a man wants to pursue his women. He wants to have to make a sale. He doesn't want the merchandise all wrapped up and tossed in his lap every time he leaves an opening. He wants to feel that *he's* the salesman.

"A smart girl, a girl who knew more about men than Rosalind, would have had Stanwick Carlton absolutely crazy about her. He was for a long time, and then she was too easy, too accessible. I tried to warn her about it but she laughed at me. She said they were going to be married and live happily ever after. You know what happened."

"What happened?"

"After a while he got tired of it. She was always there, always adoring him, always ready to obey his slightest wish. She wouldn't even look at any other man or let any other man look at her. She didn't have sense enough to ever play hard-to-get."

"And so Minerva entered the scene?"

"That's right—Minerva. She was shrewd and fast and hot. I'm not kidding. I know what I'm talking about. One woman can tell a lot about another."

"All right, she'd played around. So what?"

"She came to Colorado. She sized up the situation in an instant and *she* started playing hard-to-get."

"So Stanwick Carlton immediately married her?"

"Don't be silly, it wasn't that way at all. He became interested in her, and she simply tilted her chin, looked over her shoulder at him, and moved away. He had to take the challenge. He wanted to show her, I guess, that he could dent her armor if he wanted to, then he was going to go back to Rosalind. The first thing he knew, he was completely snared and there was a runaway marriage. I don't think the poor chap knew anything at all about what really happened to him until he woke up, safely married, after what the papers called a whirlwind courtship. A whirlwind courtship!'' she added scornfully. "I'll say it was. Only he wasn't the one who did the whirlwinding.''

"Go on,'' I said.

"They'd been married two years. I knew that Minerva was going to play around. I kept an eye on her. She came here and visited an old friend of hers, a girl by the name of Bushnell. They had a vacation at the beach and—well, did some stepping around. Then Minerva went back to Colorado. This time when I knew she was going to visit in California again I had things arranged so I could keep an eye on her.''

"Playing detective, eh?''

"That's right, and it was simple, dirt simple. She got in touch with Dover Fulton as soon as she hit town, and the first night she was here she had dinner with some other man. She has been seeing a lot of Fulton. Last week they went out to that auto court and registered as man and wife. They stayed there until after midnight. Then she drove him back to town. He picked up his car at the parking place and went on home.''

"I presume all that marital infidelity made you sick at your stomach.''

"Don't be a sap,'' she said. "I loved it. It gave me all of the aces in the deck. I just wanted to know how to play them.''

"So what?''

"So last night, when I knew they were going out to the same auto court where they'd been before, I—well, I decided I'd frame them good and proper and let them have their names in the paper.''

"So what did you do?''

"Picked you up. Got you to take me out to the auto court, register as Dover Fulton and wife, and I saw to it that you were driving Dover Fulton's car. Then I sneaked out and telephoned the police that the car had been stolen. I knew that one of the first things the police do under those circumstances is check up on the motor courts because every motor court has to keep a register in which is entered the make of car and the license number. I knew that the police would have a line on Dover Fulton's car before midnight.''

"And you felt they'd pick on me as a fall guy?''

114

"Be your age! I didn't want *you* in the picture at all. I wanted to get with someone who was smart enough and suspicious enough so that when I walked out on him, he'd—well, he'd smell a rat and get out too. I saw you pull out and start walking.

"The police would locate the stolen automobile at the Kozy Dell Slumber Court. Then I intended to ring up Mrs. Fulton and tell her not to let her husband fool her, that that business about the car being stolen was just a stall; that actually he'd been there at the court, registered with this woman for two weeks in succession. The fact that his car had been recovered there would make her go to investigate and then, of course, the woman who ran the place would have to identify Dover Fulton as the one who registered as Stanwick Carlton."

"And of course you intended to let Stanwick Carlton know about what his wife had been doing?"

"You're damn right I did."

"Sweet little thing, aren't you?"

"I'm not sweet," she said. "I'm a cat; I've got claws. I'm fighting for Rosalind. As a matter of fact, Stanwick loves Rosalind and always has loved her. This Minerva woman just came in and helped herself to a piece of cake. She saw a good eligible male that she could grab by the use of a little applied psychology. She applied the psychology. Rosalind was a sweet, innocent little lamb who didn't stand a chance. I tell you, this Minerva was a woman who knew *all* the answers."

I said, "And after you went out and ditched me, did you hear the sound of the shots?"

For a moment her eyes faltered.

"Did you?" I asked.

Her fingers dug into my arm.

"Did you?"

"Yes."

"Where were you?"

"In one of the garages. I waited until I saw you get out of the cabin. Then I decided I'd hitchhike my way and—and I heard the sound of shots."

"Have any idea what they were?"

"I—I thought they were shots, but if I'd known what cabin they came from, I—well, I'd have—well, I guess I wouldn't have, either."

115

"No," I said, "I guess you wouldn't. How many shots were there?"

"Three."

"You're certain?"

"Yes."

"What time?"

She said, "It was exactly seven minutes past ten. I looked at my watch."

"And then what?"

"Donald, I'm going to tell you the truth. I was frightened. I hid. I watched. I tell you, I saw people moving around in that cabin *after* the shots and I saw a car drive away. Then I beat it. I could hardly walk. My knees wouldn't work."

"Then what?"

"Then I hitchhiked. I gave the usual story about being out with a man who had made me walk home. The man who was driving the car was very gallant."

"He drove you here?"

"Don't be simple, Donald! I didn't want to leave a back trail. I had him take me to a downtown hotel. I told him I lived there. Then after he'd gone, I picked up a taxicab and came out here."

"And I suppose you handed the man a story that was very well embellished with all of the lurid details."

"Naturally," she said. "When a man picks up a woman at a time like that he expects at least a good story."

"At least?" I asked.

She laughed. "You're a sweet, naïve man, Donald."

"And he made passes at you?"

"Of course he did, Donald. Don't be silly. I'm attractive, and he thought I went out for a good time but just didn't like the man I was with."

I said, "How did it happen that you wrote down Kozy Dell Slumber Court on the back of that menu, and—"

"Donald, I didn't."

"Didn't what?"

"Write that."

"It was in that pack of cigarettes that you—"

"I know it was, but I didn't write it, Donald."

"Who did?"

"If I knew that I'd know a lot. I'm trying to find out. You

see, Donald—No, I'm not going to tell you until—until I know you better.''

I said, ''You're a scheming little bitch, aren't you?''

She swung around on the bed so her eyes locked with mine. ''Yes,'' she said. With that, she cupped her hands on my cheeks, drew my face toward hers and kissed me.

It was a kiss to remember. It lasted a long time. Then she suddenly pushed me away.

''Now,'' she said, ''you know *all* the answers, don't you?''

There was a provocative challenge in her eyes.

''Yes,'' I said. I got up off the bed and started for the door.

''Where are you going?''

''First,'' I said, ''I'm going to get a friend of mine on the phone—Sergeant Sellers. He's on Homicide, and he thinks I'm a damn liar. I'm going to let you talk with him.''

''Donald, you can't go out that way.''

''All right, I'll go out this other way.''

''No, no, not that way, either. Look, Donald, my sister is in the front room.''

''Where's Mrs. Arthur Marbury?''

''She's out tonight. Donald, darling, please—give me a break. I'll go—anywhere.''

''What do you mean, anywhere?''

''Exactly what I said. If you want to turn back the hands of the clock by twenty-four hours, it's okay by me.''

''You mean—''

''My God, do I have to draw you a diagram, or something?''

I said, ''Get your clothes on.''

''I'll hurry and get dressed,'' she said. ''Look, Donald, go in the bedroom at the front end of the hall. That's my sister's bedroom. Wait in there. I'll come in as soon as I'm dressed. Then we'll go in together and I'll introduce you to sister. I'll make her think that you came to get me and that I let you in the side door by the patio. She's reading a novel and—''

''And suppose she should quit reading a novel and—''

''She won't, Donald, you'd love my sister. She's a sweet, innocent girl. Her heart's been absolutely broken, and the only thing she does is read. She reads all the time. She doesn't go out. She's eating her heart out. It's the most pathetic thing.

Donald, when you see her you'll realize the truth of what I'm telling you. You won't hold it against me what I've done. And I'll—I'll show you I'm really a good scout, Donald. Honest I will. I've been thinking about you. I couldn't sleep last night. I didn't want to play you for a—well, you know—do the way I did."

She took my arm, pushed me out of the door, pointed to the door down the corridor. "Right in there, Donald, and wait. It won't take long. I'll be with you."

I walked a few steps, waited until she'd closed the door, then tiptoed to the end of the corridor, down a short flight of stairs, and peered through a curtained, arched doorway into a living-room furnished in Mission style.

A brunette was spread out on a chaise longue, a book in her hand, a cigarette in her fingers. She was reading so intently that her eyes seemed to bore holes in the page. Apparently there was no one else in the house.

I went back to the bedroom door Lucille had indicated. It was a bedroom very similar to the other, except that the windows opened on the side of the house that was toward the adjoining lot. A cord had been pulled which stretched the drapes all the way across the windows on the side.

It was a girl's bedroom, with toilet things spread out on the dresser, a nice bed, a deep, comfortable chair with a floor lamp behind it, a table with some magazines and a book.

I settled down in the chair to wait, then I remembered the lipstick on my face. I went over to the mirror, took my handkerchief and rubbed off the sticky red stain which had smeared around my mouth.

I looked around for a telephone. There was no phone in the bedroom.

I settled down in the chair, glanced at a magazine, then picked up the book.

It was a story of two kids who were in love. I glanced through the volume, then I became interested and started to read.

It opened up as a darned sweet story. Then a woman who was a shrewd, unscrupulous bitch entered the picture. The man became all confused. She was taking a green kid who didn't know too much about life and rubbing all the new off his soul. The thing he had felt for the other girl was some-

118

thing so much deeper than sex it wasn't even funny. The book had been read until the binding was limber. The cover had been wrapped in Cellophane. You'd have thought it was the kid sister's Bible.

I moistened my lips, felt uncomfortable for a minute, and couldn't realize what it was. Then I knew it was the taste of Lucille's lipstick that somehow still clung to my lips.

I got my handkerchief and scrubbed hard and then I went back to the book.

I was vaguely conscious that time was passing. I thought Lucille was taking a long time getting her clothes on. Suddenly it occurred to me that she might have gone out through the French doors into the patio. I didn't know what good it would do her. I'd found her now and knew who she was. Her kid sister was sitting in the front room, reading a novel—all I had to do was walk out there, introduce myself, or I could go back the other way, out through the bedroom—

The door was open. Someone was standing there.

"Well, it's about time," I said.

I heard a choking scream, and looked up.

It wasn't Lucille who stood in the doorway, but the brunette, the kid sister.

Looking at her startled, white face, the big black eyes, the hollow cheeks, I could see from the family resemblance that she was Lucille's sister. She was younger than Lucille, and she was fragile and sensitive. There was a soulful quality in her eyes, and she was getting ready to scream again.

I got up, and said, "I'm waiting for Lucille. She's dressing. She told me to wait here."

That calmed her down. "But how did you get in?"

"Lucille brought me in through the side door."

"Through the *side* door?"

I nodded.

"I didn't hear anything."

I said, "You were reading a book and you were completely hypnotized by it."

"I was reading, but I wasn't—well—"

I said, "Lucille motioned me to silence and put me in here. She said she wanted to change."

"I can't understand her putting you in *here*. This is my bedroom."

119

I said, "Well, Lucille should be dressed by this time and we'll let her make the explanations."

"Where is she?"

"Down the corridor somewhere," I said, indicating the end of the house vaguely. "I suppose her room is down there."

Rosalind was looking at me with startled, frightened eyes. She didn't know whether to run screaming, or to walk down the corridor.

I moved toward her and that touched off the reaction. She fairly flew down the corridor. "Lucille!" she cried. "Lucille!"

She flung herself at the door of Lucille's bedroom and opened it, then stood motionless in the doorway.

I grinned and said, "It's okay, Rosalind. You'll get to know me better after a while."

She took one step into the room, then I heard her scream, a shrill knifelike scream of terror. Then she was yelling at the top of her voice, "Help! Police! Police!" The whole neighborhood could hear her.

I stepped to the doorway so I could look over her shoulder. Lucille had taken the robe off. She'd also taken off the filmy other thing that had been around her when I first saw her. She had on just the bra and black panties.

She'd been choked to death with one of her own stockings. It was knotted tight around her throat and the girl was lying sprawled in death, her body a delicate, graceful, beautiful thing, her face mottled and disfigured.

"Police! Police! Murder!" screamed Rosalind.

A man's voice from the house across the way called out, "What's the trouble?"

"Help, police! Murder!" Rosalind screamed.

I heard a door bang, a man's steps running across cement.

I turned quickly, walked down the corridor, down the half dozen steps to the living-room, across the living-room to the door on the side of the patio, out into the night and to the sidewalk.

I needed a hell of a lot of time to think and I wasn't going to get it there in that house, not with the only story I had to tell.

CHAPTER TWELVE

The Check That Bounced

IT MADE A SWELL STORY FOR THE NEWSPAPERS. They had it all doped out.

The girl had been standing in front of the mirror, dressing, intent only upon making the best appearance for a date she had that evening. It was a warm night. The French doors were open to the patio and because the bedroom had complete privacy, the girl had neglected to pull the shades.

A sex maniac, perhaps a Peeping Tom, had been making regular rounds of the neighborhood. He had looked through the window of the bedroom and saw the half-clad girl in front of the mirror.

He had started across the patio, directly toward the bedroom, but had stepped into the soft loam of a new lawn that had recently been planted. The soil had been thoroughly wet down by the gardener that evening and the man had sunk halfway to his ankles. He had taken a few steps, then had turned and retraced his steps to the cement. Then he had walked directly toward the bedroom. The cement retained tracks of the loam-covered feet.

He had tiptoed up the stairs.

The girl had been standing there in her lingerie in front of the mirror, making herself beautiful, planning the clothes she was to wear, putting on facial creams, powder, and lipstick, fixing her eyebrows and eyelashes.

Suddenly she had become uneasy, conscious of some presence behind her. She had started to turn.

It was too late.

One of her own silk stockings had been thrown over her head and around her throat, twisted tight; a cruel merciless knee had pushed into her back, against her shoulder blades. She had tried to scream but no sound would come. The silk stocking had been twisted tighter, tighter, tighter.

There had been a futile, feeble struggle.

Suffocating, she had tried to flail with her arms and legs, but the cruel knee in her back crushed her to the floor. Sinewy, strong hands twisted the silk stocking tighter and tighter. There had been a few convulsive motions, and then silence.

The silence of death.

And then the murderer had turned her over on her back, had bent over her and had kissed her. The smeared lipstick on her lips told the story of that last kiss.

The kiss of death.

It was a natural for the sob sisters and the tabloids. There were photographs of the woman, photographs of the body in its flimsy underwear sprawled on the floor.

And then the newspapers had gone on from there.

The murderous bandit had gone down to the next room, the bedroom of the sister. He had entered that room, apparently in search of another victim, or perhaps waiting for the younger sister to come to bed.

And while there, he had become engrossed in reading a book.

The literary bandit!

It was a natural for sensational exploitation.

The book was, as it chanced, a favorite of Rosalind Hart, and one which she kept constantly in her room. It was protected from wear by a Cellophane cover, and, as it happened, police, knowing that the murderer had handled this book, were able to process it almost immediately upon their arrival at the scene of the crime and had obtained not only a perfect set of fingerprints, but a complete outline of the hand of the man they wanted.

The sister of the murdered woman had stated that when she entered the door of the bedroom, the man who had been reading the book was wiping his lips with a handkerchief, apparently getting rid of the incriminating lipstick which had come from the lips of the dead girl. The murderer had been so startled by the intrusion of the sister that he had dropped the handkerchief as he jumped to his feet. Police, recovering that handkerchief, had made an analysis of the smears of lipstick which appeared on it, and had proved conclusively that this lipstick came from the murdered woman. There was a laundry mark on the handkerchief which was slightly smudged, so that temporarily the police were not able to trace it, but they hoped to be able to reconstruct that laundry mark and use it as an additional clue.

Reading the papers, I felt as though I were teetering on the brink of a precipice, standing on rotten rock and looking down into a deep canyon.

The memory came back to me of the time years before when I'd been taken on a tour through a state's prison and had been ushered into the execution chamber, shown the square trap of the scaffold, a bit of mechanism which at first glance looked like a part of the floor, but which was precariously balanced so that it only needed the slightest touch of the tripping button to send a heavy trap door plunging down with that ominous *bang* that is so hideously familiar to those who have ever witnessed an execution, a reverberating, silence-shattering noise that will forever after be indelibly impressed upon the mind of the witness—a noise which is synchronized so that the audience watching the execution doesn't hear the sickening snap of the bone in the neck of the condemned man as he catapults to the end of the rope and the hangman's knot behind his ear dislocates the cervical vertebra, pulling the spinal cord loose, letting the neck stretch until it is no bigger than a man's arm, while the rope bites into the quivering flesh.

I felt as though I was standing on one of those insecure square platforms while an executioner slipped a black bag and a rope over my face, tightened it around my neck.

Just as a matter of form I checked the agency parking lot.

Agency car number two, the one I had been driving when I ran out of gas, the one I had abandoned when I stole the other car, was in its accustomed place.

I turned on the ignition and checked the gas tank. It was full. The attendant didn't know when it had been parked there, some time during the night. It had been there when he'd opened up.

I didn't ask any more questions.

I walked into the office, the morning newspaper under my arm, trying to appear nonchalant.

Elsie Brand, my secretary, looked up from her typing with a smile.

"Have a nice weekend?" she asked.

"Fine," I told her.

"You're looking mighty pert this morning."

"Feeling like a million dollars," I assured her. "You're looking like a movie star. Bertha in?"

She nodded. "She wants to see you."

I said, "I'll be there in case anyone wants me."

I went on into Bertha's private office.

Bertha shot me a look from her glittering little eyes, then whirled around in the swivel chair. The chair squeaked protest as she motioned me to the client's chair in the corner of the room.

"Kick the door shut, lover."

I closed the door.

"How are we coming? What have you done about getting a cut out of that eighty thousand bucks, Donald?"

I said, "How about the suitcase?"

"Bless your soul," she said, "the suitcase was easy. You just tell Bertha what you want her to do, and she'll do it."

"Where is the suitcase?" I asked.

She pushed the swivel chair back, brought a little suitcase out from under the desk.

"How did you get it?"

"I went to Stanwick Carlton and told him that I was trying to get some sort of a report on the case; that I didn't think the police theory was the right one; that I thought perhaps the whole thing was a frame-up to cover something else that was bigger."

"What, for instance?"

"My God, I didn't tell him," Bertha said. "I flung glittering generalities around. The poor guy was heartbroken. I let him cry on my shoulder and then poured hooch into him. He already had a start. I told him I wanted the suitcase. He gave it to me and kissed me. My God, lover, the son-of-a-bitch kissed me!"

"But you got the suitcase," I said, reassuringly.

Bertha swiped the back of her hand across her lips and said, "You're damn right. I got the suitcase."

124

I went over and took a look at it. "Has this been changed at all since—"

"How the hell do I know?" she said. "You know what the police do. I asked Stanwick Carlton if he'd looked in it, and he said no, he couldn't bear to."

I opened the suitcase and said, "They'll have taken the bullet out, of course. See what you make of this, Bertha."

"What *I* make of it? It's just a damn suitcase."

I said, "We may not have much time to work on this thing. We've got to find out something more than the fact that it's just a suitcase. Why was the bullet fired into it?"

"Because the man who was shooting at the woman missed her and the bullet hit the suitcase."

I started taking out the folded garments, putting them carefully on Bertha's desk, stacking them together so that the hole made by the bullet would coincide. I finally used the handle of the pen out of Bertha's desk to mark the location of the holes.

A blouse was neatly folded. The bullet hole zigzagged in through it without matching any of the folds.

I said, "Someone refolded the blouse."

"Probably the cops," Bertha said.

"It's a neat job of packing," I pointed out.

"Uh huh, I guess so."

I said, "Let's try refolding this blouse so the bullet holes all match up."

I tried half a dozen different folds. It didn't match at all.
Bertha became interested.

I said, "How else could we fold this? How would a woman pack it?"

"Hell, I don't know," Bertha said. "I usually throw them in and tramp a hundred and sixty-five pounds of pressure on top of them and then close the lid of the suitcase. You know me, lover. I have got past the coy age. I don't give a damn what I look like, just so I'm clothed."

I said, "We haven't got too much time on this thing, Bertha."

"That's twice you've said that. What the hell has time to do with it?"

I said, "I may have to be gone for a while."

"Working on this case?"

I nodded.

"Well, you bring home the bacon," Bertha said. "You know me, lover, and the way I feel about things. With eighty grand kicking around loose we certainly should be able to chisel in on enough of it to—"

"To pay eighty percent of it over to the government," I said.

I knew that was good for a reaction.

Bertha quivered with white fury, sputtered for words.

I put the garments back inside the suitcase, closed it, and took it back to my own office.

Elsie Brand looked up as I came in, ceased pounding the typewriter long enough to regard the suitcase curiously. "Going someplace?" she asked.

"Perhaps."

"Isn't that a woman's suitcase?"

I nodded, said, "Come on into the private office for a minute, Elsie."

She pushed back from the typewriter, followed me into my private office. I closed the door, said, "Elsie, we only have a few minutes. We're going to have to work fast. You're a woman who has gone to an auto camp with her lover. The door has been closed. You're in the privacy of the auto camp. What would you do?"

She blushed.

I said, "No, no, now get down to earth. You'd start taking off your clothes. What would you do with them?"

"Hang them up, of course."

I said, "Take a look at this suitcase. You can't tell much about the way it's been packed, because things have been changed around, but let's take a look at the order of the garments. There's a bullet hole through some of these. Here's some underthings and some stockings, with a bullet hole through them. Here's some handkerchiefs. Now, we come to this blouse. It's a problem. Can you fold it so that the bullet hole matches up after the blouse has been folded? You can see the bullet went through the blouse four or five times."

"On account of the way it was folded," she said.

"Fold it back the way it was, then."

Elsie spread the blouse out on my desk, starting folding it,

126

trying to get the bullet hole to line up when the blouse was folded. She couldn't do it.

Elsie studied the blouse closely, raised the place where the arms joined the blouse to her nostrils, put the blouse down, started folding it again, then shook her head and said, "It wasn't packed. It had to be folded like this."

She took it and folded it into a crumpled, disorganized package, then, using the pen holder from my office pen set, just as I had done in Bertha's office, worked around until she had the holes all lined up.

"Would a woman have packed it that way?"

She shook her head, and said, "This was a soiled blouse. It had been worn. But still she wouldn't have packed it so carelessly that—"

"Wait a minute. What do you mean it had been worn?"

"I mean it was soiled. She'd been wearing it."

I said, "If you were going to keep a rendezvous in a motor court with a man you loved, if you were stepping out on your husband, would you carry soiled clothes along?"

"Certainly not. You mean this bag was all she had?"

"That's right."

"What did the man have?"

"Nothing."

Elsie started looking through the bag, making an inventory.

"Turn your back a minute," she said. "This is going to be intimate."

I turned my back, but said over my shoulder, "You don't need to be so delicate about it. The police have pawed through everything in there."

"Not with me looking on, they haven't."

I walked over to the window and smoked a cigarette.

Elsie said, "Come on back. I think this was the blouse she was wearing at the time—well, you know, at the time she went to the motor court."

"I think so too, Elsie. I can't prove it, but I think so."

"And when she folded it, she had to fold it like this," Elsie said.

I saw the way she had wadded the garment up. The bullet holes were now all in a proper line, but the garment was half-folded, half-rolled and compressed into a small space.

I said, "Would you have folded it that way?"

She shook her head.

I said, "Okay, I think I've got the answer. Now, look, Elsie, things are going to get tough."

"How?" she asked.

I said, "They're going to get plenty tough. I'm out working on a case. It's such an important case that I'm not even going to let you know where I am. But you remember to tell everyone that I was in this morning. I didn't seem in any particular hurry and that I went to work on a case. You—"

The door burst open. Bertha Cool, standing in the doorway, was sputtering with indignation.

"What happened?" I asked.

"Why," she said, "that damn bank! I'll pin their ears down. The—Why, what the hell do they think they're doing?"

"What bank?" I asked. "And what's it all about?"

"That check Claire Bushnell gave us. They have the crust to tell me that they're going to charge my account with it, that they accepted the check only on the contingency of a check Claire Bushnell had deposited for collection being good."

"And that check wasn't good?"

"That's what they say."

"Who signed the check Claire deposited?"

"They won't tell."

I said, "All right, Bertha, I'll handle it."

Bertha said, "What the hell does that bank think it's trying to put across?"

I said, "There's no harm in trying."

"Well, they tried the wrong person. They're barking up the wrong tree. I'll—I'll—"

"You have the money, haven't you?"

"We did have it."

"Then what happened?"

She said, "They're trying to get my bank to draw it out of my account, on the theory that the whole thing was handled as a collection. Can you beat that?"

I said, "Where did you deposit the check? Did you go to the bank on which it was drawn and cash it?"

"No, don't be silly. I went to our bank. I had the bank

telephone to find out if the check was good. They looked it up and said it was, so I deposited it. On the strength of that telephone call, our bank gave us the credit."

"And then what?"

"Then this morning, when the check went over to clear, the account of Claire Bushnell had been debited on account of a check which had been deposited by her being no good. Donald, lover, they can't do this to us."

I said, "If you sent the check in for collection through our bank, they're absolutely right. They don't have to pay it, if there aren't funds enough to cover."

"But they said it was good over the telephone."

"So it was, Saturday morning," I said. "This is Monday. The situation is different now."

"Damn!" Bertha said. "That's hell. We've already done all the work for the little shyster."

I said, "I'll see what I can do. Don't let anyone know what I'm working on. Don't dare to tip anyone off to where I can be found. This thing is loaded with dynamite and I've got to be very, very careful."

"I won't tell anyone a thing," Bertha promised. "But you go get hold of that Bushnell girl. She's got some money somewhere. She has some rings or something she can pawn. She has this rich aunt. Let her go strike the aunt for some money."

I smiled and said, "You mean, let the aunt pay for having her boy friend shadowed?"

Bertha said, "I don't give a damn what you have to do, we want that check made good. Two hundred dollars. We can't let that slip through our fingers!"

I said, "I've got to do some looking around before I can help us much on this. You tell everyone that I'm working on a routine job and expect to be back any minute."

"What are you so fidgety about this morning?"

"I'm not fidgety," I said, "I'm trying to get this thing lined up before—"

"Before what?" Bertha asked.

"Before the police start tracing the course of that bullet through the suitcase."

She said, "You're nuts. That other thing is all washed up

except insofar as that one question of insurance is concerned. Don't fall down on that job, Donald. Eighty grand!''

I said, "Keep your mind fixed on that eighty grand, Bertha, it may help. Remember that's the main thing, that insurance.''

"Well, don't let it obscure your mind on this two-hundred-dollar check," she said. "We don't want to let these banks start slipping stuff like that over on us, lover. I'm so mad I could put cream and sugar on tenpenny nails and chew 'em up for breakfast food. You handle it, lover, but don't let that bitch use sex on you.''

"No?" I asked, smiling.

"No," Bertha screamed. "And don't joke about it, Donald. You know *damn* well there *ain't* two hundred dollars' worth of sex in the world!''

And Bertha went out, slamming the door behind her.

"Bertha and Claire Bushnell may have different ideas about the value of sex," I said.

Elsie Brand lowered her eyes. "And you?"

"I'm not an appraiser," I said.

Elsie's eyes remained demurely downcast.

After a moment, she said, "Did you read the papers this morning, Mr. Lam?"

I nodded.

"About the murder of the beautiful blonde, the one who was found choked to death with a stocking?"

"Yes, why?"

She said, "You know, I've always wondered how in the world people were ever able to find anyone from the descriptions that police give."

"What do you mean?"

"Why," she said, "the police have given out a description of the man they're looking for in connection with that murder. You should read it.''

"Why?"

She laughed, and said, "Honestly, it sounds exactly as though they were describing you! My heavens, when I read the thing I thought something about it was vaguely familiar, and wondered if perhaps I knew this murderer, and then I read it again and saw that it was a description that fitted you right down to the ground. And that made me laugh. It just shows how completely unreliable these things are."

"Darned if it doesn't," I told her, and started for the door.

"You'll be back?" she asked.

"Oh, yes, I'll be back," I called over my shoulder.

I took a taxi out to a drugstore in the two thousand block on Veronica Way, then walked back to 1624.

I jabbed on the bell button, giving the code signal that had been successful yesterday.

Claire Bushnell's voice came down the speaking tube. "Who is it?"

"Lam," I said.

"Oh. . . . I can't see you now."

"Why not?"

"I'm just getting up. I slept late."

I said, "Put on a robe and let me in. It's important."

She hesitated a moment, then buzzed the electric release.

I opened the door and went up.

Claire Bushnell's door was slightly ajar. I pushed it open and went in.

Her voice called from the bedroom, "Sit down and make yourself at home. I'll be out in a few minutes."

"Don't be so damn modest," I said. "Put on a robe and come out. I want to talk with you."

She opened the door a crack. "Who's being modest?" she demanded. "Hang it, I'm trying to make myself presentable. Don't you know that a woman looks like hell when she wakes up in the morning?"

"How would I know?" I asked.

"Try taking a correspondence course," she said, and slammed the bedroom door.

I sat down and waited.

It was fifteen minutes before she came out, and then she was wearing slippers and a fluffy negligee, but her hair had been combed, her face made up, and there was carefully shaped lipstick on her mouth.

She said, "You certainly do come at the most inopportune times."

I looked her over and said, "You're gilding the lily."

"What do you mean?"

131

"You don't need the war paint. You could just tumble out of bed and win a beauty prize."

"A lot you know about it. How about some coffee?"

"Suits me."

She opened a door, disclosing a kitchenette that had been built into a closet, just a small gas plate, some shelves, dishes, and a pocket-size electric refrigerator. "I can't give you much else. I don't eat much for breakfast."

"It's okay, I've had breakfast. I'm just being sociable."

"What brings you out here so early?"

I said, "That check you gave us."

"The two hundred dollars?"

"Yes."

"What about it?"

"It bounced."

She had been pouring coffee into a percolator. Now she whirled, still holding the coffee can in her hand. "What are you talking about?"

"It bounced."

"Why, that check was good as gold!"

"There seems to be a slight difference of opinion," I told her. "The bank seems to think otherwise. Apparently you had deposited a check and drawn against it with this check you gave us. The check you deposited was no good."

"Donald, that's absurd! That check was perfectly good."

I said, "Ring up your bank, if you doubt what I'm telling you."

She slowly put down the coffee can as though in a daze, then said, "Good grief, I'd never thought of *that!*"

After a while I said, "Bertha Cool's worked up about it."

"*She* would be."

"What can you do about it?" I asked.

She studied me thoughtfully. "Nothing, I guess. Not now."

"You can't raise any money?"

"Not a cent."

"You must have *some* money in the bank."

"Well, what if I have?"

"And a few things you could hock."

"Well, I'm not going to."

"Your dear auntie doesn't seem as important to you now as she did Saturday, does she?"

132

"Shut up. Sit down and wait for the coffee."

"Who was your check from?" I asked. "The one that bounced."

"What do you want to do?" she demanded. "Stay for coffee or get thrown out?"

"Stay for coffee," I said.

She put water in the percolator, lit the gas plate, brought out an electric toaster, unwrapped a half loaf of bread, opened the little refrigerator and took out a package of Nucoa.

"Seen the paper?" I asked.

"No."

I handed her the morning paper and said, "You might as well get caught up on the news while the coffee's percolating."

She said, "Oh, I'd rather talk with you. I can read the newspaper any time. You're—you're interesting, and you're going to try to pry something out of me, aren't you?"

"I've already pried it."

She opened the newspaper, glanced at the headlines, looked down through the front page, paused briefly on the account of the murder, then turned to the back page, looked at the pictures of the girl lying on the floor of her bedroom, clad in panties and bra.

"How perfectly terrible!" she said.

"What?"

"For a girl to be strangled that way."

I didn't say anything.

"Probably some sex maniac," she said, and shivered. "I hate to think of things like that."

I took a cigarette case from my pocket. "Want one?"

"Please."

She took a cigarette, guided my hand with the tips of her fingers as I held the match. Then I lit up one of my own and walked over, to stand looking out of the window.

Abruptly I turned around.

She had opened the paper to the sporting page and was studying up on the racing news.

I turned back toward the window.

I heard the paper rustle as she folded it. "Like the scenery?" she asked.

"Uh huh."

"I'm glad you do," she said. "Some people prefer the animate scenery."

I said, "You're a lot more cordial this morning than you were yesterday."

"Perhaps I like you better."

"Perhaps."

"Perhaps I feel better."

"Perhaps."

"Perhaps you just imagine I'm nicer."

"Perhaps."

"Good heavens," she said, "won't you argue with me?"

"No, I'll leave that to Bertha."

"All right, I'll take care of Bertha."

I said, "You might sing a different tune if Bertha swears out a complaint for you on the ground of giving a check for which there were not sufficient funds."

"I had sufficient funds when I gave the check. It isn't my fault if something happened."

"Not the way the bank talks. The bank says they only took that check you deposited for collection; that you had no right to draw on it until after it had cleared."

"They didn't tell me that when I deposited the check. They took it in and credited my account in the passbook. I can show you."

"Let's take a look."

She hesitated a moment, then got up and went into the bedroom.

A moment later she came gliding back, the fluffy negligee swirling around about her. She handed me a small bankbook, opened it, and with a tinted fingernail, pointed to the last deposit, a simple credit of five hundred dollars, with the initials of the man who made the entry in the book.

I moved the finger back a bit and looked up the page. There were deposits of two hundred and fifty dollars made with regularity, once each month.

She suddenly realized what I was doing, and jerked the book away.

"Alimony," I said. "I presume you lose it if you get married again."

Her eyes were flaming. "You're the nosiest, most impertinent man I ever met!"

"That alimony of yours," I went on, "is just about enough for a girl to live on if she's economical. You might try matrimony once more and get a bigger slice of alimony next time."

She said, "Someday I'm going to slap your face, Donald Lam."

"Don't do it," I told her. "It brings out the primitive in me. I might sock you."

"The primitive in *you*," she said scornfully. "You haven't any primitive."

"Still thinking about that ten-dollar bet? If you could get me to make a pass at you, you'd have ten dollars more you could credit for this month."

Her face showed a change of expression. "I'd forgotten about that bet," she said, and then added after a moment, "I'm sorry I made it."

"So am I."

"Do you," she asked throatily, "want to call it off, Donald? Just forget about it?"

"No," I told her, "I need the ten bucks."

Her face flamed with anger. "Why you—" and then she laughed and said, "You have a great line, don't you?"

"No line at all," I told her. "I'm working."

"And you never let pleasure interfere with business, I take it."

"Exactly."

"I'm not certain I like people like that."

I said, "You can throw me out after I've had my coffee."

"I will, at that."

The coffee started to percolate, and she fed two slices of bread through the toaster. I passed up the toast but had two cups of coffee in the intimacy of the little living-room. Her eyes were studying me as she ate.

I said, "I'd like the truth, Claire."

"I haven't lied to you."

"You told me you thought that young man was trying to sell your aunt some stock, or something."

"I was afraid he might have been."

"And that you were afraid he might be planning to marry her and cut himself a piece of cake."

"I was."

135

"But you didn't part with two hundred dollars to find out about him just for that."

She didn't say anything.

I said, "Let's quit beating around the bush, Claire."

"You're the one who's beating around the bush, making all sorts of wild guesses, trying to find out something that happened, torturing your imagination and—"

I said, "Look here, Claire, let's be frank with each other. You perhaps have a chance to inherit some money from your aunt. I don't think it's as big a chance as you've been leading us to believe, and I doubt very much if there's as much money there as you told Bertha Cool there was."

"So what? That's my business."

"It's your business up to a point," I said. "But when you came into the office, you started talking about having a man shadowed so you could find out who he was. He was a man who was calling on your aunt. You gave quite a story about *why* it was you wanted him shadowed. It's a story that doesn't hang together. Then Bertha made you a figure of two hundred dollars. For a girl in your position that was a lot of money. You didn't try to bargain, you didn't try to haggle. You put it right out on the line.

"Now then, it turns out you haven't as much money in your bank account as you thought you had. There was a five-hundred-dollar check which you felt certain was deposited on Saturday. That must have been before you went to see Bertha Cool because Bertha Cool rushed your check down to the bank before closing hours. Our bank telephoned your bank, and your bank advised that the check was good, that it had sufficient funds on deposit at that time.

"The position your bank now takes is that it had taken a check for collection and had temporarily credited your account, but that when it found out the check was no good it had debited your account with an amount of five hundred dollars, which made your two-hundred-dollar check no good."

"My Lord," she said, "you keep going over it and going over it. Suppose all that's true, then what?"

I said, "The inference is pretty obvious. The check which you thought was good as gold, but which you now realize you can't collect, wasn't just an ordinary check. It wasn't just an ordinary business transaction. If you had thought a five-hundred-dollar check which you had deposited in your account was perfectly good, and then I came to you this morning and told you that it wasn't good, you would, under ordinary circumstances, insist that you were going to take steps to collect the five hundred dollars and that then you'd make our two-hundred-dollar check good. The reason you're not doing that is because you know that for some reason it has suddenly become hopeless to try and collect that five-hundred-dollar check.''

''All right, what if that *is* the case? Lots of times people take checks and find out they're no good, that they've been bilked.''

''You weren't bilked,'' I said. ''You took a check that was really good as gold, and the reason that it isn't good now is not because there weren't any funds to cover it. It's because the bank has found out that the person who issued that check is dead.''

She was raising her coffee cup to her lips as I spoke. Now she lowered it back to the saucer, looked at me wordlessly.

I said, ''In other words, the check for five hundred dollars, was a check Minerva Carlton gave you. Minerva Carlton met you that Saturday morning before you went to the agency. Minerva Carlton told you that she wanted to find out about this man who was calling on your Aunt Amelia. Minerva Carlton told you she was giving you a check for five hundred dollars which you could apply on expenses, that you were to go to our office, give a great story about why you wanted to find out who this man was and all about him, and she gave you that check so you'd have money enough to pay expenses.

''Mrs. Carlton knew that she couldn't go to our office and tell any story that would hang together and wouldn't arouse suspicion. She knew that *you* could. The probabilities are that your aunt doesn't ever intend to give you a cent and you don't ever expect to get a cent from her. But you fixed up that story so it would sound plausible and would start us working on the case. The two-hundred-dollar check that you gave us didn't mean a damn thing to you because you were going to pass the expense on to Minerva. Now then, suppose you tell me the rest of it.''

She said, scornfully, "You certainly *do* have a wild imagination, don't you?"

I said, "You'd better tell me the story; otherwise, I'm going to pass my information on to the police."

"And what can the police do?" Claire Bushnell asked scornfully.

I said, "The police can serve a subpoena on your bank. They'll find out all about that five-hundred-dollar check, who gave it to you, and then they'll subpoena you as a witness before the Grand Jury."

She played with the handle of her coffee cup, her eyes downcast.

I said, "I haven't got all day to wait."

She sighed, said, "Give me a cigarette, Donald."

I gave her a cigarette and held flame to it. She took in a deep drag, blew out smoke, studied the end of the cigarette thoughtfully as though trying to find some way out of the predicament, then said, "Okay, Donald, you win."

"Tell me about it."

She said, "Minerva and I were pretty close friends. We used to play around a lot together, went out on dates. We understood each other perfectly and used to have a lot of fun. Minerva didn't care too much about the men, but we used to get a lot of kick out of going out and seeing what would develop. We both of us liked adventure."

"That was while she lived here and was working for Dover Fulton?"

"That's right. She was his secretary."

"And then what?"

"And then Minerva went to Colorado. She had some rich relatives there. She met Stanwick Carlton. She thought she could land him. Minerva didn't care particularly about him as far as falling in love was concerned, but Minerva knew he was a good matrimonial catch. She set her cap for him and landed him."

"And then what?"

She said, "Minerva got tired of being a drab respectable housewife—she was smart enough to know that her days of playing around were all over, but she did like to have someone with whom she could discuss the old days. She used to come and visit me and we'd sit and talk until the small hours, reminiscing and recalling adventures we'd had.

"Then Minerva had a vacation and decided she'd spend it with me at the beach. She wanted to come down to sea level because the altitude in Colorado was getting on her nerves. She came down and visited me and we went to the beach together."

"And started playing around?"

"Don't be as dumb as that," she said. "We did a little flirting, but that was all. Minerva was married. She had everything, social position, money, a good home, servants, everything in the world she needed. I don't think she was too terribly happy. Minerva liked laughter and action and white lights and she liked to have people make over her. And she liked a lot of variety, but she realized she had to settle down sooner or later. She'd settled down and that was that."

"But people made passes at you?"

"When?"

"Down there at the beach."

"You mean at me?"

"No, at both of you."

"Of course, they did. I never knew a man who didn't make a pass at me sooner or later."

"And what did Minerva do?"

"Strung them along, kidded them a little bit. We had escorts. We had swimming companions, and we had one fellow who was completely gaga over us, that is, he was over Minerva, but it didn't do him any good."

I said, "Minerva had her picture taken with her head lying on his bare chest."

"How do you know that?"

I said, "I saw the picture."

"Donald Lam, did you steal those films? I'll bet you did. I looked all around for them and couldn't think where I'd put them. I—why, you—"

I said, "Of course I picked up the films. You were holding out on me."

"I don't like that."

"That's all over with. Let's keep on the main subject. Did Stanwick Carlton suspect what was going on on that beach vacation?"

"I tell you, nothing was going on. We strung a couple of saps along and that was that."

"And was one of them Tom Durham?"

"I never saw this man you say was Tom Durham in my life except the one time when I was there at Aunt Amelia's place and he came in, and as I told you, Aunt Amelia didn't introduce him."

"Then why would Minerva want him shadowed?"

"She didn't want him shadowed. She wanted to find out just who he was and just what his relationship with Aunt Amelia was."

"How did she know he knew your Aunt Amelia?"

"I don't know a thing in the world about it, Donald, honestly I don't. Minerva Carlton came to me Saturday morning. She'd been in touch with me two or three times while she was here. On Saturday morning she seemed a little triumphant, as though she'd had something that was bothering her, but was getting the better of it. She was all excited. She gave me a check for five hundred dollars and told me that she wanted me to go to your office and get you to find out who a man was and all about him, but that he mustn't know he was being investigated. She said that he knew Aunt Amelia, and that was the first I knew of him. After she'd described him, I knew that he was the man I'd seen there at Aunt Amelia's."

"And you don't know what he wanted with your Aunt Amelia?"

"Heavens, no. Minerva said he'd be there at four."

"You don't know whether he was trying to sell her stock or trying to marry her, or—"

"I don't know. He may have been a life insurance salesman for all I know. I handed you a song and dance so that you could go to work, and in case anything happened there wouldn't be any trail that would lead back to Minerva. She was desperately anxious about that. She said that if anything happened and the thing was botched up in any way, she must have it so that the lead could only go back as far as me. It must never be traced to her."

I said, "And all this time, Minerva was holding out on you."

"What do you mean?"

"She was having a big love affair with Dover Fulton and she never let you know about it."

She said, "Donald, that's the thing I can't understand. I'm almost certain Minerva would have told me if—well, if there'd been anything like that. She didn't need to hold out on me. She knew that. I simply can't understand that business with Dover Fulton."

"Where were you on Saturday night about ten o'clock?" I asked.

"I was—I was out."

"Girl friend?"

"None of your business."

"Boy friend?"

"Go jump in the lake."

"I hope you can prove an alibi," I said.

"An alibi? What do you mean?"

"That's the time the murder was committed."

"What murder? What are you talking about? That murder was committed *last night.*"

"You mean the stocking murder."

"Yes."

"I don't."

"What do you mean, you don't?"

I said, "I'm talking about the murder of Minerva Carlton."

"Did you expect me to show a lot of surprise?" she asked.

"No."

"I know definitely that it wasn't a suicide," she said. "Minerva wasn't that type. Minerva wouldn't kill herself and I don't think Dover Fulton meant anything at all to her emotionally. I know she admired and respected him, but I happen to know that beyond the usual kidding that takes place in an office, Dover Fulton never so much as made a try for her while she was working for him."

"Was Dover madly in love with her?"

"That's the part I can't understand. I don't think he was. Minerva and I were very close. I don't think she'd have held out on me on anything."

"You mean you knew her *that* well?"

"Of course."

I said, "In case anyone should be looking for me, I've been here and gone."

"Someone going to be looking for you, Donald?"

"Perhaps."

"Your office?"

"Probably."

"What is your partner going to do about that check I gave you?"

"Probably take it out of your hide."

"Donald, I've explained now. You can see it isn't my fault."

I said, "If you could find any possible explanation that would talk Bertha Cool out of two hundred bucks you'd be able to talk the explosion of an atomic bomb into a hiccup."

And having left that thought in her mind, I went out to wrestle with troubles of my own.

CHAPTER THIRTEEN

Murder for Breakfast

I HAD ONE MORE LEAD. Bob Elgin had called Waverly 9-8765. The address on the registration certificate of the car that had followed me the night before had been Sam Lowry, 968 Rippling Avenue.

It was about a hundred to one shot, but it paid off.

I looked Lowry up in the phone book. He didn't have a phone. I checked on Waverly 9-8765. It was a pay-station telephone in an apartment house, and the address was 968 Rippling Avenue.

I went over there. It was a last desperate chance and time was running out. When those two photographers woke up and read the morning paper they'd be almost certain to remember the address they'd given me. After that I'd have only as long as it took Frank Sellers to throw out a dragnet.

The Rippling Avenue address turned out to be a nondescript apartment house, and the cards showed Lowry had an apartment on the second floor.

I rang the bell.

It was quite a while before anything happened. Then a man's voice called from the head of the stairs, "Who is it?"

"Message for you," I called up.

The electric door catch buzzed the door open. I went on in and walked up the stairs.

The man who was standing at the head of the stairs was a well-put-together, broad-shouldered individual, somewhere around twenty-eight or twenty-nine. He looked thoroughly capable of taking care of himself under any circumstances. He had the thick neck which usually indicates a wrestler or fighter. His dark hair was tousled in uncombed disarray. He was wearing pants, slippers, and the upper part of a pair of pajamas. His nose had been broken, and in healing had given his face a flattish, Mongolian appearance, but there was lazy good nature in his grin. "What's the idea?" he asked.

I closed the door behind me and said, "I'm sorry if I got you up."

"Oh, it's all right. I usually get up around this time, anyway. What's the idea of all the commotion? Who's the message from?"

"The message," I said, "is from me."

The good-natured grin faded from his lips. He stood with his feet apart, blocking the stairway. His shoulders settled into solid hostility. "I'm not sure I like that, buddy," he said.

"The name," I told him, "is Donald Lam."

He puckered his forehead, trying to remember where he'd heard the name before.

I refreshed his recollection. "You were playing tag with me last night."

Suddenly his face lit up. He grinned, and the grin showed a gap where a couple of teeth had been knocked out on the left side of his upper jaw. "Well, well, well," he said, "so that's the way it is! Come on up and have a chair."

He stood to one side and thrust out his hand.

I shook hands with him. The grip made my bones ache. "Get your car back all right?" he asked.

"Fine," I said.

He said, "We put some gasoline in the heap and found out where you kept it. I put it down in the regular stall so it would be there for you this morning. I had to leave the keys in it, but I didn't think anyone would steal it."

"No, it was there, all right."

"What did you do with my car?"

"Left it parked down by a streetcar track. I figured you'd report it as stolen."

He frowned a little at that and said, "You must think I'm a bum sport. Hell, I wouldn't have done that to you."

He led the way to his apartment.

I said, "I tried to call you up, but no one answered. I got the number, Waverly 9-8765."

"The hell you did! How?"

"Oh, I have ways of getting that sort of information."

He laughed. "It's a pay-station down at the end of the hall. Usually you can ring in on it unless someone happens to be in the booth, but the apartment house manager has the apartment right next to it. She's a good scout. If she's up and around she'll answer and then call whoever is wanted to the phone. If she isn't up, she'll let it ring."

"What would you have done if you'd caught me last night?" I asked.

He grinned and said, "I'd have massaged you with a bundle of fives. Maybe changed the contours of your face a little bit, depending on whether you were difficult or not."

"And what are you going to do this morning?"

"Hell, I'll buy you a cup of coffee. How about it? I've been reading the papers in bed and now I'm damn hungry."

"I've just had three breakfasts and two extra cups of coffee on top of all that."

"Well, stick around and make yourself at home. I may have to get an okay before I let you go. You seem like a good egg at that."

"What was the trouble last night?"

"You know."

"No, I don't," I told him.

"Well, you should."

He moved around with easy grace. He put on a pot of coffee, stuck his head in the bedroom door and yelled, "Hi, Babe."

A woman's sleepy voice called, "Who is it?"

"You'll never guess," Lowry said. "Get decent and come on out."

I heard the sound of feet on the floor. The bedroom door opened. A cute little redhead stood on the threshold. She was wearing a bathrobe that evidently was one of Sam Lowry's. She had the sleeves turned up some six or eight inches. The bathrobe was wrapped around her once and a half and hung down on the floor. It made her seem unusually small.

"Take a look at him," Lowry said. "This is the guy that slipped a fast one over on us last night, the one we lost in the freight cars."

"Well, I'll be damned," the redhead said. "And he comes around this morning?"

"Sure."

145

"What's he want?"

"Damned if I know. Get your teeth clean, honey, and wash the sleep out of your eyes. We'll have some breakfast and talk it over."

She said, "Okay," and slammed the door. A moment later I heard water running in the bathroom.

"Cute kid," Lowry said.

"She is, for a fact."

"Hell, you haven't seen her. Wait until she comes out from under that bathrobe. Nice disposition too. Cute little devil. Cute as they make 'em. How do you want your eggs?"

"I've had three breakfasts, thanks."

"That's right. You said you had. I have to eat good breakfasts. It takes food to keep me going. She's a cute kid, but she's not much on cooking."

"Why don't you teach her?"

"Oh, I will after a while, but I don't mind."

He unwrapped some sliced ham, tossed it in a frying pan, put the frying pan on the gas plate, and said, "I have to hand it to you. You're a fast thinker."

"Not so fast," I said. "I was lucky."

"I laid myself wide open," he admitted. "It was a damn fool thing to do. I never thought of you pulling a stunt like that. Where were you? Under the rods?"

"That's right. Under the rods on the freight car."

"Cripes, but you think fast. Just the way you run out of gas with a glimpse of my headlights in your rear-view mirror and you were wise. You must have made a dash for it the minute your car stopped."

"What did you want?"

"Hell, you know what I wanted. I wanted the pictures, and I wanted to beat you up a little bit. Just enough to teach you that it isn't wise to stick your nose into things that are none of your damned business."

"Why?"

"Well, now," he said, adjusting the flame under the frying pan to just the right height, "that's a matter of professional ethics. You'd better talk that over with someone else."

"I'd like to talk it over with you. Why did Bob Elgin tell you to work me over?"

"Now, don't make any cracks, buddy. It's early in the

146

morning and I haven't had my breakfast and I'd hate to have to work you over on an empty stomach."

I said, "It's okay by me. I've got what *I* wanted."

"I figured you would have by this time or you wouldn't have shown up here. You aren't that foolish. In fact, you're smart. What did you want that stuff for?"

"I'm investigating an insurance matter."

"What does the photograph of a couple of cheaters have to do with insurance?"

"It might have a lot."

"Well, you can tell me about it while I'm eating."

The ham started to sizzle, and he turned it with a fork. The bathroom door opened and the redhead came out. She was wearing tight-fitting slacks and a sweater.

"See," Lowry said proudly, "what did I tell you?"

I nodded.

"You take over cooking the ham, honey," Lowry said. "I'll take a crack at the bathroom."

She walked over to the gas plate, smiled at me, then turned her back and readjusted the flame under the frying pan.

Lowry called over his shoulder, "You don't need to touch that fire. It's just right the way it is."

She didn't pay any attention to him, but bent over so she could look at the flame under the frying pan.

"See what I told you?" Lowry called from the bathroom door. "It's a swell figure. Look at her bending over!"

"Oh, you!" she said in a voice that showed she wasn't in the least displeased.

Lowry closed the bathroom door.

She got the fire to suit her, then turned around and smiled at me. "You're nice," she said.

"I try to be," I told her.

She said, "I'm glad we didn't find you last night. Sometimes Sam gets too rough. He doesn't know how strong he really is."

"I can imagine," I told her.

She smoothed the sweater down, caught my eye and smiled. "What's the weather like outside?"

"Nice."

"Sunshine?"

"Not a cloud."

147

"Going to be hot?"

"I don't think so."

"Take a look at that table," she said, showing me a fine-looking, highly polished table that looked out of place in the apartment. "Isn't that a peach?"

"It certainly is."

"Sam got that for a birthday present for me. It's Myrtle wood from Oregon. I bet you never saw anything so slick."

"I never did."

She spread a thick pad on it, then put on a table cloth. "You're company," she explained, smiling. "You're going to get to eat breakfast off of it."

"That's fine, only I've had—"

"I know, but you'll have some coffee with us."

I watched her moving around. She was a cute package and she knew it. She liked to have me watch her.

She said, "So you got what you wanted, all right?"

"Uh huh."

"You were pretty smart, all right. Sam had to laugh when he realized what you'd done."

She turned the ham once more. "How do you want your eggs?"

"None for me. Thanks. I simply couldn't eat a thing."

The redhead said, "How about some news?"

I said, "I can get you a morning paper and—"

"Phooey! They're too much trouble to read. Let's listen."

She went over and turned on the radio, catching a radio broadcast that had apparently been on the air some two or three minutes when she turned it on. "I'll make it loud so Sam can hear in the bathroom," she explained and twisted the dial which controlled the volume.

The announcer had finished with a discussion of the foreign situation, made a few comments on current labor troubles, and then launched into local news.

It was a little set, but it had good reception, and the voice of the announcer came in very clearly as he said, "The latest bulletin on the murder of Lucille Hollister, who was stocking-strangled by a sex maniac last night, is a tribute to the detective ability of Sergeant Frank Sellers of the Homicide Squad.

"Detective Sellers, playing a hunch, checked back on the activities of a private detective who was known to have been working on a case in which the Hollister girl had some undisclosed interest.

"Only a few moments ago, police were able to announce with positive certainty that the murderer for whom they were looking was a private detective by the name of Donald Lam, who together with his partner, B. Cool, transacts business as a private investigator under the firm name of Cool & Lam. Not only did the sister of the murdered girl positively identify photographs of Donald Lam as those of the man whom she had seen in her bedroom yesterday night immediately after the commission of the murder, but fingerprints which were left on the Cellophane cover of the book the intruder was reading have been positively identified as those of Donald Lam.

"Moreover, the proprietor of a suburban motor court has now identified the dead girl as being a young woman who appeared with Donald Lam at the motor court, at a time when the detective, registering under the name of Dover Fulton and wife, secured one of the cottages.

"Sergeant Sellers modestly disclaimed credit for any unusual detective work. The break, he said, came when, checking the description of the murdered girl, he found that it tallied almost identically with the description that had been given of the young woman who had been registered at the motor court as Mrs. Dover Fulton. Knowing that this young woman had been associated with the private detective, Sergeant Sellers made a quick trip to the motor court, got the woman who ran the place to rush to the morgue, where she positively identified the body. Thereupon Sergeant Sellers immediately started checking with Rosalind Hart, sister of the murdered girl, for the purpose of ascertaining whether Donald Lam might have been the intruder whom she saw waiting in her bedroom.

"In commenting on the motivation for the crime, Sergeant Sellers said today, 'Lam has always been exceptionally brilliant, but there has been some suspicion as to whether he was entirely normal. His partner admitted that, while women seemed attracted to Lam, and almost invariably made advances, Lam was at times cold, to the point of indifference.'

"Police have not as yet prepared a description for broadcast, but on our next news program, on the hour, we will assist the police by broadcasting a detailed description of the suspect. In the meantime police are alerting all radio cars and watching all exits from the city. Sellers feels positive that Lam will be apprehended within the next few hours. 'However,' he announced grimly, and I quote, 'it is pretty well established that the man is now desperate, and unless he is surprised and overpowered there will probably be trouble when we try to make the arrest.' "

The voice of the announcer then started on another subject and the redhead calmly walked over and switched the radio off.

Sam Lowry came out of the bathroom, wiping lather off his face with a wet towel. "Well, now," he said, "isn't *that* something."

I lit a cigarette.

"What do we do?" the redhead asked.

"You got a gun?" Lowry asked me.

"No," I said.

"Are you guilty of the murder?"

"No."

"How did you happen to leave your fingerprints there?"

"I'll explain that when the proper time comes."

"It's a damn good time right now," Lowry said.

He moved around so that he was between me and the door. "Sam Lowry," the girl screamed, "don't you get me in line of fire! You got your gun?"

"I don't need a gun," Lowry said.

I kept on puffing at the cigarette.

"I'm going to phone the cops," the girl said.

"Wait a minute, wait a minute," Lowry told her. "Get smart, will you?"

"What's the matter?"

Lowry said, "There's going to be a reward for this bird if they don't have him by tomorrow morning. Suppose he just vanishes slick and clean? You know what happens in these sex murders. Police start beating the drums, and the city puts up a reward."

The redhead looked at me with loathing and said, "You look like such a normal chap. How in the world could you do *that* to a woman? What satisfaction do you get out of anything like—?"

"Shut up," Lowry said. "I'm getting an idea. Stand up, Lam."

He came toward me, treading lightly on the balls of his feet, his shoulders weaving. "Don't try anything now, buddy," he said. "Just don't try anything. Just stand up and turn your back."

I stood up and turned my back. He ran his hands over my clothes carefully, said, "What do you know about that, Babe? He's telling the truth. The guy really hasn't got a rod."

I sat down in the chair.

"Don't you leave that man alone with me for as much as one second!" the girl said.

Lowry nodded, surveying me appraisingly with eyes that glittered from over high cheekbones which had been permanently swollen by the impact of fists during a pugilistic career.

I said, "I didn't kill her."

"I know," Lowry said, grinning. "She kissed you and then all of a sudden she was possessed by an overpowering impulse, and grabbed up one of her stockings, wrapped it around her neck and choked herself to death. You watched in horrid fascination, powerless to stop her. I know just how it was, buddy."

The redhead said, "If you let that man even get close to me, Sam Lowry, I'll kill *you.*"

"Don't worry, Babe," Lowry said, "he isn't going to get close to you. Watch that ham. You're burning the hell out of it."

"You do your own cooking," she said. "I can't—"

"You go ahead and cook the ham," he told her. "I'm going to keep an eye on this bird. If you don't do a good job with that cooking, I'll walk out and leave you two alone."

The threat was enough. She grabbed a fork, lifted the ham out of the frying pan.

"Now pour in some water, some milk, and a little thickening, and make some gravy," Lowry said.

"I know how to make it. Heaven knows I have enough times."

"Okay, I'm not going to argue about it. Just snap into it."

The girl made the gravy. Lowry licked his thick lips, and said, "I think I can make something out of this, Lam."

I said, "You hold me, and when you finally turn me in to get a reward I'll tell the police all about how you kept me here."

He laughed, and said, "Your word isn't going to be worth a damn now. You'll be trying to tell police you didn't kill the girl, and your fingerprints will show all over the back of the book. The lipstick smears were all over your handkerchief. Anything you tell the police isn't going to do you a damn bit of good. I can make a trade all right, and I think I can collect some dough."

"Well, don't think you're going to leave me here with him," the girl said. "I—"

"Shut up, Babe. I've got to do a little heavy thinking. What did you want those pictures for, Lam?"

"I was working on a case."

"What kind of a case?"

"Oh, just one of those love-pact things! A murder and suicide."

"That one out in the motor court?" the girl asked.

I nodded.

She was looking at me with wide, round eyes. She said, "This girl went out to the motor court with you, and you registered as husband and wife?"

"That's what the police say."

"You wanted to get her in there so you—" she said. "You wanted to get her close up and tie a stocking around her neck, and—"

"Shut up, Babe. Pour that gravy out, and rinse out the pan, then put some eggs in. Sure you don't want any, Lam?"

I shook my head.

"Okay. Just four eggs, Babe."

"I'm not hungry any more," the girl said. "I feel sick to my stomach."

"Get those eggs in the frying pan," Lowry commanded, moving threateningly toward her.

She shut up and started cooking.

Lowry said, musingly, "This is going to take a little figuring."

"If you think you're going to move one step out of this apartment while he's here, you're crazy," she said.

"That's what's bothering me," Lowry admitted. "How I

can swing this thing. I want to get hold of Bob Elgin, but— I don't want him to find you here."

There was silence for a while. Then Lowry said, "I could give you the rod, Babe. You could hold it on him. You could sit right there, and—"

"I tell you, I won't be in this room with him when you're not here. I don't care how many rods you give me."

Lowry tried thinking things over.

I said, "You could tag along with me, Lowry, and make some dough."

"How come?"

I said, "Why don't you grow up? You don't want to be a night club bouncer all your life."

"It ain't what you want in this world that makes you fat. It's what you get," Lowry said.

"Perhaps you and I could get our heads together."

The girl put breakfast on the table. Lowry started eating.

"You watch him," Babe said indignantly to Lowry. "He's smooth. You start making any kind of a deal with him and I walk out of your life so fast you just hear me whiz as I go through the door."

"What's the deal?" Lowry asked me.

I said, "There's eighty thousand dollars' insurance at stake. The insurance company would like to refund one year's premium and be in the clear. It would hate like hell to be stuck for eighty thousand bucks."

"Who wouldn't?" Lowry interjected, shoveling ham into his mouth.

I said, "I'm going to stick them. I was working on that angle of the case. I went to see the girl, but she was dressing. She told me to wait in the other room while she got some clothes on. Someone followed me. I think it was you."

"Not him," the girl declared. "You can't pull that stuff on us. I was with him every minute of the time from the time you stole our car. We had to flag a passing motorist, get some gas for your car, drive it into town, and park it and then take a taxi out here."

I said, "Somebody else knew about that address."

"What address?"

"The girl's address. The one that was murdered."

He grinned and said, "You've got a nice story there. Let's

153

see how it goes. You got in the girl's bedroom and she was dressing. Is that right?''

"That's right."

"And she kissed you while she was undressed?"

I nodded.

"And then you were too modest to sit in the room while she was dressing, and she was too bashful to have you in there, so she sent you into her sister's bedroom."

"Believe it or not, that's it," I said.

He laughed. "What would you think of a girl like that, Babe?" he asked the redhead.

"Don't drag me into this," she declared. "When I think of the chances a girl takes! Gosh, to think of that poor kid!"

I said, "I'm going to change my mind and have some eggs after all. Don't bother. I'll cook them."

I started to get up out of the chair.

"You sit right where you are," Lowry said, "and don't make a move. Babe, if he wants a couple of eggs, cook them for him."

She pouted, and said, "I don't want to cook for any sex killer. Why don't you let him cook them himself?"

"He got hungry too suddenly," Lowry said, his eyes cunning. "He wanted to do the cooking. Let him get hold of a frying pan full of hot grease and you know what could happen? He could fling that in my eyes and then what would happen to you?"

"Oh, oh!" she said.

I said, "Suspicious, aren't you?"

"You're damn right I'm suspicious." Lowry grinned. "I've had one experience with you. You're smart."

The redhead got up and cooked a couple of eggs. I sat there and watched them sputtering in the frying pan. She didn't make a good job of cooking them. There was too much crust on the bottom and there were lots of bubbles cooked into the sides so that it was a nasty mess swimming in grease.

"Take the pepper off the table, honey," Lowry said.

"I want pepper on my eggs."

"I'll pepper the eggs," Lowry said. "You get your hands on that pepper shaker and you might find some way of unscrewing the top and getting a fistful of pepper.

"And don't reach for that coffee," he said, as I started to

reach for the pot of hot coffee. *"I'll* pour the coffee. No, I won't either. Babe, *you* pour the coffee."

Lowry moved his chair back a few feet, and said, "Don't make a move, Lam. Don't try any smart stuff. I'll be right back."

He stepped into the other room, leaving the door open, and a moment later came back carrying a revolver. "Now," he said, "this will get you over any ideas you might have of throwing hot coffee in my eyes."

I choked down the greasy eggs, had some toast and coffee. The coffee was fairly good, but I was having trouble with the food.

Lowry watched me eat, and laughed. He said, "You're having to swallow twice with every mouthful."

"What's the idea?" I asked. "Are you trying to criticize Babe's cooking? I don't seem to stand much chance of getting along, no matter what I do."

He watched me while I finished eating the eggs and sipped my second cup of coffee.

He said, "You sit right there in that chair. No matter what happens, don't move out of that chair. Do you understand?"

I yawned, and said, "It suits me all right. I was going to give your wife a hand with the dishes."

"His *wife,*" the redhead said, and then laughed.

"It's okay, Babe. Let it ride," Lowry said.

I said, "Why do you suppose I came up here this morning, Lowry?"

"I'm damned if I know."

"I've made a deal with Elgin. There's eighty grand involved. We only get a cut of it, but it's a nice hunk of change at that. I guess Elgin will be along pretty quick—unless he intended to cut you out. He wouldn't do that, would he?"

Lowry looked at me with eyes that glittered with cold suspicion. "What the hell do you mean, cut me out?"

"I just asked you."

"How the hell do I know what he'd do?"

We sat silent. The redhead put water in the dishpan. Both of us sat watching the lithe motions of the girl as she took the dishes from the panful of soapy water, rinsed them, and then put them on the drainboard.

I looked at my wrist watch and said, "Damn it, it's funny

you haven't heard from Elgin. I thought he was going to be here."

"Did he *say* he'd be here?"

I said, "I gave him the whole dope and told him I needed a man who could hold up his end in case the going got tough. I told him what his cut would be. He gave me your name and address. I told him you'd tried to meet me before, and he laughed and said, 'People whom you wanted to meet didn't always want to meet you,' or something like that. I've forgotten just what it was. I told him I was on my way up here. I certainly thought he'd either be here or get in touch with me."

There was another period of silence.

I said, "You don't suppose he could be giving us *both* a doublecross, do you?"

"Hell, I'm not his partner," Lowry said. "I'm his bouncer."

"You were supposed to be in on this deal."

"How much did you say was involved?"

"Eighty thousand smackers."

"How come?"

I said, "Take yesterday's paper. Figure it out for yourself. Dover Fulton was found dead. If he committed suicide, his policies don't pay off because they're less than a year old. He gets nothing except a return of the first year's premium. If he didn't commit suicide, the policies carry a double indemnity provision. The face of the policies is forty thousand, twice forty is eighty."

"Eighty grand!" Lowry said, and licked his lips.

I said, "Our share of that would be around twenty grand. Your cut would give you a chance to get in business for yourself, and buy some swell clothes for the redhead. She could go in pictures if she had the right backing."

"Do you think I could?" the girl asked.

Lowry said, angrily, "You just go ahead and talk to *me* about the deal, Lam. Don't spend my money for me. I'll do my own spending."

The redhead said, angrily, "I believe you *would* cut me out if—"

"Shut up, Babe," he ordered. "I want to think."

In the period of silence which followed we could hear the

ticking of the cheap tin alarm clock. The redhead finished the dishes and hung up the dish towel.

I held out my coffee cup, and she refilled it with the thick, black coffee that was at the bottom of the percolator.

"Warm it up for him, Babe," Lowry said.

"This is all right," I told him. "I like it this way."

I sat holding the cup of coffee over the table.

Abruptly Lowry said, "I've *got* to telephone Bob Elgin, honey."

"You're not going to leave me here alone with him."

"Now look, kid, I'll leave you the rod. You sit across the room, out of the way. If he makes a move, plug him. You've got every right in the world. He's a murderer, the police are looking for him, and he's trying to escape. If anything happens and you shoot, remember that I was going down the hall to telephone for the bulls."

"I don't want to be left alone with him."

"It's the only way," Lowry said. "I've *got* to telephone."

"Let *me* telephone."

He laughed and said, "You know what Bob would say if he knew you were here."

"Well, what are you going to do if he comes up?"

"You're going to duck out the back way."

"I'll duck now."

"Not until after I put through that phone call. You've got to watch this guy."

"I tell you I don't want to be left alone with him."

"Now look, honey, you sit over here right by the door to the hall. If he makes a move, you shoot. It isn't as though I wouldn't be right near here. I'm just going to be down at the end of the hall. I can hear you if you shoot! Heck, I can even hear you if you scream. I'll be back in a jiffy. If you do shoot, don't fumble around. Blow the bastard wide open."

"I'd like to blow him wide open anyway," she said. "When I think of that girl, with her cute figure, and—I tell you, it makes me sick to my stomach."

I said to Lowry, "Of course, Bob may not have figured on cutting you in on the deal, but I thought he did."

"He *should*," Lowry said.

I said, "The way I figured the thing, Bob Elgin knew

enough about the setup to know about this deal at the motor court. He knew who went out, and—"

"Say, wait a minute," Lowry said, "you aren't getting Bob wrong, are you? He runs a clean place down there. He doesn't let any mobsters hang around the place. An occasional skirt can cut herself a piece of cake, but that's as far as it goes."

I said, "Well, he acted as though he knew all about this deal, and he said you and I could clean it up. Maybe I told him too much."

"You take the rod, honey," Lowry said. "I'm going to go call Elgin."

"You don't have anything to call him about, not so far," she said. "All you've heard is talk."

I could see he was impressed by that. He settled back in his chair. "I guess the guy is a smooth liar, at that."

I said, "What did you expect? Sleight-of-hand tricks, or television? I'm telling you."

"Just what are you telling us, again?" she asked. "Why don't you get down to brass tacks?"

I said, "Okay, I will. Tom Durham and Bob Elgin have a racket. I don't know what's in it for either of them, and I don't care. I don't know what Durham was playing for on this mixup that goes back to the so-called suicide pact Saturday night; but I do know that they're in the picture somewhere. I have a chance for salvage, an opportunity to get a cut out of eighty grand. Bob Elgin was interested in it. He told me to come here—Hell, I don't know, he could be doublecrossing all of us. I hate to sit here and take the rap."

"You're going to be sitting places for a long time," Lowry said.

"Not if I can help it, I'm not. I'm going to wrap up a cut of eighty grand and get out from under on this Hollister killing."

"Are you trying to tell us you didn't do that?"

"Of course I didn't."

Lowry said, "I'm going to call Bob, and that's final. You take the rod, Babe."

Lowry passed the gun over to the girl. She took up a position between me and the door.

"I'll leave the door open," Lowry said.

158

He looked the situation over, then nodded to the girl, and beat it through the door.

The girl sat there, the door half open, the gun pointed at me. I could see the skin was white across her knuckles. "Don't you make a move," she said. "I believe I'd really *like* to pull the trigger, you filthy beast! And you looked so decent, too."

I said, "I told you I didn't have anything to do with that killing. It wasn't a sex killing, anyway."

"You had lipstick on your handkerchief."

"She kissed me."

"What were you doing in her bedroom?"

"Talking to her."

"She wasn't dressed."

"She invited me in."

"That sounds like a likely story."

I reached over to my coffee cup, let my hand slip, and tipped the coffee all over the table cloth.

The instinctive reaction was too strong. She came up out of the chair like a shot. "You clumsy fool!" she said. "Put something under it, so it doesn't reach the table."

I took a handkerchief from my pocket, made futile attempts at sopping up the mess.

"No, no!" she said, *"underneath* it! Quick! Before it reaches the table."

She came flying across the room, and as she got on the other side of the table I tipped the whole thing over on top of her, reached across the tilted table top, grabbed her gun wrist, twisted the arm, took the gun, and said, "Not a sound. Out the back way. Quick!"

She was so white the makeup showed as orange patches on each cheek.

"Down the back way," I repeated, and then added, fiendishly, "Do you want a stocking tied around your little white neck, a nice stocking that would shut off the air? My, you'd look pretty choking to death, you—"

That did it. She started to scream. I clapped my hand over her mouth, and said, "One word out of you and I'll wrap that stocking around your neck. Out the back way!"

She was trembling violently. I took my hand from her mouth, patted her reassuringly on the shoulder, and said,

159

"Shucks, Babe, I haven't the heart to go ahead and torture you this way. Take me out the back way. I didn't know anything at all about that Hollister killing."

"Don't—don't choke me. I'll do—anything. Anything you want. I—"

"Don't be silly," I said. "I never choked anybody in my life, but I want out of here fast, and I want to take you with me so you don't run down the hall and tell Sam. Now let's go."

She led the way through a back door, into a screened back porch. We went down the first of the stairs, our feet echoing on the wood. I shoved the gun back under my coat.

Halfway down, I said, "You can go on back now, Babe. I'm sorry I had to play it this way, but I needed to get out. I hadn't counted on that radio broadcast coming in just when it did."

She said, "You aren't going to—to take me with you—to do things—to choke me?"

I laughed, and said, "Forget it. Here, here's the gun." I broke the gun open, took the shells out, handed her the empty gun and then handed her the shells. "Don't try shooting until you get the shells in," I said, "and by that time you'll have thought better of it. There's no need attracting a lot of attention and getting your name in the papers. After all, Bob Elgin wouldn't like it if he knew *you* were here. Good-bye, Babe."

She hesitated for a moment, then her lips twisted in a half smile. "Good-bye," she said. "I guess you're—pretty damn smart—and a good egg, after all."

I ran down the rest of the stairs. I looked back and saw she was holding the gun, still making no effort to load it.

CHAPTER FOURTEEN

Bertha Crashes Through

THIRTY MINUTES AFTER I MADE MY GETAWAY from Lowry's apartment, I was playing tunes on Claire Bushnell's doorbell.

She let me in.

I said, *"I'm* back."

"So I see. You certainly do pop in and out, don't you?"

"Uh huh! Seen the late newspapers?"

She shook her head.

"Been talking with people?"

Again she shook her head, said, "I've been doing my nails."

I said, "Okay, Claire, I'm working for you. You're putting me up."

"What do you mean?"

I said, "I have some people looking for me. I don't want to see them. I want to stay here."

"For how long?"

"The rest of the day, anyway. Perhaps all night."

"My God, you certainly *do* move in!"

"Don't I?"

"You can't spend the night here."

"Why not?"

"There are other tenants. It would look bad."

I said, "It wouldn't look bad if they didn't see me."

She couldn't think of the answer to that one.

She walked over to the window, stood looking out for a moment, then turned back to face me.

"Donald," she said, "I know."

"Know what?"

"I heard the radio."

161

I moved, so that I was between her and the door. "So what are you going to do?"

She came toward me, her eyes steady. "You didn't do it."

"Thanks."

"Why do you want to hide, Donald?"

"I want to clear this thing up before they get me. If they catch me I'll go in a cell and be held without bail. I can't do anything from a cell."

"And if they don't catch you?"

"I *may* be able to clear things up."

"You can't clear them up here, Donald."

"I could make a start, and when I had a chance to make a stab at the thing, I could be in a position to move. In a cell I couldn't move."

"How do I know that I wouldn't wake up with a stocking around my neck?"

"You don't."

She moved closer to me. Her hands were on my shoulder. "Donald, look at me."

I met her eyes. She said, "Tell me what happened with that—that other girl."

I said, "I moved around the house, reconnoitering. I found her in the back bedroom. The shades weren't drawn on the windows. The French doors were open. It was a warm night. She was dressing. She saw me. I went in. I think she was a little frightened."

"Of you?"

"She'd been doing something that she was afraid of. She knew something she didn't want me to find out."

"What did she do?"

"She tried the vamp act. I can't tell, it *may* have been sincere. Then she told me to go in the other room and sit down and wait for her. I did."

"And the other room was the sister's bedroom?"

"That's right."

"Why didn't you wait for the police to come?"

"Because then I'd have gone to jail and wouldn't have had any chance to clear the thing up."

"Couldn't the police have cleared it up?"

"I don't think so."

"You understand that running away puts you in a position where you don't stand *any* chance."

"I don't stand any chance, anyway," I told her. "I either have to clear the thing up or I'll get the death penalty as a sex murderer. What's more, they'll bring up every unsolved murder they've had in the last five years and pin them on me as well. They'll try to write a solution to the whole smear of stuff by making me out a fiend."

"And you think you can clear it up if you have a chance?"

"There's a good gambling chance that I can. It's the chance I have to take. It's the only one I have."

"How can you clear it up, Donald?"

I walked over to a chair and sat down. She hesitated a moment, then came over to sit down opposite me. "I like you," she said. "I'm going to take a chance. That is, I *think* I'm going to take a chance, but I want you to start talking. I want the facts."

I said, "I started out with Tom Durham. You wanted me to find out about him. You came to the office with a nice story about the reason you wanted him shadowed. That wasn't the real story. You wanted him shadowed because Minerva Carlton wanted to find out about him."

"I told you that."

"How did Minerva know Durham was seeing your aunt?"

"I don't know."

I said, "I *don't* think Tom Durham intended to marry your aunt."

"He'd be foolish if he did."

"And I don't think he was trying to sell her any stock."

"Well, he certainly wanted something."

I nodded. "I think Tom Durham is a blackmailer. I think Tom Durham is blackmailing your aunt. Now put your mind on that and tell me how he could blackmail her. What he could possibly have on her."

She frowned and said, "Blackmailing? Aunt Amelia?"

"That's right."

She shook her head and said, "Amelia wouldn't blackmail."

"Then he was *trying* to blackmail her."

"She'd have called the officers."

163

"I don't think so. I think the evidence indicates he must have had something on her, or thought he did."

"I haven't the faintest idea what it could have been."

"Is your aunt at all vulnerable?"

"I don't see why. She's not accountable to anyone for her actions."

"There's nothing in her past?"

She shook her head.

"How about her dead husband?"

"Nothing there. His memory is nothing to her. He bored her."

"She got some money from her last husband?"

"To tell the truth, Donald, I don't know. She's always been exceptionally secretive about finances. I think there was some money but I don't know how much. If there was money, it was mostly insurance."

"And how did your uncle die?"

"He died very suddenly. Some sort of food poisoning, I think."

I said, "That *may* be it."

"Donald, what are you saying?"

I said, "I'm thinking out loud. I'm exploring the possibilities. How long ago did he die?"

"Three or four years."

I said, "I think your aunt's being blackmailed. How long has she had that maid with her?"

"Susie?"

"Yes."

"Years."

"Susie was with her when her husband was alive?"

"Oh, yes."

"And did Susie like the husband?"

"Susie has always been very, very devoted to Aunt Amelia. There's some sort of a strange bond between them."

"And your Aunt Amelia's married life wasn't particularly happy?"

"I'm sure I couldn't tell you, Donald. I didn't see too much of her. She irritated me and—well, that's the way it was. I do know that Aunt Amelia always wanted to be free. She was looking for romance."

I got up and moved over to look out of the window, lit a

cigarette, paced the floor for a few minutes, then went back and sat down.

"Why do you think my aunt was being blackmailed?"

"Because I think Tom Durham was a blackmailer."

Claire Bushnell said, "Well, I don't know as there's any way that we can find out anything about it. Of course—Well, come to think of it, there *was* something rather peculiar about my uncle's death; that is, it was sudden, and Aunt Amelia didn't seem to have any of the symptoms that he had. I remember she *said* she had been a little ill, but, to tell you the truth, I didn't think too much about it."

I said, "Minerva Carlton was being blackmailed. That is, someone was putting a bite on her. I think it was Tom Durham. I think she also found out that Tom was trying to blackmail your aunt. I think she wanted to find out all she could about Tom, and because Tom was trying to bleed your aunt white, it gave Minerva a good opening to get a private detective agency to work on the job through you."

"What makes you think Minerva was being blackmailed?"

I said, "Everything points to it. I—"

The bell rang.

I said, "Let it ring for a while. Try not answering it."

Whoever was downstairs kept playing a persistent, steady tune on the doorbell.

After a while I said, "Okay, find out who it is. If it's the police you'll have to let them in. Can you lie about my being here?"

"Like a trooper," she said, picking up the cigarette ends I had left in the ash tray and with the tip of her finger putting little smears of lipstick on the ends.

I laughed, and said, "You must have been caught in *that* trap before."

"What trap?"

"Having cigarette ends in an ash tray that didn't have lipstick on them."

"Is that nice?" she asked, pouting.

"No," I said.

She went over to the speaking tube and whistled down. "Who is it?" she asked.

Bertha Cool's voice came booming up the speaking tube. "This is Bertha Cool. I want to see you *right* away!"

Claire Bushnell looked at me questioningly.

I said, "Wait a minute. Tell her you're—No, that's all right. Tell her to come up."

Claire pushed the electric door release. "Now what do you do?" she asked. "Hide?"

I nodded. "I'll be in the closet back of the wall bed. Tell Bertha you haven't seen me."

"Okay," she said.

I moved over to the door which concealed the wall bed, pushed it open, stepped inside, and Claire Bushnell pushed the door closed. I heard the latch click into place.

A few moments later I heard Bertha Cool's voice. "Hello, Miss Bushnell."

"Hello, Mrs. Cool. What brings you here?"

"We're working on a case for you. Remember?"

"Yes indeed. Do come in and sit down."

I heard the floor creak with Bertha's weight moving across it, then she settled herself in a chair with a plunk and said, "Your check bounced, dearie."

"What do you mean?"

"The check that you gave us for two hundred dollars. It wasn't any good. Damn it, I told Donald to tell you. I thought I'd find him here."

"Why—why it *must* have been good. I had money in the bank."

"The bank says you didn't. The bank says a check that you had thought was deposited was taken for collection. It was a check on an out-of-state bank. It was no good so they debited your account."

"Well, I like that! That check is just as good as gold."

"Whose check was it?"

"I'm afraid I can't tell you that, Mrs. Cool, but I'll certainly be glad to go to the bank with you."

I couldn't see Claire Bushnell's facial expression, but the tone of her voice was perfect. She was a darned good little actress. Thinking back on the smooth manner in which she'd smeared lipstick on the ends of my cigarette butts, I began to wonder just how much experience our client had had in the art of deception.

"We want you to make the check good," Bertha said.

"But the check *is* good, Mrs. Cool."

"The bank says it isn't."

"Well, I'll take that up with the bank."

"I don't give a damn who you take it up with or what you have to say," Bertha said vehemently, "but before I leave, I want something that'll balance that two-hundred-dollar red ink entry on our bank account, because I deposited your check in good faith."

"Well, of course I—if the person who gave me the check—well—that *would* leave me in a position where I'd be temporarily embarrassed."

"You will be embarrassed in a lot more ways than that if you don't meet that check," Bertha Cool said grimly.

"But I'm sorry, Mrs. Cool, I haven't a thing."

"The hell you haven't."

"What do you mean?"

"Be your age, dearie," Bertha said. "Go to your boy friend and—"

"I haven't a boy friend."

"Get one, then."

"I—I—well, you see, I—"

"You haven't seen Donald Lam today, have you?"

"No."

"My God," Bertha said, "what a mess! The police are spreading it all over the country that he's guilty of a sex murder. The little bastard!"

"A sex murder!" Claire Bushnell exclaimed.

"That's right. This girl who was choked to death with her own stocking, lying half-nude on the bedroom floor."

"Why, Mr. Lam seemed like a—why, I wouldn't have thought anything like *that* of him."

"Well, I don't know," Bertha said judicially. "I've always been fond of him, all right, but there's something wrong with him. Women throw themselves at him and he doesn't go overboard the way he should. Come to think of it—well, looking back on things, I *am* starting to wonder a little bit."

"Why, Mrs. Cool! How can you say anything like that about your partner?"

"Damned if I know," Bertha said. "I'm just talking."

"Weren't you working on a lot of cases together?"

"Certainly."

"Well, couldn't you tell from the way he acted?"

"Hell's bells," Bertha said, "our arrangement was a business partnership. I didn't sleep with him."

"That isn't what I meant," Claire Bushnell said.

"Well, I thought I'd head you off," Bertha said, "because that's what you were going to get around to. So you haven't seen him?"

"No. . . . Have you been in your office, Mrs. Cool?"

"Off and on," Bertha said. "I had to go out to San Robles on a job out there. I kept the radio tuned in on the news broadcasts and heard about Donald on the radio. I came back to the office, and everybody had heard it. The girls were having hysterics."

"What girls?"

"The secretaries," Bertha said. "That Elsie Brand, the one that's Donald's private secretary, was fighting mad. She was white-faced she was so damn indignant. She said that she'd stake her life Donald was absolutely innocent, said she'd buy him a dozen stockings and turn out the lights with him any time."

Claire Bushnell took advantage of the situation to rub it in on me. She said musingly, "Well, of course, there *is* something funny. I had a talk with Mr. Lam yesterday. He came in the apartment and caught me rather informally."

The bell rang again insistently, stridently, and kept on ringing. Claire Bushnell went over to the speaking tube. I heard her say, "Who is it?" then there was a long moment of silence.

"Well, who was it?" Bertha Cool said. "My God, you're white as a sheet."

"A man by the name of Sellers," she said, "Sergeant Sellers, of the police."

"That'll be Frank," Bertha said. "He's a good egg. He's on Homicide. I wonder what the hell he's doing here."

I sat tight. A few moments later I heard the bang of Sellers's imperative knuckles on the apartment door, and then Claire went across and opened it. Sellers said, "You're Claire Bushnell?"

"That's right."

"Hello, Frank," Bertha said.

"Hel-lo, Bertha!" Sellers exclaimed. "I sure hated to do it, Bertha, but that's the way the chips fell."

"Well, I don't blame you," Bertha said. "If what I heard over the radio is right, I guess the little bastard is caught dead to rights. I guess that's been the trouble with him all along. One of those over-developed brains. He always did keep to himself, sort of."

"Never had any normal relations with women?" Sellers asked.

"How the hell would I know?" Bertha demanded truculently. "Women fall all over themselves falling in love with him. . . . Take that little secretary he's got. She's nuts over him, and Donald treats her as though she might be his kid sister. Her eyes light up like automobile headlights every time he comes in the room. She follows him all around with those eyes. Donald doesn't even seem to notice it. But he's always been nice to her, always tried to give her the breaks. He fought to get her raises in salary and make the work easier for her."

"Typical symptoms," Sellers said with all the smug finality of an amateur psychoanalyst. "Hell, I should have smelled it a long time ago."

"May I ask *what* you're talking about?" Claire Bushnell said.

"Her partner, Donald Lam," Sellers said. "He's a murderer—sex murder. What do you know about him?"

"Why, I've met him," Claire Bushnell said.

Sellers said, "Hell, let's quit beating around the bush. Where is he?"

"What do you mean?"

"You know what I mean," Sellers said. "You've got him up here, hiding."

"Why, what are you talking about?" Claire Bushnell exclaimed indignantly.

"Phooey," Sellers said. "I knew damn well that as soon as this thing broke Donald would be too smart to come to the office. He'd go someplace where he didn't think anybody would look for him and telephone Bertha to come and join him, so I simply stuck around and shadowed Bertha. When she started out here, I tagged along. I knew damn well she came out here to meet Donald Lam. He's either here now or else he's going to come in later and meet Bertha Cool."

Bertha said, "You're nuts, Frank. I haven't talked with Donald. I don't know where the hell the little runt is."

"You're not kidding me a damn bit, Bertha," Sellers answered. "You may think he's a murderer or you may not, but you've got business together and you sure as hell aren't going to let him get locked up until you've had a chance to find out everything he knows about that case he's working on, so you can carry on and make some mazuma out of it."

Bertha said, "It would have been a good idea; if I'd known where to get in touch with him I would have. I came out here because this little lady gave us a two-hundred-dollar check that bounced."

"Yeah, I know," Sellers said. "I'll just look around."

"Look around," Bertha Cool told him. "If you want to make a bet, I'll bet you don't find him, because he isn't here."

"What'll you bet?" Sellers asked.

"Fifty bucks," Bertha said quickly. "Come on, is it a go?"

I could see that that bothered Sellers. He hesitated for a minute, then said, "I'm not betting, but I'm taking a look around, just the same."

"You can't search my apartment," Claire Bushnell said.

"Oh, oh," Sellers observed. "*That's* the pay off!"

"Well, you can't. You haven't a warrant and you just can't come barging in here. How do *I* know you're an officer?"

"Bertha knows I'm an officer," Sellers said. "Why don't you want me to search the place, sister?"

"Because it's my place. I don't like the idea of police barging in here and going through it just any time they happen to feel like it."

"Still want to bet?" Sellers asked Bertha.

There was a long interval of silence, then Bertha said dubiously, "I'll bet you ten bucks."

"Make it twenty-five," Sellers said.

"No, ten," Bertha said. "That's my limit."

"You've come down forty bucks."

"You've changed *your* tune," Bertha told him.

"Okay," Sellers said, "I'll bet you ten bucks. Get out of my way, sister. What's behind this door?"

I could hear her struggling with Sellers. Sellers merely laughed.

"Damn you!" she panted. "You can't do that. You—"

"Out of the way, sister, out of the way," Sellers said.

The door latch clicked. The door swung open and the wall bed pushed me out to one side.

"Well, well, well," Sellers said. "First rattle out of the box. Come on out, Lam."

I walked out into the room.

Bertha jumped up, her eyes blazing. "Why you damned little son-of-a-bitch!" she screamed at me. "You've cost me ten bucks!"

Frank Sellers threw back his head and roared with laughter. "This is good," he said. "This really is good."

"Why you ungrateful little—" Bertha's voice choked with emotion.

Claire looked at me helplessly.

I said, "It's all right, Claire. I'm sorry. I came up the stairs. You must have been out telephoning or something. The door was open. I came in here and waited for you to come back and then the doorbell began to ring. I didn't know who it was so I slipped in here and pulled the door shut behind me."

Sellers said, "You must have got here just before Bertha did, then."

"That's right," I said.

Sellers quit laughing. He got up off the davenport, walked over to the door and said, "Show me how you pulled this thing shut after you got in here, Lam."

I knew I was trapped. There wasn't any handle on the inside of the door.

Sellers grinned, and said, "That makes it nice. Stick your wrists out, Donald."

"Wait a minute, Frank. I want to go over this—"

"Stick your wrists out," he said, his voice suddenly ringing with brutalized authority.

I knew that tone of voice. I knew the gleam in his eyes. I put my wrists out and Sellers snapped on handcuffs, then he searched me for weapons and said, "All right, now sit down.

If you have any talking to do, start talking. You're under arrest. You're charged with the murder of Lucille Hollister. Anything you say can be used against you. Now talk your damn head off, if you want to."

I said, "I didn't kill her."

"Yeah, I know. You just came in and found her dead and smeared lipstick all over your mouth and then went into the other kid's bedroom and waited for her. I'd never have thought it of you, Donald. I always knew you were a queer piece of fish but I never thought you were like that."

I said, "Let's go back to the beginning on this thing, Sellers."

"Oh, nuts," Sellers said, and then added hastily, "But go ahead. Keep talking."

I said, "All you're listening for is for me to say something that will incriminate me. Now, give a guy a break. Get your mind free and clear of all that prejudice. Forget you're a cop and let's see what we can make out of this."

"It's your party," Sellers said. "Go ahead and serve the refreshments."

I said, "Let's go into the history of the thing, Sellers. Lucille Hollister was crazy about her young sister, Rosalind. Rosalind was in love with Stanwick Carlton. Stanwick Carlton's wife may have done a little playing around. Lucille thought she did, anyway. She wanted to bust up Stanwick's marriage."

"Who told you all this?" Sellers asked.

"Lucille."

"When?"

"Just before she died."

Sellers's eyes lit up with the gleam of a hunter finding a fresh trail. "So you admit you were in the bedroom with her just before she died."

I looked him in the eyes and said, "Yes."

"Why did you kill her, Donald? Was it a sex murder?"

"Don't be silly," I said. "In the first place, I didn't kill her. In the second place, it wasn't a sex murder. Someone killed her to keep her from talking."

"About what?"

"That's what I'm trying to tell you, what I'm trying to find out."

"Go ahead," Sellers said, and then turned to Claire Bushnell. "You heard him admit that he was with her just before she died."

Claire Bushnell, white-faced, tense, nodded.

I said, "That accounts for Lucille Hollister. She was trailing Minerva Carlton, but on this trip Minerva Carlton wasn't playing around."

"I see," Sellers said sarcastically. "She went in that auto camp with Dover Fulton because he wanted to teach her how to play tiddlywinks, and she took her blouse off so the sleeves wouldn't get wrinkled."

I said, "Minerva Carlton was playing a deep game. She came to Claire Bushnell, here, and gave her a check for five hundred dollars and instructions as to what Claire was to do. Claire was to get Bertha Cool to find out about a man who was calling on Claire Bushnell's aunt."

Sellers glanced at Claire Bushnell.

She nodded.

Sellers, interested now, said, "Go ahead, Lam. What's the sketch?"

I said, "I got on the job. I shadowed this man to the Westchester Arms Hotel. He was staying there. He was registered under the name of Tom Durham. Now why do you suppose Minerva Carlton wanted him shadowed?"

"Hell, I don't know," Sellers said. "I'm not a mind reader."

I said, "When Lucille Hollister went to the motor court with me, she opened her purse and took out a package of cigarettes and some matches. She left both cigarettes and matches on the table. The matches had the imprint of the Cabanita Club."

"So what?" Sellers asked.

"And," I went on, "when she took out the cigarettes she had evidently forgotten that she had used the cigarette package as concealment for a little piece of paper. It was a piece that had been torn from the menu of the Cabanita Club, and on it had been written, Kozy Dell Slumber Court."

"And that was the place where Lucille Hollister steered you?" Sellers asked.

"That's right."

"The place where Dover Fulton and Minerva Carlton committed suicide?"

"The place where they were murdered," I corrected.

Sellers said, "Well, well, the party's perking up. You mean they were murdered, with the door locked from the inside?"

"That's right."

"Keep talking," Sellers said. "We may have you on two more counts of murder, just in case we can't convict you on the first one."

I said, "The door was locked from the inside, all right, but who knows *when* it was locked?"

"What are you getting at?"

I said, "There were several shots fired."

"That's right. One in the suitcase, one in Dover Fulton, one in Minerva Carlton."

"That's four," I said.

"Four!" Sellers said. "Are you nuts? That's three."

"Four."

Sellers said, "What are you trying to do, start an argument?"

"How many shells were fired out of Dover Fulton's gun?"

"Three."

"Only two loaded shells were left."

"Well, that's because he usually carried it with an empty space in the cylinder under the hammer. Lots of people do that because it's safer."

"So there was one empty chamber, three fired shells, and two full shells in Dover Fulton's gun."

"That's right."

"Four shells were fired," I said.

Sellers began to look at me with a certain element of respect. "Of course, Lam," he said, "you *could* be right. What do you know about it?"

I said, "I'm putting two and two together."

"And making four," Sellers said, grinning at his own joke.

"And making four," I told him. "If Dover Fulton had been shooting the gun in a suicide pact, how could he have fired the shot into the suitcase?"

"He could have shot at the girl and missed her the first shot."

174

"Missed her by that wide a range? The suitcase was down on the floor."

"Hell," Sellers said, "she could have been bending over the suitcase, just getting ready to put something in it, and he decided he'd surprise her."

"That's fine," I said. "She's down by the suitcase, on her knees, just getting ready to open it. Dover Fulton shoots at the back of her head. He's going to catch her by surprise."

"Well," Sellers said, "it *could* have been that way."

I said, "All right, figure the surprise element. Then what does she do?"

"Well, naturally, she'd jump up."

"And turn to face him," I said.

"Well, so what?"

"Then the second shot would have been in the *front* of her forehead."

"Not necessarily. She turned to face him, then saw what was happening and started to run."

"And then he shot her right in the back of the head."

"That's right."

"In other words," I said, "he misses her slick and clean when she's down on her knees and he's standing right close behind her, but when she jumps up and starts to run, he makes a perfect bull's-eye."

Sellers scratched his head and said, "Well, hell, I don't know what happened, but that's an explanation."

"It's an explanation that doesn't explain," I said. "I'll tell you what happened: There were three shots fired in that room. The other person who was in there knew he had to account for three shots. He wasn't in a position to account for them, so he picked up the gun and the suitcase. He carried both of them off, far enough away so the report wouldn't be heard. Then he fired a bullet into the suitcase. Then he brought the suitcase back to the cabin, left the suitcase, planted the gun in Dover Fulton's hand, locked the door from the inside, and climbed out of the window."

"I don't get you," Sellers said. "Why did he go to all that trouble? Why did he do all that?"

"Because he had to account for the third bullet. He had to put it in the suitcase."

175

"But that makes *four* bullets, the way you're talking now," Sellers said.

"Exactly."

"Any why did he have to shoot a fourth bullet in order to account for the third bullet?"

"Because," I said, "he was wearing the third bullet."

Sellers looked at me for four or five seconds, his eyes blinking as he tried to digest the idea. Then he said, "It's a theory, all right. Nothing but a theory, but it's a theory."

I said, "There's a lot more to it than a theory. Where were the woman's clothes when you found the bodies?"

"Part of them were on and the rest of them were—let's see, I guess the rest of them were in the suitcase."

I said, "That does it. A woman who is undressing in a motor court on a weekend party wouldn't take off her blouse, roll it up, and then jam it in the suitcase. At the time of the shooting, that suitcase was lying open. Her blouse was on the chair by the suitcase. The murderer got in a panic and wadded that blouse into a bundle and jammed it in the suitcase, then closed the suitcase."

"You seem to know a lot about it," Sellers said, and then added significantly, "You should. You were there, camped in the motor court at the time."

Sellers thought that over, then said suddenly, "By gosh, we're beginning to get somewhere now! I want you folks to remember every word this guy's saying. He was there at the time. If it was a murder, he did it."

"I didn't do it," I said, "because I'm not wearing that third bullet."

I said, "Take a look at the photos that show the interior of that room where the bodies were found. Look at the towels hanging on the towel rack."

"What about them?"

"One bath towel," I said, "two hand towels."

"Well?"

"Standard equipment is two bath towels and two hand towels. What happened to the other bath towel?"

"Hell, I don't know," Sellers said. "It's not up to us to go around checking linen."

I said, "The murderer had been wounded, and the murderer wrapped a bath towel around the wound to stop the bleeding. It probably didn't bleed too much, but that's what the bath towel was used for."

Sellers said, "It's a wild theory, Lam. Just a wild, wild theory."

"Sure it is, but it's worth investigating."

"You're damn right it's worth investigating," Bertha Cool said. "Think of what it does to the insurance company, Frank."

"How come?" Sellers asked.

"Suicide within a year, the policies don't pay anything," Bertha pointed out, greedily. "Death *not* by suicide, they pay forty thousand dollars; death by accidental means gives them double indemnity or eighty thousand bucks."

Sellers whistled.

Bertha said, "We're in on that—that is, *I'm* in on it."

"Go ahead," Sellers said to me, "Keep talking, Lam."

I said, "It wasn't a love nest affair at all. Minerva Carlton was being blackmailed. The blackmailer wanted a big shakedown, too much for her to pay. If he didn't get it, he threatened to go to her husband and spill the beans."

"*If* she was being blackmailed, that's probably the way it was," Sellers said.

I said, "She decided to slip a fast one over on the blackmailer. She went to Dover Fulton. He had been her former boss. She liked him. She may have been sweet on him at one time, I don't know. But anyway she went to him, and they agreed to fix things up so that Dover Fulton posed as her husband. The blackmailer had never seen Stanwick Carlton. Fulton posed as Stanwick Carlton, probably said in effect, 'So what? My wife's been indiscreet, but I forgive her!' So they kissed and made up in front of the blackmailer, and Fulton, who was posing as Stanwick Carlton, said, 'Now go jump in the lake!' "

"Could be," Sellers said after thinking it over. "You'd want proof."

I said, "I was trying to get proof when you put these on me." I held out my hands with the handcuffs on them.

"You're damn right I put them on you," Sellers said. "You were caught redhanded in a murder."

"I didn't kill her."

"Then you shouldn't have run away, my lad. You know

177

what happens when you try to make a break for it. You thought you could walk out and get by with it. You didn't think anyone who had seen you could identify you. But I just happened to play a smart hunch. I remembered the description of the little blonde number you gave me tallied absolutely with the dead girl. I got—"

"Yeah, I know," I said. "It all came over the radio."

Sellers glared at me. "And I checked up on the book, incidentally, and your fingerprints are all over the Cellophane cover."

"Sure," I said, "I was out there."

"That's the second time he's admitted it," Sellers said to Bertha Cool and Claire Bushnell. "Remember it."

I said, "There's pretty good reason to believe that whatever the blackmail consisted of, it centered around the Cabañita Club. You know what happens around those places. The playboys go out when they're on the loose. Occasionally some smart egg with a good memory and an eye for faces sticks around and gets a line on who's doing the celebrating. If it happens to be a married man from out of town, or someone who lives in the city and is doing a little weekend playing, the blackmailers look them over. Nearly all of those places have blackmailers who hang around, or I'll put it another way: Lots of blackmailers drop around to those places and keep looking the crowd over, trying to pick up the license number of an automobile, or something that'll mean a little cash. It's usually a job of slim pickings, but I think that this blackmail centers around the Cabanita outfit. I think that Tom Durham is mixed up in it, and I think that Bob Elgin knows who Tom Durham is and where he can be found.

"Durham was staying at the Westchester Arms Hotel. He checked out right after the killing. I thought at the time it was because he'd found out I was shadowing him. I think now it was because he knew there'd been a shooting. I'd like to look him over. We might find a .32 bullet parked somewhere in his anatomy."

Sellers said, "Okay, I'll keep it in mind and see what can be done."

I said, "I started prowling around the Cabanita last night. I started getting pictures that had been taken. People didn't like it. They tried to work me over. I barely squeezed out from under a good beating. I had some pictures and an address. The address was that of the blonde girl who was killed last night. I went out there to check, to find out what was at that address. I found out. Somebody was following me, or else someone knew I was going to be there."

"That's what *you* say," Sellers said.

"And that," I told him, "is why I want to get this thing cleared up. It's my only chance for my white alley. Let's go down and talk with Claire Bushnell's aunt before she has a chance to think up a good story. She was being blackmailed. I think the blackmailer would keep in touch with her, probably by telephone. I don't think Tom Durham is doing much traveling around today, because I *think* he's got a .32 bullet in him somewhere. All you need to do is to stop by Amelia Jasper's house on the road to headquarters and give her a grilling."

"Yeah, and lose my badge for it," Sellers said. "What do you think I am? A sucker that's going to break in on somebody's rich aunt and say, 'Look here, Madam, you're being blackmailed'?"

I said, "You're going to let me do that. I wouldn't ask you to do it. All you need to do is to sit and listen."

Sellers thought it over, then shook his head and said, "It's a gag. You're going to headquarters."

"By that time the trail will be cold and you'll *never* find out anything."

"I've caught me a murderer," Sellers said, grinning with self-satisfaction. "That's all right for one day's work. Come on."

Bertha said, "For the love of Mike, Frank, give *me* a break. You're busting up my partnership and smearing the thing with a lot of publicity that's going to cost me all kinds of dough. I'm on the trail of an eighty-thousand-dollar insurance job. If what Donald says is right, I stand a chance of throwing the hooks into the insurance company and cleaning up a little gravy."

Frank Sellers hesitated. At length he said to me, "If you doublecross me on this thing I—"

"Since when did anybody doublecross you?" Bertha demanded.

179

Sellers looked at me and frowned. "It's not you, Bertha. It's this guy. You never know what he's figuring."

I held out my manacled wrists, and said, sarcastically, "Yeah, it looks like I'm smart."

Bertha said, "We could give you a cut in case we—"

"Don't be a fool, Bertha," I interrupted. "Frank isn't thinking about money."

Sellers gave me a grateful look.

I said, "You have an opportunity to straighten up that killing out at the Kozy Dell Slumber Court. You have an opportunity to put a whole bevy of feathers in your cap. You have a chance to break up a blackmailing ring, and you have a chance to show how that Hollister girl was actually killed, why she was killed, and who killed her."

"A lot of people would say I had the answers to that last right here, right now," Sellers said, but his tone lacked the positive conviction he had shown earlier.

"And," I went on, "you've got a widow out there in San Robles who has two kids. Those kids have got to grow up, they've got to go to school. They've got to go through college, if they really want to make a dent in the world. It takes education these days, and education takes money. There's a woman out there who doesn't know where her next dime is coming from. Now, then, if you could play things my way, and she could have eighty thousand bucks—"

"You've made a sale," Sellers said. "Let's go."

We all got up, and I said, "What about the handcuffs?"

"Just let them ride." Sellers grinned. "Don't bother about them. You can walk all right if you just keep your hands in front of you and right close to your belt."

"I could do a lot more good if you would take them off."

"Good for whom?" he jibed.

"The trouble with you is you have a mind of a cop. Come on, let's go."

We piled into the elevator, rattled down to the ground floor, and then all climbed into Frank Sellers's police car.

"What's the address?" Sellers asked.

"226 Korreander," Claire Bushnell said.

Sellers pushed the car into speed.

I said, "You'll do better if you don't use the siren."

Sellers gave me a withering glance, then devoted his attention to driving.

He slowed the car to a conservative thirty miles an hour before we got to the two hundred block on Korreander, then slid to a stop in front of the white stucco house.

We all piled out and trooped up the stairs to the porch. Sellers rang the bell.

Susie, the loose-jointed maid, came striding deliberately down the hallway. She opened the door, and for a moment I thought she recoiled at the sight of Frank Sellers. Then she let her face petrify in expressionless lines of wooden indifference.

"Hello, Susie," Claire said. "Is Aunt Amelia in?"

The maid hesitated.

Frank Sellers pulled back his coat, showed his star. "She in?" he asked.

"Yes."

"Come on," Sellers said, and pushed his way in, without waiting for any announcement to be made.

Susie glowered at him, but stood helplessly where she had been pushed to one side. Just before we got to the living room her presence of mind reasserted itself and she raised her voice and called in a high, shrill tone, "Oh, Mrs. Jasper! Claire and the police are here to see you."

Sellers, with one hand gripping my arm, pushed the door open with his left hand and we entered the sitting-room.

Amelia Jasper looked up from her wheel chair and transfixed us with her most winning smile. "How do you do!" she said. "Won't you all be seated? Hello, Claire, honey. How are you today, dear?"

"Fine, thank you."

"Well, since I can't get up you'll have to act as hostess, Claire. That sciatica again, a flare-up from that horrid automobile accident. I *do* wish I could do something to get over the pain. I've taken aspirin until I'm sick—but do sit down. Pardon me if I seem a little groggy. I've taken so much drug."

Her eyes fluttered half shut, then she caught herself and raised the lids.

We started to sit down, and then she caught sight of the

181

handcuffs. "Why, Mr. Lam!" she said, and then added, "Surely you're not—Why—"

Susie Irwin, the maid, finished the sentence from the doorway. "I heard it on the radio, ma'am. I wasn't going to say anything. He's the one that killed that Lucille Hollister last night. You remember you were reading about it in the papers, the stocking murder."

"Donald Lam killed her!" Amelia Jasper exclaimed, incredulously. "Why, I thought he was so nice. Why—Why— And you bring him here!"

"In order to try and clear a couple of angles of the case," Sergeant Sellers apologized.

"Well, I don't want that man in my house. I don't want to be near him. I read all about that crime in the newspapers, the horrible, sickening details. I—I'm sorry, but I just—"

"Just a couple of questions, Aunt Amelia," Claire said. "Just a few things that the police want to clear up. If you can answer the questions quickly, why then they'll be out that much sooner."

"Well, I don't want them here at all," Amelia Jasper snapped. "And what possible questions could I answer? I saw this man just once when—"

Sergeant Sellers interrupted. "We want to know something about a man by the name of Durham."

"What about him?" Amelia Jasper demanded, truculently.

"We thought that there might be some connection between him and this man, Lam."

"Well, there certainly isn't," Amelia Jasper said. "Mr. Durham is a very nice young man."

"How long since you've seen him?" I asked.

She glared at me, and said, "I don't have to answer your questions."

I said, "The reason I'm asking is because I think Durham may have been mixed up in some trouble out at the Kozy Dell Slumber Court."

She tilted her chin in the air and ignored me.

"And," I went on, "I think he's a blackmailer."

"A blackmailer!" she said, scornfully.

"Has he been blackmailing you?" I asked.

She ignored the question.

"Has he?" Sellers asked, bluntly.

"I don't see why I should answer a lot of questions about my personal affairs in front of a man who is the lowest type of murderer, a man who tried to insinuate himself into this household under the guise of being a writer who was going to help me get satisfaction from the insurance company. Good Heavens, it's just the biggest wonder that *I'm* not lying there on the floor with a stocking around my neck!"

"Was Durham trying to blackmail you?" I interrupted.

She ignored me.

"Was he?" Sellers asked.

"I don't know what gave you that idea."

I said, "If he wasn't blackmailing you, what *did* he want? Come on, let's not stall around. Give a straightforward answer. What was he doing here?"

She said, "We had some business that we were talking over."

"What sort of business?" I asked.

"A mine," she said.

"What kind of a mine?"

"A lead mine."

"Located where?"

"Colorado."

"Are you sure it was a lead mine?" I asked, and managed a triumphant smile.

That smile bothered her. She thought she'd walked into a trap. "Well," she said, "there was lead in it, mixed with the gold."

"Well, which did you intend to make the money out of, the lead or the gold?"

"I don't know. I didn't follow it that far. I didn't go into it that deeply."

"Then you weren't interested in making an investment?"

"No."

"Then why did you see so much of Durham? Why had he been coming back here? Why—?"

"I'm not going to be cross-examined by you in my own home," she said. "This is outrageous! Sergeant, I'm going to report you for this."

Sellers squirmed uncomfortably.

She turned on me. "You're a horrible beast!" Then she swung back to Sellers and shuddered. "A sweet little girl like that, and at the very moment she was putting her hands up to his cheeks to draw his head down so she could kiss him, and he—"

"Wait a minute," I said. "How do *you* know she put her hands up to my cheeks to draw my face down to kiss her?"

"It said so on the radio."

"No, it didn't. How do you know? And it wasn't in the papers either."

I leaned forward in my chair to hold her eyes.

She became confused. "I don't know," she said. "I told you I'd taken so much dope I—"

"*I* told you," Susie Irwin said. "*I* heard it on the radio."

"And how did you hear it on the radio?" I said. "Where was the announcer concealed? How did he know how I was kissed?"

"I guess the police made the announcement. I don't know. Probably they had some witness."

"That's right," Amelia Jasper said, "Susie told me."

I settled back in the chair, and said, "That does it. I've been dumb."

"What does what?" Sellers said, irritably. "And as far as being dumb is concerned, *I'm* the one that stuck my head into a noose."

I said, "Don't you get it now?"

"Get what?"

I said, "Durham was a blackmailer, all right, but he wasn't the brains of the outfit, and he wasn't blackmailing this woman. Get a doctor out here and take a look at that sciatic rheumatism of hers and you'll find it's caused by a .32 caliber bullet."

Amelia Jasper screamed angrily, "Take that man out of here! I demand it."

"Go on," I said. "Get a doctor."

Sellers hesitated a moment, then said, "You're nuts, Lam. You can't pull things like that. You're talking in order to get yourself an out."

"Don't be a fool," I told him. "You can see the whole play now. That sudden flare-up of sciatic rheumatism is due to the fact that the first shot that was fired in the Kozy Dell Slumber Court went into her hip."

"Sergeant," Amelia Jasper said, her face a mask of fury,

"I demand that you all leave my house immediately. I have stood all of the insults I intend to take. Susie, will you go to the phone and telephone police headquarters in the event—"

"I'm sorry," Frank Sellers apologized.

He reached over, caught my coat collar, and jerked me to my feet. "Come on, Lam. You've master-minded me into a helluva situation. On your way. This is what comes of trying to give you and Bertha a break."

He slammed me around until I started to fall and I unconsciously flung out my hands to catch myself. The steel of the handcuffs bit into my wrist, made me numb with the pain.

Sellers said, "I hope you'll excuse it please, Mrs. Jasper. I was just trying to get the case cleared up. This fellow sold me a bill of goods."

"Open the door for them, Susie," Mrs. Jasper commanded.

The maid strode down the corridor.

I turned to Sellers, and said, "You damn fool. Can't you see what happened? She—"

Sellers slapped me across the mouth. "Shut up!"

He started me down the corridor. Claire Bushnell was crying.

Bertha Cool came lumbering along in the rear. Susie stood triumphantly in the doorway, holding it open.

I turned my head and said, pleadingly, "Bertha."

Sellers slapped the side of my head so hard he almost broke my neck.

But in that brief glimpse I had behind me, I had seen Bertha Cool turning back.

We were halfway to the front door when the scream came from the living-room. Then there was a sound of a chair overturning, the sound of struggle, another scream, and Amelia Jasper was crying for help.

Bertha Cool's voice said, "That does it. You damn liar. Keep still or I'll break your neck. . . . Frank, come back here!"

Sellers hesitated for just a moment, then spun me around and pushed me down the corridor on a run.

The wheel chair had skidded to one side of the room and tilted over to its side. A bloodstained bandage was unwound

185

and lying on the floor. Bertha was calmly sitting on Amelia Jasper's shoulders, holding one leg in a grip of iron.

Amelia Jasper was kicking with the other leg, screaming and shouting for help.

Sellers shouted, "You can't do this, Bertha. You can't do it."

"The hell I can't," Bertha said, grimly. "I've done it. Look at the bullet hole."

Sellers grabbed Bertha's shoulders. "Let her up, Bertha. You can't do that."

Bertha said, "I tell you, I've done it."

Sellers grabbed Bertha's shoulders and tried to move her.

She gave him a push that threw him off balance, and he swung around crazily for a minute, trying to regain it.

In the doorway, Susie Irwin, the maid, stood grimly efficient, holding a blue-steel revolver. "Put your hands up, everybody," she said.

The grim, sinister purpose of her voice knifed through to everyone's consciousness.

"That means you, too, Sergeant," she said. "Get 'em up."

Sellers turned too quickly, and Susie Irwin pulled the trigger. The room was filled with sound, and Sellers, as one dazed, looked at the blood streaming down from his shattered right hand.

The grim reality of the situation suddenly impressed itself on everyone. Susie Irwin meant business.

Amelia Jasper struggled to her feet.

"Come on, Amelia," Susie said.

Amelia ran, a hobbling, one-sided gait. Quite evidently every step was painful.

Sellers tried reaching for his gun with his left hand. He couldn't make it. Bertha Cool lumbered to her feet, charged down the corridor like a tank going into battle.

Susie Irwin stopped at the front door, turned, and took deliberate aim.

I stuck out my foot and tripped Bertha Cool. She went down with a bang that shook the house. Susie Irwin pulled the trigger, and the bullet went swishing through the air right where Bertha Cool's ample chest would have been if I hadn't tripped her.

The front door banged.

There was the sound of a motor.

Sergeant Sellers yelled at Bertha, "Get my gun out of the holster over on the right, put it in my left hand."

Claire Bushnell was the one who got his gun out for him. Sellers, holding the gun in his left hand, dashed to the open front door.

He was in time to see the tail end of his police car skidding around the corner.

He stood dazed, angry and swearing. Then he turned to me. "You're responsible for this. I'll be the laughing stock of—"

"Shut up," I told him. "Take these handcuffs off and start broadcasting an alarm. You're on the verge of promotion and you're too dumb to realize it."

187

CHAPTER FIFTEEN

The Prize Boob

FRANK SELLERS GLOWERED AT ME and awkwardly wrapped a handkerchief around his right wrist, using it as a tourniquet to stop the bleeding of his hand.

"That's what I get for listening to you," he said savagely.

"What is?"

"A woman has caught me with my pants down, shot me, and made a getaway in my police car. I'm a hell of a looking spectacle right now."

I caught Bertha's eyes. "See if you can't find him a towel to wrap around that arm, Bertha."

"I'm doing all right," Sellers said. "I'll take care of myself. Get hold of a taxi, Bertha, and we'll drive to Headquarters in that. Dammit, now I'm going to be the laughing stock of the whole department. Shot by a woman!"

I said, "Try and find a *bath* towel, Bertha."

"A *bath* towel," she said. "You don't want to put anything around it. Just tie something above it the way he's done. That handkerchief is working all right. It'll stop the bleeding and—"

I said, "If I have to spell it out for you, try and find a bath towel that has Kozy Dell Slumber Court embroidered on it."

"Well, why the hell didn't you say so?" Bertha said.

"I'm saying so now," I told her.

Sellers said angrily, "You get me a taxicab. Hell, I'll get one myself."

He walked over to the telephone, picked up the receiver, laid it on the little table, dialed a number with his left hand, then picked up the receiver and said, "Hello, this is Police

Sergeant Frank Sellers. I'm at 226 Korreander, and I want a taxi out here right away. Now rush it out here, will you?"

He waited a moment for confirmation, then grunted and slammed the receiver back into place.

Bertha, prowling around through the house, was banging doors behind her. Claire Bushnell, sympathetic and frightened, was hovering around Sergeant Sellers.

"Can I take a look at that hand?" she asked.

"Fortunately," Sellers said, "I think it missed most of the bones except the thumb. That thumb's pretty messy." He turned to me and said, "I'm going to get both you and Bertha for this, Lam. Bertha pushed me off balance or I'd have—"

I said, "Bertha probably saved your life."

He looked as though he wanted to bite my head off.

We heard Bertha's steps coming rapidly down the corridor. Then she was triumphantly displaying a blood-stained bath towel that had the words Kozy Dell embroidered on it in red thread.

"Here we are, lover," she said. "I found it in a soiled clothes hamper in the bathroom. The woman certainly was careless, just threw it in the soiled clothes."

I said, "She felt pretty certain no one would ever be here to look for it. Wrap it up in some paper, Bertha. First, better put your initials on a corner with a fountain pen so that you can testify as to where you found it."

Sellers said, "Don't bother. If there's any evidence, I'll take charge of it."

I said, "We don't want to get any blood on it, Sergeant. You're bleeding from that wound in your hand. We want to keep the blood that's on there as evidence."

He glared at me and said, "I'm not buying any more of your schemes, Donald. You're going to Headquarters. You're going to be booked. That's what I should have done with you in the first place. And then I'm going to settle an account with those two women."

"Sure," I said. "Newspaper reporters will be around you thick like flies. They'll want to know all about the story of how you got shot."

"Okay. I'll tell them."

I said, "Bertha saved your life. She pushed you out of the line of fire."

"What the hell are you talking about?"

"About Bertha saving your life," I said. "And if you think that's going to look well in print, just—"

"Bertha didn't save my life," he yelled. "She gave me a shove that had me off balance when that hatchet-faced number took a pop at me. Bertha, if you ever lay your hands on me again, I don't care if you are a woman, I'll bust your damn jaw."

"Just try it," Bertha said, belligerently, and then added, "that is, if you feel lucky."

I said, "All right, if you want to get tough about it, Frank, let's put the cards right on the table. You go up to Headquarters now and you're in the worst mess of your life. You've arrested me, but you can't hold me."

"Says you!"

"For a while," I said, "but there's enough evidence now so a lawyer can get me out."

"I don't see it," Sellers said. "You find out that Amelia Jasper has a bullet hole in her thigh—so what?"

I said, "Okay, you haven't got a case against her yet. But you haven't got a case against me—not now."

"The hell I haven't."

"No, you haven't, Frank. The fact that this woman made that statement about the girl putting her hands on my face shows that she knew what happened. She was watching from outside the window."

"*Did* the girl put her hands on your face?"

"Yes."

That gave Sellers something to think about.

I said, "It's now pretty well established that Amelia Jasper was out there at the Kozy Dell. She was putting the bite on Minerva Carlton. Minerva was in a spot. Someone had stuff on her that she didn't want her husband to find out. So she ran in a ringer. Dover Fulton was called in to pose as her husband."

"You've gone over all that before."

I said, "Something went wrong. Here's what probably happened. Dover Fulton pulled his gun. Both of these women were there. One of them rushed him and Amelia Jasper turned her back. Susie, the grim-faced maid, probably hit Fulton over the head with something. Fulton convulsively pulled the trigger of the gun; the bullet went into Mrs. Jasper's hip. Minerva Carlton started to run. Susie picked up the gun and put a bullet through the back of her head. By that time, everybody was in too deep to quit. They rubbed Dover Fulton out and then decided they'd have to make it look like a murder and suicide. But they had an extra shot to account for. They finally figured out the scheme of putting that extra shot in the suitcase.

"The suitcase was lying open on the floor. The blouse probably was on top of it. Minerva Carlton had taken off just enough clothes to make it appear she was delightfully informal with her husband in the motor court. Amelia Jasper grabbed a bath towel and wrapped it around her leg to stop the flow of blood. She closed the suitcase, and in order to get it closed, simply wadded the blouse, which had been carelessly tossed on top of the clothes in the suitcase, into a ball and slammed the suitcase shut. They got out of there, went a mile or so down the road, perforated the suitcase, took one empty shell out of the gun so it would look as though Dover Fulton had been carrying the gun with one empty shell under the hammer, then went back to the auto court, put the suitcase in place, locked the door from the inside, crawled out through the window and went away."

Sellers said wearily, "I get so damn tired of listening to your theories that don't have anything to back them up."

I said, "This isn't a theory. This is what happened. I'm telling you because it's an interview I'm going to give to the press."

"Give it and be damned."

I said, "It means that you've got off on the wrong foot. Instead of actually solving the murder of Lucille Hollister, you've got the thing all balled up and have let a woman shoot you in the hand and steal your car. That's certainly going to put you in the position of being the prize boob. When you pose for the flashlight pictures of the newspaper photographers you can just see the headlines: WOMAN SUSPECT SHOOTS OFFICER, STEALS CAR, ESCAPES!"

Frank Sellers thought that over. He conjured up a picture of how that was going to look in print and didn't like the picture.

I said, "You're in this thing now to a point where you've got to straighten it out. Take half an hour with me and—"

"All right," he said wearily, "let's have it. You've got some wild-eyed plan in view. Let's hear what it is. At any rate, I'll listen."

I said, "Take these handcuffs off and—"

"Not by a damn sight!"

I said, "Let's use our heads. This man, Tom Durham, was mixed up in it. We know that because Minerva Carlton wanted to find out about him. He was the contact man. He must have been. Now then, Amelia Jasper and her maid, Susie, are mixed up in blackmail, and by this time, murder. They may make a run for it, but before they do, they're going to pick up Tom Durham, who is also on the lam. And, unless I miss my guess, they're going to give Durham a story to tell. And after Durham has told that story, then the two women will switch their own stories, stand together on it, appeal to the chivalry of an American jury, and convict Durham of first-degree murder."

"You talk and talk and talk," Sellers said. "Where the hell's that taxicab?"

Almost as though the cab had been waiting for the words, we heard the sound of a horn out front.

Sellers lumbered to his feet, said, "Okay, everybody, let's go."

Sellers hooked the fingers of his left hand around my arm, said, "On your way, Smart Guy."

I held back long enough to say, "It's all right with me if that's the way you want to play it, but if you play it smart you can come back to Headquarters driving your own police car, with the Lucille Hollister murder solved and the killing in the Kozy Dell Slumber Court all cleaned up."

I thought I felt some of the tension go out of his fingers.

I said, "What the hell. You've got your gun. You can hold it in your left hand. If I try to get away, you can drill me. Take those handcuffs off and I'll take you to Tom Durham."

The taxicab honked his horn again.

"And to where your police car has been parked," I added.

He said, "Look, if you know so much, you're going to begin by taking me to where the police car is. The bracelets look good on you. Try to hold out on me and you'll swallow your teeth! One of you janes go tell that taxi driver to quit blowing that horn.''

Claire Bushnell ran out to the taxicab.

I said to Sellers, ''Tom Durham checked out of Westchester Arms about eleven o'clock, just about the time he could have got back from the expedition to the Kozy Dell Slumber Court. That's a peculiar hour to check out. The good trains have all pulled out by that time. The night planes are beginning to take off; but Durham didn't go in one of the limousines that runs to the airport. He didn't take a taxi. The doorman's certain about that. He didn't remember Durham, but he remembered Durham's suitcase, a massive affair with two hasps and two padlocks.

''The bellboy says Durham paid his bill at the cashier's desk and then the boy took the suitcase out to the front door. The doorman remembers seeing the boy put the suitcase down. He had a glimpse of Durham, then he helped some people into a taxicab, and when he turned around, Durham was gone.''

''Walked around to another entrance and got a cab,'' Sellers said.

''I don't think he did.''

''Where do you think he went?''

I said, ''Let's make a bargain. If your car is parked around the Westchester Arms Hotel, will you take the handcuffs off and give me a break?''

Sellers hesitated. I could see the thought of losing that car really bothered him.

I said, ''Remember, I'll take you right to where your car is parked and—''

''You get busy and dig up my car,'' he said. ''When you've found that car for me, you can do more talking. I hate to go in and report that car stolen.''

I said, ''Okay. Let's go.''

We marched out to the waiting taxi.

''Westchester Arms Hotel,'' I said, ''and when you get there, cruise slowly around a two-block square until I tell you to stop.''

CHAPTER SIXTEEN

Basement Brawl

TWO BLOCKS FROM THE WESTCHESTER ARMS, we found Frank Sellers's police car parked by a fire hydrant.

Sellers's exclamation of satisfaction was ample indication of the load that had been lifted from his mind.

"Stop right here," he told the cab driver.

The cab driver lurched the car to a stop.

Sellers opened the door with his good hand, walked over to the police car, saw that the keys were in it, locked the ignition switch, pulled the keys out, put them in his pocket, grinned, and walked back to the cab.

"Bertha," Sellers said, holding his injured right hand so that there was little possibility of bumping it against the car door, "the keys to those handcuffs are in my right-hand vest pocket."

Bertha pulled his coat back, fumbled for the keys. Sellers winced as the pressure of the coat caused motion in his right hand.

Bertha fitted the keys to the handcuffs on my wrists, took them off.

Sellers said, "Understand, Lam, you're still under arrest. I'm just giving you a break."

The cab driver said, "Who's going to pay me?"

"They are," Sellers said.

It spoke volumes for the condition of Bertha's mind that she opened her purse, took out the sixty cents that was due the cab driver and added fifteen cents with it.

"Now what?" Sellers asked. "Do we wait for them to come back?"

"They aren't coming back," I told him. "They're smart

enough to know that the quickest way they can get picked up is to be driving a stolen police car.''

"All right. What next?'' Sellers demanded impatiently.

I said, "You come along with me.''

Sellers frowned, hesitated, all but refused point blank, then fell into step at my side.

"No funny stuff,'' he warned.

We walked in silence to the Westchester Arms Hotel.

"You certainly don't think they're staying here?'' Sellers asked.

I said, "They're hunted, they're desperate, they're trying to make a getaway. When Tom Durham checked out of that hotel, *he* was in a hurry and *he* was trying to make a getaway. He and his suitcase disappeared. They might as well have been swallowed into thin air. We're dealing with a regularly established blackmail ring. It isn't a casual act of isolated blackmail. It's part of a pattern.''

"All right, get to the point,'' Sellers said.

I said, "Come on. This way.''

I opened the door of the cocktail lounge.

The manager was standing near the center of the room where he could see both the door into the hotel lobby and the street door.

He came toward us, bowing, then he spotted Sellers, saw the bandaged hand, and then in a flash, recognized me.

I said, "I guess you remember me, don't you?''

He tried to look blank.

I said, "You gave me some water with an olive in it and charged me for a cocktail.''

He said, "Where's the evidence?''

"Down the drain, I guess.''

He said, "Don't be a damn fool.'' His eyes were fixed with fascination on the bloodstained bandage around Frank Sellers's right hand.

I said, "Okay, we're going to order a drink, and I want this one to be better than the others.''

I moved over to a booth. The four of us sat down, Sellers with obvious reluctance.

The manager melted away.

I said, in an undertone, "Follow him, Claire, quick! If he

goes to a telephone, try and watch him and see what number he calls.''

Claire Bushnell slid out from behind the table, and, looking demure as befits a modest young woman who is searching for a rest room, started tagging along behind the manager.

"You think *he's* in on it?" Sellers asked skeptically.

I said, "Something happened in this vicinity when I was trying to follow Tom Durham. What's more, Dover Fulton and Minerva Carlton were in here having drinks just before they went out to the Kozy Dell Slumber Court.''

"That's a damn slender thread on which to tie a conclusion,'' Sellers said angrily.

I said, "It's a thread that was stout enough to get your car back.''

There wasn't any answer he could make to that.

I said, "I figure it had to be either here or at the Cabanita. I tried this first because it's nearer and was an easier place to get rid of the car; but I'm not certain but what we'll find the answer in the Cabanita.''

Sellers moved his hand and winced with sudden pain. The numbness was beginning to leave and the slivers of bone in his shattered thumb were grating every time he moved the elbow.

Bertha watched him sympathetically. "You'd better have a good shot of hooch,'' she said.

Sellers said, "You've got something there. Let's get that waiter.''

"I'll find him,'' I said. "What do you want?''

"Double brandy,'' Sellers said, and dropped his head back against the cushion. His face suddenly went white and his eyes closed. There were marks of pain around the corners of his mouth.

I slid out of the booth and had taken half a dozen steps before Sellers opened his eyes and suddenly straightened.

"Hey,'' he said, "not you! Bertha can go. You come back here.''

Somewhere a woman screamed.

It was a peculiar muffled scream which seemed to come from back of the bar somewhere.

I made a dash for the bar. The bartender said, "You can't go in there.''

I spotted an open door and a flight of stairs. I made a sprint. The bartender grabbed and caught the shoulder of my coat. I kicked him in the kneecap and when his hold loosened, dashed on down the stairs. The bartender had sufficient presence of mind to slam the door shut behind me so that any noise made down below wouldn't be heard in the cocktail lounge.

I reached a basement storage room. There were cases of liquor stacked all around, racks with wine bottles. There was no sign of Claire Bushnell.

The manager of the cocktail lounge was in the process of gliding through another opened door at the far end of the room. He saw me, and an expression of black anger came over his face.

"What do *you* want?" he demanded.

"Where's the girl who screamed?"

"I don't know. She ran back upstairs. This is private. Get out."

"Where are you going?" I asked.

He heard the sound of commotion at the head of the stairs, said suddenly, "As far as I'm concerned, this is a stick-up. I'm going to defend myself."

His hand darted under his coat.

I grabbed a champagne bottle by the neck and hurled it.

The bottle missed his head, but struck against the concrete wall. The champagne, spurting out from the broken bottle, drenched his face and had him blinking hard.

He kept his right hand under the lapel of his coat. His left hand angrily brushed his eyes.

I charged across the room at him.

Behind me, I heard the crash of a door being kicked open, the sound of heavy steps on the stairs.

The manager of the cocktail lounge suddenly thought better of it. He jerked his right hand out from under his coat.

Sergeant Sellers and Bertha Cool came barging down the stairs.

"What the hell's coming off here?" Frank Sellers asked, his face white as a sheet.

"Where's the woman?" I asked.

"She went back up the stairs," the manager said.

Claire Bushnell thrust a cobweb-streaked countenance out

197

from behind a wine bin. "Nuts!" she said angrily. "I was going to see where he went. I ran back up the stairs when he turned on me and then when he ran back I sneaked on down and got behind the wine bin."

"Say, what *is* this?" the manager demanded. "I'm going to make a protest to police headquarters. It's lucky there wasn't a shooting. I thought this was a holdup. I was getting ready to defend myself. Sergeant, I'm going to hold you responsible for this."

Sellers seemed as tense as a marathon runner trying to hold out until he reached the tape. He came slowly forward and said, "Lam, I've had enough of this—"

I whirled, ducked under the arm of the manager of the cocktail lounge, sprinted through the open door.

I heard Sellers bellow with anger, "Grab him!"

There were feet pounding after me.

I heard the manager shouting, "You can't go in there," and then adding, "I'll catch him."

I was in a place that had been fixed up as an apartment, evidently living-quarters for a janitor in the hotel. The furniture was cheap and shoddy, but there was the odor of fresh tobacco smoke in the room and a cigarette in an ash tray was sending up wisps of smoke.

I bent down to look under the bed.

I saw skirts, a woman's leg, and then met the glare of Amelia Jasper's angry eyes.

The sound of motion caused me to look up.

Tom Durham was swinging a club. I got my head out of the way and grabbed for his foot. The club numbed my shoulder. Durham went down on the floor with me, and we went whirling around, over and over.

Amelia Jasper came scrambling out from under the bed and grabbed a fistful of my hair. The manager of the cocktail lounge kicked me, and then Bertha hit the scrimmage like a battering ram.

I heard Sergeant Sellers yell, "Break it up! Break it up there!" Then I saw Bertha's muscular leg, felt her toe whiz past my head, smack into Durham's jaw, and heard Bertha saying angrily, "That's the worst of these modern styles. You have to fumble around with a couple of yards of skirt every time you want to kick some son-of-a-bitch in the face!"

CHAPTER SEVENTEEN

Requiem For A Racket

BERTHA COOL SURVEYED ME DISTASTEFULLY as I walked into the office.

"Where the hell have *you* been?"

"Tying up a few loose threads," I said.

"Loose threads, my eye!" Bertha stormed. "You've been out with that Bushnell wench, billing and cooing. *She* thinks you're a hero."

I said, "I thought it would make things better for Sellers if I wasn't available for an interview with the press."

Bertha snorted and said, "I knew you were falling for her like a ton of bricks."

"What happened?" I asked.

Bertha said, "You were right all the way along the line, lover. The manager of the cocktail lounge had a lease on an apartment in the hotel basement which had originally been made for the assistant janitor. It went with his lease on the cocktail lounge. He was in on the blackmail racket.

"It looks as though Bob Elgin was mixed up in it too. You know the way it is around these night clubs. There's opportunity for some nice blackmail if the people want to do it. They didn't want to take over the real dirty work, but Amelia Jasper did. That's the way she's been making her living for the past five years.

"It's strange the way she happened to start on Minerva Carlton. It seems Claire Bushnell made some crack about the swell time the two girls had been having at the beach. She thought she was just entertaining her Aunt Amelia. Amelia urged her on, got all of the facts and—"

199

I said, "Did anybody confess? Did Sellers get a confession?"

"Did he get a confession!" Bertha said, with a glint of admiration in her eyes. "You should have seen that boy work! Him with only one good hand! But he pulled a piece of rubber hose and he scared the pants right off that crowd."

"Who squawked?"

"Oddly enough," Bertha said, "it was the man who weakened first."

"Tom Durham?"

"Yes."

"All right, what's the low-down?"

"They were shaking down Minerva Carlton. They threatened to tell her husband. Tom Durham met her in the Cabanita. Minerva said she'd be at the Kozy Dell Slumber Court Saturday night and would pay off. She wrote the name on the back of a menu. Lucille managed to get placed in the same booth after they'd left and grabbed the menu. They didn't show the first time—scared, I guess. Mrs. Carlton repeated the next week. She got Dover Fulton to pose as Stanwick Carlton, her husband. When the blackmailers showed up, she laughed at them, said her husband knew all about her 'indiscretion' and had forgiven her; that he'd arrived unexpectedly from Colorado and she'd confessed the whole thing to him because she had to. She seemed radiantly happy.

"There was some argument, and Durham, mad at having lost a touch, started a swing at Fulton. Fulton drew his gun, took a shot, missed, and hit Amelia Jasper in the fanny.

"Before Fulton could fire again, Durham had the gun wrenched away from him.

"Fulton made the mistake of being game. He made a lunge and Durham let him have it right between the eyes. Minerva Carlton turned and started to run and he hit her in the back of the head. He's a crack shot."

"And the suitcase?"

"Just as you said. They knew they had to account for the third bullet."

"And what about Lucille Hollister?"

"They wanted to do business with her. She'd been keeping an eye on the blackmailers. They were watching the house where she was staying, intending to get her when she came out. You blundered into the picture and the two women followed you around to the back, later on into the bedroom.''

"You mean Amelia Jasper and Susie?"

"That's right. My God, but you're dumb! Can't you even look behind you and see whether or not a couple of amateurs are trailing along behind?"

"Not when a girl's undressing in a bedroom window," I said.

Bertha sighed and shook her head. 'That's what comes of having a man for a partner. I should buy you polarized glasses.''

"You should for a fact," I said. "They followed me, is that right?"

"No. They were watching the house."

"I know, but after I showed up, they followed me."

"That's right. They'd been afraid of Lucille. They didn't know just where she entered the picture. They thought she was a detective. They found out, of course, from reading the newspaper accounts of the shooting in the Kozy Dell Slumber Court that you'd been there and had a woman with you. They read her description. They knew that Lucille had been hanging around the clubs and cocktail bars where they were working. They didn't know just *what* she wanted. They were close enough so they could hear her bedroom conversation with you through the open window. She signed her own death warrant when she said she'd seen people moving around in the cabin where Minerva Carlton and Dover Fulton were killed after the three shots had been fired.''

Elsie Brand tapped on the door and said, "The adjuster from the insurance company is here. He wants to see Donald Lam.''

A beatific grin suffused Bertha Cool's features.

"Send the gentleman in here where we can *both* work on him," she said softly.